Murder in Bloomsbury

ALSO AVAILABLE BY D. M. QUINCY

Murder in Mayfair

Murder in Bloomsbury

An Atlas Catesby Mystery

D. M. Quincy

NEW YORK

This is a work of fiction. All of the names, characters, organizations, places, and events portrayed in this novel are either products of the author's imagination or used fictitiously. Any resemblance to real or actual events, locales, or persons, living or dead, is entirely coincidental.

Published in the United States by Crooked Lane Books, an imprint of The Quick Brown Fox & Company LLC.

Crooked Lane Books and its logo are trademarks of The Quick Brown Fox & Company LLC.

Library of Congress Catalog-in-Publication data available upon request.

ISBN (hardcover): 978-1-68331-465-3
ISBN (ePub): 978-1-68331-466-0
ISBN (ePDF): 978-1-68331-467-7

Cover design by Lori Palmer
Book design by Jennifer Canzone

Printed in the United States.

www.crookedlanebooks.com

Crooked Lane Books
34 West 27th St., 10th Floor
New York, NY 10001

First Edition: February 2018

10 9 8 7 6 5 4 3 2 1

To my husband, Taoufiq—
For believing in me and encouraging me
to write my own stories before it ever
occurred to me that I actually could

Chapter One

"Sir? Are you awake?" The distant voice, halting and uncertain, cut through the morning stillness, penetrating Atlas Catesby's deep slumber. "He says it's urgent."

Atlas rolled over, his body heavy with lethargy. It took a moment for his valet's voice to pierce his slumber-slogged mind. He swallowed against the dryness in his throat, his voice scratchy. "What is it?"

"I'm sorry to disturb you, sir." Jamie spoke hesitantly. Just a few short months ago, he'd been a houseboy in a modest country home and was still adjusting to his newly elevated status as a gentleman's valet.

"Then why are you?" Trying to recall what day it was, Atlas pressed a palm flat against his left temple, where sharp pain hammered like a righteous blacksmith behind his eye.

"There's a message for you. It was just delivered."

So early in the morning? "What time is it?"

"Half past ten, sir."

Atlas blinked and tried to order his mind. He rarely slept late. The reason for his current somnolent state, for the relentless drumbeat in his head, slowly took shape in his memory. Last evening's events flowed back like a lazy river, filling the fuzzy spaces in his mind. He remembered a prodigious amount of wine as well as the source of the cinnamon scent that still lingered in the air. Her uncomplicated feminine smile had beckoned him to bed, a balm for the inner bleakness that had permeated almost everything since his recent return to London.

He slid a hand across to the other side of the bed, only to find an empty space where she should have been. The cool bedclothes suggested the spot had been abandoned hours ago. Relief loosened his muscles, even as a stab of guilt assailed him.

The door creaked as Jamie pushed it farther open. His eyes widened at something on the worn parquet floor.

"Begging your pardon, sir." He flushed, painful florid splotches painting his full cheeks. The boy's curious gaze darted to the mahogany-framed bed and bounced away from it just as quickly.

Atlas lifted his weight onto one elbow, squinting as a sharp blade of morning light cut across his face. Following the trail of Jamie's gaze, he spotted the cause of his valet's discomfiture. A woman's stays were strewn on the floor next to the pantaloons Atlas had carelessly tossed aside during the previous evening's urgent, slightly drunken coupling.

Atlas felt the heat rise in his own face. He was still unaccustomed to having servants underfoot during his most private moments. And the boy had never witnessed his master in intimate company with a woman, not since coming into his employ almost a year ago. Granted, Atlas had been gone most of that time, but still, he did not make a practice of taking respectable women to bed in order to slake his lust.

"Leave the message on the table." He spoke curtly, suddenly feeling self-conscious of his nudity beneath the bedclothes, even though, as his valet, Jamie had certainly seen him stripped to the skin before.

The boy seemed to find the bedpost's ornate carving extraordinarily interesting, for his gaze never left it. "It's just that . . . you see . . . there's . . . ," he stammered.

Atlas suppressed a curse. How long was Jamie going to remain in the chamber? "What is it? Spit it out."

Jamie cleared his throat, shifting from one long gangly leg to the other but showing no apparent inclination to quit the room. "There's a footman here. He insists on waiting for your answer or for you to accompany him."

"Accompany him where? Whose footman is he?" Few people knew he was in town, save his friend, the Earl of Charlton, who employed Jamie whenever Atlas traveled abroad. "Is the note from Charlton?"

"No, sir."

"Then who?"

"I'm sure I couldn't say, sir. But his livery . . . it's the same as the bloke that came last fall."

Atlas froze. *It couldn't be.* "Black-and-gold livery?"

"Yes, sir." Jamie nodded eagerly. "That's it."

A bittersweet sensation sliced through his lungs. Black-and-gold livery could only belong to the Duke of Somerville. Lilliana's brother. Not *Lilliana*, he reminded himself harshly. *Roslyn.* Lady Roslyn Lilliana Sterling. The woman he'd been trying to forget for the past nine long months.

Slipping out from under the bedclothes, he touched his feet to the frayed carpet. Unmindful of his bare state, he strode across the chamber and reached for his crumpled clothes.

"I wonder what the devil he wants." Atlas pulled on his trousers, half skipping on one foot to maintain his balance. Pulling his linen shirt over his head, he slipped out to his sitting room and crossed barefoot into the entry hall, where the duke's servant awaited him.

The polished brass buttons and gold braiding adorning the young man's uniform glittered like twinkling stars against the fine black wool fabric. The footman wore the livery to excellent advantage; he was tall and well made, as were all the footmen in Mayfair's finest homes. Only the best accoutrements would do for the metropolis's highest born.

And few births were superior to Somerville's. Even among dukes, he stood at the highest rung, just below the royal dukes. Although, if the rumors were to be believed, Somerville was wealthier than the royals.

Atlas took the note and broke the seal. He hadn't recognized the emblem on the previous occasion when the young duke had written to him, but now the glossy smooth wax medallion made him think of the man's sister.

Somerville had, of course, used an entire sheet of paper to write the short note. Cost was no issue. The missive, written in fluent, confident strokes, bade Atlas to attend his grace at his earliest convenience. Nothing else. No explanation. It was practically a command.

Irritation simmered along the surface of Atlas's skin. He wasn't one of Somerville's lackeys. He crumpled the sheet in one large hand, intent on instructing the footman to tell his employer to go to the devil.

But—he paused—what if something had happened to Lilliana? Or one of her children? His resolve to stay away, to put Lilliana from his mind, evaporated like morning dew once the sun broke.

He gave the footman a sharp nod. "Inform his grace that I'll attend him this afternoon."

* * *

Atlas was shown to the Duke of Somerville's library, a massive two-story chamber tastefully accoutred in soft blues and vivid golds. Books lined the walls in every direction, the shelves almost reaching the ceiling's ornate gilded plasterwork.

"You came." The duke's clipped voice echoed off the high timbers. He sat in an elegant mahogany armchair—upholstered in velvet the color of a pale sky—at the center of the cavernous room. With a pale manicured hand resting on each of the chair arms, he looked rather like an emperor perched on his throne.

"Did you assume that I wouldn't?"

Somerville regarded him with intense dark eyes. He was a young man in his midtwenties, but he'd been duke for well over a decade, having come into the title at age twelve after the death of his parents in a tragic carriage accident. "I thought it was a distinct possibility."

"One rarely defies a ducal summons."

"Something tells me you would if you cared to." The duke rose and crossed over to a rosewood table bearing a silver tray holding a decanter filled with amber liquid and several glasses. As always, he was impeccably dressed, today in superfine royal-blue wool perfectly tailored to his slender form.

Atlas didn't bother to deny his ambivalence. "Curiosity got the better of me."

"Drink?" Somerville filled two glasses without waiting for his response and turned toward his visitor. "I seem to recall you enjoy a fine brandy."

Atlas accepted the proffered glass. "And I seem to recall that you have the finest brandy there is."

"I'd settle for nothing less." Somerville led the way to the chamber's two facing velvet stuffed sofas. Settling on one, he gestured for Atlas to take the other. "There's no reason to allow war with the Corsican to interfere with our savoring of the finest things in life."

Atlas took a seat and brought the glass to his lips, inhaling the rich aroma before sipping the brandy's sweet heat. "Excellent as always," he said, still wondering why he'd been summoned. Although he'd shared the man's brandy on a handful of previous occasions and was privy to his deepest, darkest, most ruinous secret, the two were not friends.

"I trust your family is well," the duke said.

"Very well. Thank you." Atlas smothered his inclination to ask specifically about Lilliana but welcomed the opening to learn how she fared. "And yours?"

"The boys keep my sister very busy. I suppose the household will be more peaceful once Peter leaves for Eton in the fall."

"You're sending the boy away to school?"

Draping one arm over the sofa's high armrest, Somerville sipped his brandy. "Naturally."

Atlas frowned, taken aback that a mother as devoted as Lilliana would send her son from home at such a tender age. Although he should not be. Since she was the daughter of a duke, her children would naturally follow the prescribed academic path expected of highborn progeny.

"Isn't Peter a little young to go away to school?"

"Not in the least. After all, he just turned eight."

"I see." Atlas's own parents had kept all four of their sons at home with a tutor until the age of fourteen, with the exception of Atlas, who'd escaped to Harrow three years earlier than his brothers under dark circumstances that Atlas preferred not to dwell on.

"I suppose you're wondering why I asked you here," Somerville said.

"Did you ask?" he said tartly. "It rather felt like a summons."

One corner of the duke's mouth kicked up. "Be that as it may, I appreciate your coming."

"Why am I here?"

"I hope you will be disposed to do me a favor."

Atlas sipped his brandy, savoring the exquisite taste. "What sort of service could I possibly provide for you?"

"Not for him." The confident feminine tones sounded from above. Atlas started. He'd know that clipped upper-class voice anywhere. "For me."

He stared up at Lady Roslyn Lilliana Sterling Warwick's regal form on the library's mezzanine level. She stood with her arms splayed wide apart, both hands resting delicately on the mahogany banister.

"The favor is for me." Chin raised, she gazed down at him with the innate haughtiness of a queen surveying her kingdom. "If you are disposed to assist me, that is."

His heart pounded hard at his first glimpse of her in many months. When he'd first known her, she'd been simply Mrs. Lilliana Warwick, a tradesman's widow. He'd entertained thoughts of taking her to wife. He hadn't understood then who she really was.

Coming to his feet, he managed to find his voice. "Lady Roslyn." He bowed. "You are looking very well."

She walked along the railing, one fine-boned hand drifting along the banister. "Am I?" She glided down the stairs in a lilac gown with a wide, rounded neckline that highlighted her porcelain décolletage and graceful neck. It had been more than a year since her husband's demise, and he was pleased to see she'd thrown off the blacks required of women in mourning.

"The boys fare well, I hope." Even to his own ears, his voice sounded distant, polite, strained. It had not always been so between them.

"They are thriving," she said. "Somerville is an excellent guardian to them."

"My sister is generous in her praise." The duke stood as his sister joined them. "I was not accustomed to the . . . erm . . . rambunctious nature of young boys, but I am learning."

As she passed Atlas to stand alongside her brother, a whiff of her perfume, the scent of jasmine and cloves that always evoked memories of her, momentarily teased him before vanishing—as ephemerally elusive as the lady herself.

He cleared his throat. "What is it that I can do for you, Lady Roslyn?"

She regarded him steadily with those autumn-hued eyes he so admired. Her dark hair, gathered up in a style he presumed to be of the latest fashion, framed sharp cheekbones and refined features set against ivory skin.

"There's been a murder," she said. "I hope you will help me find the killer."

Chapter Two

Atlas huffed an abrupt laugh of complete surprise. "Murder?"

"Yes," she said smoothly. "The victim's name is Gordon Davis. He was a clerk at a factory in Spitalfields, but he died at his lodging house in Bloomsbury."

"What possible interest could you have in this matter?" he asked. "A duke's daughter hardly travels in the same circles as a factory clerk."

A slight smile touched her lips. "My associations are not the usual ones, as you are aware."

He surmised that she referred not only to her late husband and the people she'd befriended during her turbulent marriage but also to Atlas himself. The two of them would never have met under ordinary circumstances; she was a daughter of one of England's most powerful families, while he, the lowly fourth son of a newly minted baron, was just barely a gentleman.

"What was your association with him?" he asked.

"Gordon Davis was the brother of my maid, Tacy."

"I see." That explained her interest.

"I have assured her that his killer will be brought to justice," she said. "That is why I hope you will assist me in this matter."

He stared at her. She couldn't possibly be serious. A woman of her stature couldn't traipse about town in search of a killer. The one time she had done so was an exception, an extraordinary circumstance. "The investigation of murder is best left to Bow Street."

"They're not interested." She waved a dismissive hand, her irritation apparent. "The inquest found Mr. Davis's death to be an accident."

Now he understood Lilliana's frustration. Bow Street runners received a nominal annual salary, but they supplemented their incomes with the statutory rewards they received with each arrest and successful conviction. If this factory clerk's death had been ruled an accident, then officially, there were no suspects and, more importantly, no potential monetary gain.

Atlas stole a look at the duke, whose expression remained inscrutable. Seeing no assistance from that quarter, he returned his attention to Lilliana. "While I am sorry for your maid's loss, neither of us is in any position to pursue a killer. We must leave that to the experts."

"What rot," she said coolly. "It isn't as though you haven't done it before. And quite successfully, I might add."

He had found her husband's killer, with her help, a year ago. "Those circumstances were entirely different."

"I am well aware."

"I was trying to keep my neck out of the hangman's noose." He spoke emphatically. "And yours as well, I might add." They'd both been suspects. So he, who had a talent for puzzles of all kinds, had taken it upon himself to find the murderer before the gallows found him. Or Lilliana.

"My lady's maid is distraught at the loss of her brother." She gave no indication that his show of vehemence affected her. "I have already promised to help her."

"I am sorry to disappoint you—" he began.

"So if I must investigate on my own," she continued as if he hadn't spoken, "I will certainly do so."

"You most certainly will not!" The flabbergasted retort escaped his mouth before he could even think to censor it.

She seared him with one of those haughty looks of hers. "That is not for you to decide."

Atlas looked to the duke for reinforcement. "Surely you do not approve of this madness?"

"My sister's mind is her own." His ducal equanimity still firmly in place, Somerville sipped his brandy. "Regrettably, it's a remarkably stubborn one."

Atlas released an incredulous huff. "That's all you have to say on the matter?"

"What else is there to be said?" The duke gave an elegant shrug of his well-dressed shoulders. "My sister's time among the plebeian masses caused her to develop an unfortunate affinity for them."

Atlas resisted the urge to glare at the man. He had no idea how much power Somerville exerted over his sister. The siblings had been separated as children only to be reunited last year after a decade apart. Still, he suspected his grace had far greater influence over Lilliana than he let on.

Refocusing on Lilliana, Atlas said, "If the coroner thinks this clerk's death was an accident, that could very well be the case."

She returned a skeptical look. "If he wasn't purposely poisoned, how would an otherwise healthy young man end up with a belly full of arsenic?"

He paused. "Arsenic?"

"Yes, a great deal of it from what I understand. And Tacy says her brother had enemies."

That piqued his interest. "Why did he have enemies?"

"Tacy says her brother was a handsome charmer who drew his share of jealousy."

Few people were murdered for their beauty. "Why was his death ruled an accident?"

"I've no idea." She tilted her head and spoke in deliberate tones. "It's quite a puzzle, don't you think?"

"Quite." He narrowed his eyes at her. She understood him far too well. His mind had already begun to filter through the pieces of the labyrinth she'd presented. A dead man who had enemies. A gut full of poison. He couldn't help but be intrigued. "A very interesting puzzle."

"I thought you would see it so," she said. "Will you help us now?"

His curiosity—his need to put things in order in his mind, to solve the potential puzzle she presented—overtook his sense of caution. "I suppose it wouldn't hurt to inquire a little further."

Her triumphant smile took his breath away.

⋆ ⋆ ⋆

Atlas decided to start with Ambrose Endicott, the Bow Street runner who'd almost succeeded in sending him to the gallows for the murder of Lilliana's husband. Fortunately, Atlas had managed to run the true killer to ground. Although their acquaintanceship had begun in an adversarial manner, Atlas had come to appreciate Endicott's shrewd intelligence.

He sent word to arrange a meeting, which took place the following day at the narrow house on Bow Street that served as the runners' headquarters. The current magistrate, the man Endicott reported to, lived abovestairs, while the boisterous court sessions took place on the ground floor.

Atlas made his way down the crowded, dim corridor, past Covent Garden prostitutes with brightly painted faces and raggedy pickpockets in tattered clothing waiting to go before the magistrate. The mingled odors of cheap perfume, perspiration, and unwashed bodies permeated the air, as did the vocal protestations of innocence from the inmates in the jail cells around back.

He was shown to a private room where Endicott sat at a scratched-up wooden table working on a report. The runner looked up, his fleshy face brightening when he spotted his visitor.

"Why, if it isn't Mr. Atlas Catesby, as I live and breathe." The runner heaved himself up from his compact chair to shake Atlas's hand. He was a ruddy-complexioned porcine man of about forty with sagging jowls and small black eyes set deep in his meaty face. "Back from your travels, are you?"

"Yes, I am returned recently." Atlas shook the man's hand. "Just three weeks past."

The runner gestured for him to take a seat at the table. "Where were you off to this time, if you don't mind my asking?"

Atlas settled himself on a hard chair. "I went to Jamaica."

"What is that like? Similar to the beaches in Brighton?"

Atlas shook his head. "No, quite different in fact. The sand is pure white and very smooth. The water is just about the bluest I've ever seen." As he described it, Atlas could almost feel the cool ocean lapping at his knees as the bright Jamaican sun warmed him. London's dour weather stood in sharp contrast to the island's splendid climate. "The water is so clear you can look down while standing in it and see the bright-colored fish swimming about your legs."

Endicott grimaced as he retook his seat. "I'm not overly fond of fish, at least not live ones, anywhere in the vicinity of my person."

"Then you might prefer the mountainous parts of the island and their dense forests."

"As long as there are no fish there." Endicott crossed his arms high over his ample girth. "What can I do for you? I presume this is not a social call."

"As I mentioned in my note, I am curious about the death of Gordon Davis. His fate is of great interest to a particular friend of mine."

"It was an accident. At least, that's what the coroner decided."

"But there was arsenic in his belly?"

"After receiving your note, I pulled the report and looked it over." Endicott reached for a file on the table and leafed through the individual report pages glued to narrow paper stubs. When he came to the relevant page, he tapped a pudgy forefinger against it. "Here it is. Arsenic, a great deal of it, was found in the man's belly."

"Black or white?" Chemists routinely colored the poison to prevent buyers from confusing the poison with everyday household items such as flour or sugar.

"White. It wasn't sooty arsenic, if that's what you're asking."

"Why would the coroner rule the death to be an accident if there was a large amount of poison in the man's stomach?"

"The man's friend"—he consulted the report—"one Henry Buller, testified that Davis routinely used arsenic to treat his asthma."

Atlas's brows lifted. "I wasn't aware of arsenic being used as a treatment for breathing ailments."

The detective shrugged. "I suppose some doctors believe it to be so."

"But what explains such a large amount of the toxic substance in his stomach?"

Endicott gave him a strange look. "You are aware of where the victim worked, are you not?"

Atlas wondered what he was missing. "I know he was a factory clerk."

"Yes, but do you know the type of factory?"

"No." His interest intensified. "Does it signify?"

"I'd certainly say so. Gordon Davis worked at a dye factory."

"I don't follow."

"Arsenic is routinely used in dyes and wallpapers. So you see," the runner said, "the man not only took arsenic, he was surrounded by the poison. Both at home and at work."

⋆ ⋆ ⋆

Atlas went directly from Bow Street to Spitalfields to visit the dead man's place of business.

He decided to travel on foot rather than hail a hackney. His destination wasn't far, and the weather, although on the chilly side for a late April day, was fine enough. Atlas preferred to walk whenever he was in London. His left foot, which he'd broken in several places eighteen months before, still pained him at times but, at the moment, seemed up to the demands being placed upon it.

Atlas enjoyed the solitude of walking alone; it gave him time to think. Unfortunately, the thoughts that accompanied him on the way to Spitalfields were not pleasant ones.

As he turned down Drury Lane, guilt over the evening he'd spent with Olivia Disher plagued him. He'd used his widowed landlady grievously, mostly to alleviate the unflagging morosity that had accompanied his return to London. She had been willing, certainly, and he had enjoyed her company, but he could see no future between them. And a true gentleman did not engage in a liaison with a respectable widow such as Mrs. Disher when he had nothing further to offer her.

He reached his destination forty-five minutes after starting out. Spitalfields was littered with tenement houses, workshops, and other small industries. Black slime slicked the malodorous streets, which were lined with once-gracious homes that had long since been divided into tiny rooms for poor laborers and their families.

Atlas paused before the building where Gordon Davis had worked. It was located not far from the Old Bengal Warehouse, a facility built about twenty years earlier to house the spices, cigars, tobacco, and tea imported by the East India Company. The Gunther & Archer Dye Company was a generously sized brick-front property that took up a good portion of the block. Atlas passed through the austere gateposts flanking the front entrance where a guard directed him to the front office, a tidy space accented with glass and wrought iron.

A young man at a standing desk looked up when Atlas entered. "May I help you, sir?"

"Good day." Atlas drew off his hat. "I hope so. My name is Atlas Catesby."

"How do you do, sir?" The clerk, who appeared to be in his midtwenties, was slim and small in stature with neatly combed short brown hair and even, if unremarkable, features. "I'm Henry Buller."

"Well met." He recalled that Buller was the name of the clerk who'd told authorities that Davis took arsenic. "Tell me, Henry, did you perchance work with Gordon Davis?"

The clerk regarded him with undisguised curiosity. "I did, sir." He stammered, "But he . . . ah . . . no longer works here."

"Yes, I am aware," Atlas said gently. "Did you know him well?"

Buller set his pencil down. "We worked together for almost a year and took a pint or two together from time to time."

"I am looking into Mr. Davis's death at the request of his family," Atlas said.

The boy shot a worried look at the closed door several feet behind his desk. Atlas presumed his employer sat behind it. "The coroner ruled that the death was an accident."

"Mr. Davis's sister does not believe that to be the case. She suspects he was killed. He did have a great deal of arsenic in his belly."

The door to the back office opened. A stocky, grizzled-looking man in shirt sleeves appeared. "Henry," he barked. "Have you entered my letters in the correspondence book?"

"Yes, Mr. Gunther. I'm almost done. I was just on my way to have them posted."

"Be quick about it." The gray-haired factory owner squinted in Atlas's direction, seeming to take notice of him for the first time. "Who are you?"

"I am Atlas Catesby. I was inquiring after Gordon Davis."

"He doesn't work here anymore."

"I'm looking into his death."

"Nobody here knows anything about that," the man responded in a distinctly unfriendly manner. Atlas detected a Germanic accent.

"I'm interested in learning about the arsenic you use in your dyes."

Gunther glared at him. "Davis was a clerk. He stayed in the front office. He was never around the dyes."

"Did he ever go out onto the floor?"

"Never. There was no need." He turned to look at the clerk, who still stood at his desk. "Buller," he snapped. "Get on with you!"

The younger man quickly gathered some papers. "Yes, Mr. Gunther, I'll go and deliver these right away."

Gunther said a few additional words to his clerk in German. The clerk nodded nervously and made his way out.

"You should go with him," Gunther said to Atlas. "There's nothing more to say, and I have work to do."

Seeing that there was no arguing with the man, Atlas made his good-byes and left the building, taking care as he crossed the miry street. He walked up a block and waited for about twenty minutes until he spotted the young clerk returning from his errand.

"Mr. Buller," Atlas called out.

A look of alarm crossed the younger man's face. "I really must return to work."

Atlas fell into step beside him. He towered over the clerk and, with his much longer legs, kept an easy pace beside the hurrying man. "What incident was Mr. Gunther referring to?"

Buller cut him a sidelong glance. "Pardon?"

"Before you left to deliver your letters, Mr. Gunther told you not to mention Mr. Davis or the incident to me."

Buller came to an abrupt halt. "You speak German?"

Atlas dipped his chin. "I do. I travel extensively." *And fortunately tended to pick up languages easily.* "How do you know German?"

"My mother is Mr. Gunther's cousin. That's how I obtained this situation. It's a very good position, and I don't want to lose my place at the factory by speaking out of turn."

"I have no interest in causing trouble for you, Henry, but I intend to get to the bottom of the matter of Mr. Davis's death. Just tell me what incident Gunther was referring to, and I'll be on my way."

Buller darted a nervous look around them. "I'm not supposed to talk to you."

"And no one will know that you have," he said encouragingly. "You said you were Mr. Davis's friend."

"Very well." Buller shot another furtive look around before taking a deep breath. "The factory floor manager caught Gordon stealing some of the arsenic used for the dyes."

"When was this?"

"About three weeks before he died."

"What happened after that?"

"Mr. Gunther tossed Gordon out as soon as the floor manager reported him, but then Mr. Archer hired him back."

"Mr. Archer." Atlas mused. "The man who co-owns the factory?"

"Aye."

"Why would he do that? Why retain a worker who has stolen from you?"

"I'm sure I cannot say."

"Didn't Mr. Gunther object?"

The clerk shook his head. "He couldn't say much. Even though Mr. Gunther runs the factory, Mr. Archer is the true owner. Gunther only has a thirty percent stake in the company. Whatever Archer wants, he gets, no matter how Gunther feels about it."

"Did Mr. Archer know Gordon Davis well? As the owner, is he often at the factory?"

"No, Archer comes rarely, maybe two or three days a month."

Atlas contemplated the clerk's revelations. It was deuced odd to keep on a man who'd stolen from you. He studied the clerk. "I presume Davis stole the arsenic to treat his asthma?"

Buller flushed. "I'm afraid I wasn't exactly truthful at the inquest."

"How do you mean? Are you saying Davis didn't take arsenic?"

"Oh, he took it all right. Just not for asthma."

"For what then?"

This time even the young man's ears turned a bright red. "To enhance his lustful activities."

Atlas stared at the man. "He took arsenic to heighten the pleasure he took in the carnal act?" This was a use for arsenic Atlas had never heard of.

"Not exactly. It was to make certain"—clearly embarrassed, Buller stammered through his answer—"that he would be . . . erm . . . prepared to perform when called upon."

"Did he have trouble in that area?" Atlas now felt a little uncomfortable himself. "Did his . . . er . . . equipment not work properly?"

"Gordon said everything down there worked as it should. It was just that his lady was a lustful wench, and he wanted to keep her satisfied." Buller lowered his voice. "Said the young lady wanted it two or three times a night."

Atlas heard the wondering tone in young man's voice. "Who was this young woman?"

"Gordon never said, but he was eager to marry her. He said giving her a good bedding would keep her coming back for more."

"Mr. Davis intended to wed this woman? You are certain?"

Buller nodded. "Oh, yes, he was determined. He had been jilted once before, you see, by a toff. Gordon said he had made certain that this time the betrothal would end with a wedding."

"Did he tell you anything else about this wealthy lady who jilted him? Her name, perhaps, or the neighborhood where she lived?"

"No, not that I recall. I had the impression she cried off in order to marry a title. It happened years ago." He glanced nervously in the direction of the Gunther & Archer Dye Company. "If that's all, I really must go."

"One more thing, Henry. What kind of arsenic is used in the dyes at the factory?"

Buller appeared confused. "Is there more than one kind?"

"I'm interested to know whether it's white or sooty."

"Ah, I see what you mean." Buller's wrinkled forehead smoothed. "The sooty kind, so that the workers don't confuse it with something else."

"I see. And did Mr. Davis also buy his own arsenic from other places?"

"I don't think so. Gordon said he'd taken enough arsenic from the factory to last him for several more months." He turned to go, obviously anxious about being seen on the street corner talking to Atlas. "I'm sorry I couldn't be of more assistance."

"You've been a great help, Henry," Atlas said, his mind pulling the disparate pieces of the puzzle together in a way that made sense. He waved the clerk on his way with great satisfaction.

"Far more than you realize."

Chapter Three

It was late afternoon by the time Atlas returned to his Bond Street apartments. The fashionable shopping area was at its most sedate at that time of day; the genteel ladies who frequented the exclusive establishments along the busy strand had long since retired to the protection of their homes.

Bond Street evenings were the provenance of young dandies who paraded along the stone walkways, visiting a gaming house or two or partaking in the feminine company offered at the discreet sporting hotels. The lack of signage advertising the carnal services offered within did little to hamper the brothels' ability to attract well-heeled clients.

Atlas's own apartments were located above a tobacconist on New Bond Street. Accommodations such as his were in great demand among modish young bucks, but Atlas had no interest in being fashionable. These were the first rooms he'd seen after injuring his foot in the carriage accident, when it became apparent his convalescence would take several months. At first, he'd recuperated at his sister's house, but there was only so much of Thea's managing nature he'd been able to bear before seeking a refuge of his own.

He tensed when he reached the tobacco shop's double-fronted bow window. He wondered if Olivia was still within. He'd returned from Jamaica a few weeks before to find that her husband, his former landlord, had met his demise during Atlas's absence. Now widowed, Olivia was his landlady, and he'd overstepped badly with her the previous evening. Now, he might not be able to rectify the error, but he could certainly apologize for it.

A wooden statue of an American Indian carrying a large smoking pipe greeted him as he entered the shop. Olivia stood at the long oak counter serving a patron. She wore a somber navy dress, and her fair hair, which the night before had spilled about her shoulders in generous waves, was now fashioned into a severe knot at the nape of her neck.

She turned and reached for one of the snuff-filled jars lining the shelves behind her—the movement highlighting the generous curves of her petite frame—and scooped a portion out for the man. Atlas waited patiently, pretending to examine the high-quality pipes and hand-blended tobaccos on display until the gentleman departed and they were more or less alone.

"Mr. Catesby." She smiled brightly, her manner betraying no sign of discomfort.

"Mrs. Disher," he said, feeling awkward. "I trust you are well."

"I think I know why you are here," she said pertly.

She certainly was direct. He swallowed. "Do you?"

She reached under the counter and produced a small brown packet. "The tobacco for your *nargileh* has arrived."

"Oh. I see." He exhaled. "My thanks." The tobacco was for the hookah pipe habit he'd acquired during his travels to

Constantinople, one of his favorites of all the exotic places he'd visited.

Months ago, his friend Charlton had remarked that the tobacconist's wife regarded Atlas with an especially appreciative eye. Upon his return from the islands, Atlas had learned not only of Mr. Disher's untimely death but also that Charlton had been correct about Mrs. Disher's interest in him.

"One of these days, I'd like to try that strange pipe of yours"—she handed him the packet—"to see why you favor it so. Perhaps it will prove to be an excellent addition to the smoking room." He glanced back at the wood-and-glass-paneled screen that separated the front of the shop from the smoke-hazed back room, where he spotted three patrons indulging their tobacco passions.

"You would be most welcome to do so." He cleared his throat, knowing he must disavow her of the notion that he expected their intimate relationship to continue. Remorse snaked through his guts. Now that Lilliana was back in his sphere, no matter how remotely, his dalliance with this woman felt like a betrayal.

"As to that," he began, lowering his voice, "I wish to beg your pardon in regards to last evening."

Merriment danced in her eyes. "I assure you, Mr. Catesby, you have naught to be sorry about in that area."

His cheeks heated. "I just wish to assure you that nothing of that nature will be repeated in the future."

"Be at your ease, Mr. Catesby. I don't have any expectations," she said easily. "I've just become a widow. The last thing I desire is to wed again and have another husband to answer to."

He relaxed, her lack of artifice reminding him of what had tempted him the previous evening when she'd stopped by to collect the rent. They'd gotten to chatting, and he'd invited her in for a glass of wine. He'd dismissed Jamie early, intending to focus on his latest puzzle, the most challenging one he'd attempted to date. But she'd accepted his offer, and the conversation had flowed easily from there, the evening growing late. One thing had led to another in the late stillness of the night when they'd relaxed and the usual proprieties no longer seemed to apply.

"Why, Mrs. Disher," he managed to tease, "I do believe you've used me abominably."

She leaned over the counter. "You didn't seem to mind overmuch last night."

He couldn't help but return her smile. He liked Mrs. Disher very much. She was uncomplicated, whereas he was usually drawn to more complex characters, to the unknown intricacies of everyday life that made people who they were and drove their actions. Studying these hints, putting together the clues, fascinated him. With Olivia Disher, there was none of that. In her, he found the lack of guile to be a refreshing change.

She was most undeserving of any uncharitable thoughts. She was a sunny presence who added warmth to his morose countenance. He preferred not to dwell on the cause of the peevishness that had dogged him during his entire trip to Jamaica.

Even long swims on sun-blessed beaches had done little to improve his distemper. The bleakness had persisted upon his return to London, and Olivia, with her natural warmth and good cheer, had been a temporary salve for his soul. "Well, thank you, I did enjoy last evening."

The bell above the door rang as it opened. Mrs. Disher turned her attention to the newcomer, effectively dismissing Atlas.

"Duty calls," she said cheerily and slipped away.

Relieved—although his conscience did not allow for him to feel completely exonerated where his dishonorable behavior with Olivia was concerned—Atlas left her and trudged up the narrow stairwell to his apartments above the shop.

The dark raised-panel door opened as soon as Atlas stepped onto the stone landing outside his rooms. Young Jamie, who had yet to see his twentieth year, greeted him.

"Good afternoon, sir." The boy's chest was puffed, his shoulders pulled back; he'd taken his recent valeting lessons very seriously. "The Earl of Charlton has come to call."

"Has he?" Handing off his hat and the package of tobacco from downstairs, Atlas crossed into the colorful sitting room. The apartments had come fully furnished with crimson carpets, bright-orange wallpaper, and stuffed chintz furniture. He found the earl comfortably ensconced in one of those stuffed chairs. His puce tailcoat shone bright against the furniture's sky-blue paisley upholstery as he puffed on Atlas's water pipe, the fragrant smoke floating through the air.

"Hello, Charlton."

The earl smiled as he held up the mouthpiece attached to the hookah's hose. "I hope you don't mind. I prevailed upon your valet to prepare the *nargileh* for us. Only I started without you."

Atlas shrugged out of his coat. "This is a surprise."

The earl regarded him with an arrogant lift of his eyebrow. "It shouldn't be so. We have an appointment to take dinner at my club."

"Damnation." Atlas rubbed a palm against his forehead. "I'd forgotten."

"Have you made other arrangements for this evening?" Mischief sparked in the earl's very blue eyes. "With the lovely Mrs. Disher, perhaps?"

Atlas stiffened. "I'm sure I have no idea what you're speaking of."

"I'm speaking of a voluptuous little handful who is very attainable now that she is a widow."

"You should mind your tongue when speaking of a respectable lady."

Amusement laced the earl's words. "Did you mind your tongue when you took her to bed?"

Atlas shot him a look. "Don't be absurd."

Charlton took a long drag off the hookah pipe and held the hose out for Atlas to take a turn. "I happened to be here when your lovely landlady came looking for the wrap she'd left here."

Atlas settled into the chair opposite his friend and reached for the proffered pipe hose. "Which means nothing. She came to collect the rents last evening, that is all."

"Ah. You two lovebirds really should get your Banbury tales straight." Charlton smirked. "She said she forgot it this morning. You say she came last evening. An intelligent man would draw inevitable conclusions when a bachelor entertains a widow in his rooms from the evening all the way through to the morning hours."

"Even if that were so, a true gentleman wouldn't speak of it."

Charlton rolled his eyes. "You can be dreadfully boring."

"I was referring to you," Atlas said pointedly before taking a lengthy draw from the *nargileh.* Settling back in his chair, Atlas allowed himself to enjoy the full effect of the mellow tobacco taste.

"In any case, I approve of the liaison." Charlton exhaled a breath of silvery smoke into the air. "You cannot live like a monk forever."

Having no desire to continue this line of conversation, Atlas changed the subject. "You'll be interested to learn that the reason

I forgot about our plans is because I've somehow managed to become involved in another murder investigation."

"A masterful diversionary tactic," the earl said languidly. But Atlas registered the interest that flared in his eyes. No one enjoyed a good *on-dit* more than his friend. "Do not tell me you've been accused of murdering someone again. The first time was tiresome enough."

"No, I've been asked to look into the death of a factory clerk." Atlas took another puff off the *nargileh*. "The coroner found his death to be accidental even though the man had a belly full of arsenic."

"Why would anyone willingly ingest that much arsenic?"

"There are medicinal reasons, apparently. A fellow clerk at the factory says the man used it to enhance his . . . erm . . . virility."

"Truly?" This time Charlton didn't bother to hide his interest. "I don't suppose you'd care to be more specific."

Atlas huffed a short laugh. "The dead man's name was Gordon Davis. Mr. Davis seemed to believe taking arsenic would enable him to be of immediate service when a particularly lustful lady came to call."

"Had trouble in that area, did he?"

"Not exactly." Atlas passed the hose back. "It seems his particular lady was very demanding and required multiple performances in each session."

Charlton whistled low. "Doesn't sound like much of a lady to me."

"I cannot say whether she is or not. I've yet to identify her. So far, she's something of a mystery."

They sat in companionable silence for a moment, taking turns with the hookah, until Charlton broke the silence. "You mentioned that someone had asked you to look into the libidinous clerk's death." When Atlas said nothing, his friend prodded further. "Who made this request of you?"

"The Duke of Somerville summoned me yesterday."

Charlton sat forward. "Somerville?" The earl and the duke were particular friends who traveled in the same high circles that Atlas did not. "I don't mean to be crass, but why would the duke care about a factory clerk?"

"The victim was the brother of Lilliana . . . Lady Roslyn's . . . maid. The duke's sister asked for my assistance."

"Ah." Charlton dropped back in his chair as comprehension dawned. "Rescuing the damsel in distress yet again, I see."

"Hardly." Atlas bit back a sharp retort at Charlton's assertion that he made of habit of coming to the aid of females in need.

He was hardly anyone's knight in shining armor. He hadn't even been able to save his own sister from her murderous husband. A wave of sorrow crashed over him, and he forced himself to breathe through the pain. Even after all these years, the reality of Phoebe's death hit him at unexpected times, like a runaway carriage, leaving him unable to gird himself against it.

"Lady Roslyn has just begun to go about in society again," Charlton was saying.

"I'm pleased to hear it." Atlas made an effort to focus on the conversation at hand. "That bastard husband of hers did not deserve to be mourned."

"Truer words were never said. As you can imagine, she does not want for suitors."

"Is that so?" Inhaling the *nargileh*'s smooth dulcet flavor, Atlas affected a disinterest he did not feel. "I suppose it's to be expected that she'll wed again. Is there a particular gentleman who has won her favor?"

"Roxbury spends a great deal of time in her company."

"Roxbury?" The unfamiliar name tasted like acid on his tongue.

"The Marquess of Roxbury. He's agreeable enough. She could do worse." Charlton eyed him with concern. "I do hope you'll have a care where Lady Roslyn is concerned."

Atlas did not miss the way his friend used the lady's formal name, the one she used in society. Charlton had been with Atlas when they'd first encountered the duke's sister, only they hadn't known then who she was. She'd been using her middle name, Lilliana, and that was how Atlas still thought of her. "There is nothing between us."

"There might have been had the circumstances been different."

"But they're not. In any case, I shall take care." His sense of self-preservation kicked in. He might be back in Lilliana's sphere, but that's as far as it went.

His temporary infatuation with her was over.

* * *

"I do believe it's possible that Gordon Davis was murdered."

The absolute confidence in Atlas's statement seemed to take Lilliana by surprise. "You've come to this conclusion in less than a day? Dare I ask if you've discovered the murderer as well?"

He suppressed a smile. "Not as of yet."

"Please." She swept a hand out, inviting him to take a seat. She'd received him in her sitting room, a sunny chamber she'd apparently refurbished to her own tastes after reuniting with her brother. It felt strange to be in her company after all this time. When they'd parted almost a year ago—around the same time she and the boys had come to live with the duke—she'd invited him to call on her, but he had not. There could be no future for a duke's sister and a man of modest means who was just barely a gentleman.

"What makes you so certain Mr. Davis was killed?" she asked as she settled upon her soft peach sofa.

He took the chair to her right, his brawny form filling the cream silk bergère. "The arsenic found in his body was white, the kind one could easily mistake for sugar or flour." He paused, his cheeks warming, before continuing. "The arsenic he took for his . . . erm . . . ailment . . . was sooty, as was the arsenic used at the factory where he worked."

"Ailment?" She tilted her head. "What ailment did he have?"

"There are conflicting reports. According to the coroner's report, it was asthma."

"Could it have killed him?"

He cleared his throat. "I thought I could speak with your maid. Perhaps she can tell us more about her late brother's health."

She rang for the footman and instructed him to locate Tacy and bring her to the sitting room. While they waited for her maid, Lilliana inquired about his travels.

"I was in Jamaica." He proceeded to describe the island, telling her about the local culture, mountainous forests, and pristine beaches. "The climate is beautiful there," he said in conclusion. "I was able to swim every day."

"That explains the color in your face," she remarked. When they'd first met, he'd been quite pale, a result of recuperating indoors for several months following his injury. "Very un-English of you."

"My brother the baron would agree with you. He often despairs of my heathenish tendencies."

"Will you go abroad again soon?"

"In a couple of months, I hope. I may go to India."

She uttered a sound of surprise. "That is very far away."

"Indeed. The journey can take upward of six months."

They were distracted by the arrival of the footman bearing the tea tray. The lady's maid appeared shortly thereafter.

"Tacy," Lilliana said to the woman, "this is Mr. Catesby. As you know, he has agreed to look into your brother's death."

"I'm grateful, sir," Tacy said to Atlas. "I truly am." She was a short round woman of about forty with ruddy cheeks and smiling eyes.

"I am sorry for your loss," he began gently. "May I ask you some questions?"

Tacy stood awkwardly before them, twisting a fistful of her starched apron between the hands clasped in front of her. "If you think it'll help my Gordy, I'm happy to answer anything you'd like to know."

Lilliana scooted forward to pour the tea. "Please sit, Tacy."

"Oh, I couldn't, my lady." She shook her head. "It wouldn't be proper."

Atlas leaned forward. "Did your brother have any illnesses or chronic conditions?"

"No, sir. He was healthy, he was."

Lilliana replaced the teapot on the silver tray. "What about lung illnesses, such as asthma?"

Tacy's eyebrows hooded over her eyes. "No, my lady. Nothing like that. My Gordy was as fit as they come."

Lilliana shot a look at Atlas, her surprise evident. He was not surprised, given what Buller, the clerk, had shared with him about the true reason for Gordon Davis's arsenic use.

"Were you close to your brother?" he asked.

"Oh, yes, I practically raised him after our ma died." Her eyes watered. "He was seven years younger than me. I never expected him to go first."

"I understand your loss." He spoke softly. "I lost my sister many years ago."

A sense of shared grief passed between them, even though Tacy was a servant and he a gentleman. In that moment, their common loss bonded them in a way that had nothing to do with class or wealth.

Tacy sniffled and lowered her gaze. "Yes, sir. Then you know it's a terrible thing."

Atlas nodded. "The very worst." He paused a beat before continuing. "What did your brother tell you about the young woman he hoped to marry?"

Her eyes rounded. "You heard about that?"

He nodded. "What do you know about her?"

"Very little." She spread her hands, palms up. "Except that he expected to wed her."

"Isn't that unusual," Lilliana interjected, "for your brother not to tell you more about his intended?"

"He said she was from a fine family and that their acquaintance had to be kept a secret until her father would agree to the match."

"Did he tell you anything else about her?" Atlas pressed. "Anything at all? Are you certain she really existed?"

"Oh, yes." She nodded her head vigorously. "Gordon was uncommonly handsome. All the girls were drawn to him. Young and old. High and low. He lost a position in a fine house once when the young lady of the house became too familiar with him."

"What house was this?" Atlas asked.

"Lord Merton's."

"Viscount Merton?" Lilliana asked.

The maid nodded in sharp, indignant motions. "Gordy was let go without reference. As if it was his fault the young lady behaved in a forward manner."

"I see." Atlas forced an expression of polite impassivity even though Tacy's brother struck him as an unsavory character. "One of your brother's acquaintances tells me that Mr. Davis was once betrothed to a wealthy young woman who jilted him."

Tacy blinked. "No, sir. He must be mistaken. My brother was never betrothed before."

"You mentioned to Lady Roslyn that your brother had enemies?"

She nodded vigorously. "Gordy told me as much. He said people resented him on account of his charm and good looks."

Gordon Davis had certainly thought highly of himself. "Did he mention anyone in particular who might have wanted to harm him?"

Tacy sniffled. "No, sir."

He asked the maid a few more questions. When he was done, Lilliana dismissed the woman and turned to him. "I presume you will wish to speak with Lord Merton."

"I would, yes." He grimaced. He had only a passing acquaintance with Jermyn Fenton, the Viscount of Merton. "But I can hardly ask the man about a servant who might have dallied with his daughter."

She sipped her tea. "Especially not now, with the Season getting under way in earnest."

"How does that signify?" He was not familiar with the particulars of the Season, a period of months when London's finest families engaged in a whirlwind of festivities and social engagements to entertain themselves while parliament was in session.

The Catesbys were not deeply entrenched in the upper echelons of society. Although they could trace their roots back to King Edward III—as Charlton was so fond of pointing out—the family had been untitled until about twenty years ago when Atlas's father, a celebrated poet, had been awarded a barony.

"What does the Season have to do with my speaking with Lord Merton?" he asked her.

"Lord Merton only has one daughter—Lavinia," she explained. "The girl is in her second Season and no doubt hopes to land a husband this year."

Now he understood. "Any rumors of her dallying with a servant would not assist in that endeavor."

"Precisely," she said with a sharp nod. "Therefore, you may speak with Lord Merton here."

"Where here?" he asked blankly.

"Somerville is hosting his main entertainment for the Season in a few days' time." She raised her teacup from its saucer, pausing just before it reached her lips. "He prefers to get it over with before the Season begins in earnest, now that Easter has come and gone. Naturally, you must attend."

"Naturally." He began to see where she meant to lead him. It took him a moment longer than it should have because he was unused to viewing Lilliana as part of the aristocracy, which was ridiculous considering their sumptuous surroundings. Apart from the plush furnishings, priceless paintings adorned the walls, and equally precious artifacts graced the gleaming tabletops.

Lilliana gave every appearance of being at ease in this imposing space, inhabiting it all as easily as he slipped into his comfortable old dressing gown. It was no wonder. She was the sister of a duke and, as Somerville was unwed, no doubt served as the ducal hostess as well.

"Lord Merton is to be one of your guests," he said. It was not a question.

"Precisely. And while you speak with him, I shall have a friendly chat with his daughter, Lady Lavinia, in an attempt to ascertain if there is any truth to what Tacy says about her brother and the young lady."

"It certainly seems as though Mr. Davis made a habit of dallying with young ladies who were above his station. That could certainly earn one enemies."

"More than one young lady?" She sipped her tea. "Maybe Lord Merton's daughter and the mysterious woman Mr. Davis intended to marry are one and the same."

He shifted in his seat. "I would be surprised if that were the case."

"Would you?" She regarded him with open curiosity. "Why? It makes perfect sense for the two to be the same woman."

He puffed out his cheeks and then exhaled. "It is my understanding that Mr. Davis was rather . . . erm . . . rather well acquainted . . . extremely so . . . intimately . . . with the mystery woman he hoped to marry."

"I see." She took a moment to consider his revelation. "How scandalous."

"Indeed." He gulped his tea. "I rather doubt the daughter of a peer would be left without a chaperone long enough to engage in . . ."

Her lips twitched with amusement. "Really, Atlas, you hardly have to protect me from the indecent aspects of the case. I am a widow after all." She regarded him over the rim of her porcelain cup. "Besides, the unseemly details tend to be the most intriguing. Please be frank, and do stop trying to protect my sensibilities."

He released a breath. "As you wish."

"So was Mr. Davis taking arsenic or not?" she asked. "Tacy said he didn't suffer any lung ailments."

"Yes, I do believe he was taking it. He was caught stealing the poison at the factory."

"Why would he do that?" she asked. "What was he taking arsenic for?"

He looked away, breaking eye contact. "For amorous reasons."

"Amorous reasons? I don't understand."

He stood, still avoiding her gaze. "That is just as well." The words were rather sharp. "Rest assured, I don't plan to explain it to you in any great detail. I have my limits while in polite company."

She came to her feet as well. "Are you leaving?"

"Has Tacy collected her brother's things from his boardinghouse? I'd like to have a look at them."

"No. As a matter of fact, she has asked for some time off tomorrow afternoon to go and collect them."

"I should like to go and have a look around before she packs everything up."

"Certainly," Lilliana said. "I'll come too."

Chapter Four

The lodging house where Gordon Davis had lived and died was located on a narrow lane off Great Russell Street in Bloomsbury. The neighborhood was no longer fashionable, but the size and quality of the homes—despite their definite air of decay—assured that Bloomsbury would never fall into complete disrepair in the manner of Seven Dials to the south.

A testament to the area's respectability was the fact that Atlas's sister lived several streets away. Thea, a mathematician who was always grappling with one equation or the other, preferred to reside among the upper-middle-class doctors, lawyers, and architects who inhabited some of the quarter's finer homes rather than in very fashionable Mayfair, where her husband, Charles Palmer, had wanted to take a house.

The lodging house was old-fashioned in appearance, the carpets threadbare, the curtains worn and faded from decades of use. The residence was clean and tidy, with an upright and conservative air, not unlike the landlady who greeted Atlas and Lilliana before leading them up the stairs to Davis's room.

"A terrible shock it was," said Mrs. Norman when they reached the landing. "He'd been ill for a few days, complaining of terrible stomach pains."

"Did you summon a doctor?" Lilliana asked. She looked incredibly elegant and expensive. From the first, Lilliana had always been flawless in her dress and appearance, but her husband had not provided her with gowns made of the finest fabrics, as her brother now did.

"I didn't call for the doctor until that last evening," the landlady replied. "I had been out all day, staying out much later than is my usual habit. When I did arrive home, I found Mr. Gordon had become much worse, so I insisted on summoning the doctor."

"What happened when the doctor came?" Atlas stepped onto the landing behind the women. "Was he able to provide any relief?"

"He administered morphine." The landlady led them down the wide corridor of the once-grand home, where the soft green paint was cracked and faded. Her voice became more hushed. "But it did no good. By morning, Mr. Davis was gone. I have always thought that if I'd come home earlier, as I usually did, then perhaps that agreeable young man might have been saved."

"You cannot blame yourself," Lilliana said kindly.

Atlas hesitated before asking the question that had been on the tip of his tongue since they'd arrived. "Did Mr. Davis receive many visitors? A young lady, perhaps, who might have visited Mr. Davis's room?"

The older woman pinned him with a sharp look. "Absolutely not. I run a respectable house. No ladies are ever allowed abovestairs. Unless, of course, they are married residents. We have couples here, but we do not allow children. The couples live down a separate hall."

Lilliana patted the woman's arm. "It is obvious to anyone who visits here that this is a respectable house."

Mrs. Norman appeared somewhat mollified. "Mr. Davis did not have visitors, but he was in the habit of receiving letters. A great many of them, all in the same hand."

"Did he ever mention who they were from?" Atlas inquired.

"No, not that I recall. Toward the end, those last few weeks, the correspondence slowed down considerably, which seemed to upset Mr. Davis."

Lilliana, who'd been listening intently, said, "We have heard that Mr. Davis had a special friend, a lady he hoped to marry."

"He did mention a young lady." Mrs. Norman's expression softened. "He cared for her a great deal. So much so that Mr. Davis said he would forgive her if she tried to poison him."

Atlas and Lilliana exchanged a startled look. "I beg your pardon," Lilliana said. "Did Mr. Davis believe his beloved was trying to kill him?"

Mrs. Norman pressed her thin lips together until they all but vanished. "He said he couldn't imagine why he felt so ill after drinking the chocolate she'd served him. That was when he said he loved her so much that he would forgive her even if she'd poisoned him."

"When was this?" Atlas said.

"About a fortnight before he passed."

Lilliana's delicate brow furrowed. "But why would she try to kill him if they were in love?"

Mrs. Norman clasped her hands together in front of her thick waist. "I didn't credit it at the time. I thought perhaps the illness was making him feverish and confused." She stopped before a closed door. "I cannot imagine any young woman turning Mr. Davis away. He was such a handsome and agreeable man. Charmed everyone who knew him." She paused. "Except perhaps Mr. Perry."

"Who is Mr. Perry?" Atlas wanted to know.

"One of my tenants. He lives on the east hall with his wife, where my married couples reside. The rooms are a little bit bigger there." She pushed the door open. "Here it is, Mr. Davis's room."

The landlady stepped aside to let them enter, which Lilliana did, while Atlas paused in the doorframe. The house might have been old, but it had stately bones and generously sized chambers. A neatly made four-poster bed dominated the space. The carpet was ragged but clean. The room was also furnished with a dresser and small scratched-up escritoire with a hard chair that had seen better days. Books, papers, and notebooks were neatly stacked on the table. An old stuffed chair was positioned before the empty fireplace. For a man of his station and resources, Mr. Davis had lived in relative comfort.

Lilliana crossed over to the desk for a closer look at the books and papers, but Atlas held in place, eager to learn more about the man who had found Mr. Davis less than charming. "Did this Mr. Perry have a quarrel with Mr. Davis?"

Mrs. Norman sighed. "He accused Mr. Davis of untoward behavior toward Mrs. Perry. It was all nonsense, of course. Mr. Perry is a terribly jealous man. Mr. Davis intended to marry his young lady. He would not look at another woman."

Lilliana looked up from the notebook she was thumbing through. "Mr. Davis told you that he hoped to wed. Did he say when?"

"He did not."

"Do you know if he visited his betrothed?" Atlas asked.

She wrinkled her nose. "He often went out late at night. Since he carried on a private correspondence and I knew he expected to wed soon, I never inquired too closely as to where he went in the late hours."

Atlas wanted to ask more about Mr. Perry, the jealous upstairs neighbor; however, before he could question her further, the landlady excused herself, saying she had to attend to matters in the kitchen. After she'd gone, Atlas turned to find Lilliana regarding him with twinkling eyes. "He was certainly popular with the ladies, our Mr. Davis."

He couldn't help but agree. "We may have no end of suspects at this rate."

"Indeed." She reached for a notebook and thumbed through it, methodically going through the things on Davis's table as she spoke. "Jealous husbands, angry fathers. The list of suspects could go on and on."

Atlas wondered how many women Davis had been courting at the same time. He began to see why the dead man had felt he needed to take arsenic to enhance his stamina. "Thus far, there are at least three, maybe four women we know him to possibly have been involved with."

"Four women?"

He counted them off on his fingers. "The upstairs neighbor, Lord Merton's daughter, the mystery woman he was seeing when he died, and the wealthy woman Davis's colleague said was once his betrothed but jilted him before the wedding."

"But Tacy said he hadn't been betrothed before."

"Maybe he never told her."

"Possibly five women." She looked up from the open notebook in her hand. "I believe I've found Mr. Davis's journal."

He went immediately to her side. The notebook was of surprisingly good quality, with a red morocco binding and white vellum pages trimmed in what appeared to be gold leaf.

"That's a fine notebook for a lowly clerk," he observed.

"It seems our Mr. Davis had a taste for the better things in life."

"And possibly aimed to marry money so that he could indulge those tastes." He peered down at the notebook in her hands. "What does it say?"

She thumbed through the log. "There are only a few entries. It looks like he started it shortly before he died."

He read over her shoulder, standing close enough for the fleeting scent of jasmine and cloves to tease his nostrils. There were only eleven entries, which primarily catalogued Davis's declining health in the three weeks leading up to his death. Davis wrote of suffering bouts of illness twice immediately after visiting his beloved, referred to only as *Lady L.* The last entry was dated the evening before Davis's death:

This evening I took chocolate with my beloved and reveled in what little time we can spend in each other's company . . .

"Well," Lilliana said. "This certainly corroborates what the landlady said."

He nodded gravely. "That Mr. Davis suspected the woman he loved was poisoning him." He surveyed the chamber. "Now we must see if there is anything here that will help lead us to her."

They proceeded to go through all of the dead man's personal effects, everything in his wardrobe or stored under the bed. Unfortunately, the desk drawers were locked.

"No letters," Lilliana observed.

"And no arsenic. If he took such a large quantity of the poison, we should find it somewhere in this room."

"Do you think he locked it up in his escritoire?"

"It makes perfect sense," Atlas said. "Now all we must do is find the key."

While Lilliana went in search of the landlady to ask after the keys to the desk, Atlas seized the opportunity to seek out the dead man's jealous neighbor. He wandered through the corridor until he came upon a male boarder who directed him to the area of the lodging house where the married couples resided.

He found Mrs. Perry alone in the rented room she shared with her husband. The space was larger than Davis's accommodations, but the condition of the furnishings was similar.

"I am sorry," she said after he had introduced himself, "but my husband has gone out."

Although he had hoped to speak with Mr. Perry, Atlas welcomed the opportunity to question the man's wife. The landlady had said Davis and Mr. Perry had fallen out over the latter's wife. Mrs. Perry did not look like a woman who ignited men's passions. She was a little thing, somewhat homely, very thin, with faded features except for the curved pointed nose that dominated her narrow face.

"I am assisting Mr. Davis's sister in sorting through her late brother's belongings," he told her, hoping to strike up a conversation.

"It's a very sad thing," she said. "He was such a young man."

"Were you well acquainted with Mr. Davis?"

"We spoke on occasion."

"May I ask about what?"

She tilted her head to the side as she studied him. "What is your interest in my association with Mr. Davis?"

He decided to speak honestly. "Mr. Davis's sister believes her brother's death was no accident."

Her eyes widened slightly. "Oh, I see." With a motion of her hand, she invited him to sit. He took one of the ladder-back chairs tucked neatly under the small scarred table while she slipped into the other. "I do not know if I can be of any help to you, but I shall try."

"Perhaps we could begin with you telling me what you thought of Mr. Davis?"

"He was a very agreeable young man."

Mr. Davis had certainly had a way with women. Atlas could not think of an acceptable way to ask her how agreeable she had found the dead man, so he tried a different approach. "And did your husband think well of your fellow boarder?"

"Mr. Perry mistakenly assumed that Mr. Davis had designs on me." She spoke with calm certainty. "But he could not have been more wrong."

"How can you be so certain?"

She gave a slight closemouthed smile. "Because Mr. Davis was betrothed. He had no interest in someone like me."

Davis certainly hadn't been shy about sharing his romantic hopes with people. "What did he tell you about the young woman he hoped to marry?"

"Very little, but it was apparent that Mr. Davis was very attached to her."

"Do you have any idea who she is?"

"No, none." She paused. "Though, in the last fortnight before he died, there was a change in him."

"How so?"

"Mr. Davis felt he detected a cooling in her ardor for him, and it upset him greatly."

The door swung open. "What is this?" a rough male voice asked.

Atlas stood to greet the grizzled middle-aged man who appeared to be at least a decade older than his wife. "Mr. Perry, I presume?"

"That's right." The man shut the door with a noisy bang behind him. "You're a stranger to me. Why are you alone with my wife?"

"This is Mr. Catesby." Mrs. Perry came to her feet as well. "He is looking into Mr. Davis's death."

Perry's nose wrinkled. "He was a snake, that one. Always sniffing after things that didn't belong to him."

His wife exhaled quietly, wearily. "I have told my husband that Mr. Davis was not interested in me."

"Why wouldn't he be?" her husband returned gruffly, sounding indignant on his wife's behalf. "You're the finest woman I know."

She blushed prettily at the compliment. "Mr. Perry knows he is the only man for me," she told Atlas. "As for Mr. Davis, he was looking to marry high. He said his betrothed was a gently raised young woman from a family of social standing."

"But it was probably her handsome dowry the cur found most appealing." Mr. Perry made a rude sound. "Davis was always looking above himself. He thought he could woo a woman with his pretty face and prettier manners. I suspect the fathers were not as easy to win over."

"That is true," his wife agreed. "Mr. Davis said his betrothal must be kept secret until his lady's father could be made amenable to the match."

Atlas considered her words. If Davis had been bedding his betrothed, perhaps he'd hoped to get her with child in order to force the union upon her reluctant family. "Did you ever see a young lady visit him here?"

"No," said Mrs. Perry. "Mrs. Norman is very strict about unwed boarders entertaining visitors in their bedchambers."

"I will walk you out," Mr. Perry said abruptly. Atlas thanked the man's wife for her time before following her husband out the door.

Perry remained quiet until they reached the stairs. "I saw Davis once with a young lady."

"She visited him here?"

The other man shook his head. "I saw them just the one time, walking near the Strand. It was before we had words about my wife. Davis pretended not to see me and steered the young woman in the opposite direction."

Atlas's skin tingled. Here was a possible clue as to the mystery woman's identity. "What did she look like?"

"Average. Perhaps even a little plain. But she was finely dressed and carried herself like a prize."

"Her hair color?"

"I don't recall. She wore a hat."

"If you saw her again, do you think you'd recognize her?"

"Possibly." Perry considered for a moment. "Yes, I think I could. I never forget a face. Even an unremarkable one."

Atlas asked a few more questions about the mystery lady's appearance but learned nothing more. After thanking Perry for his help, Atlas went down to meet up with Lilliana. He found her waiting for him in the front hall. "Any luck with the keys?" he asked.

"None. I hope Tacy has them. Did you have any luck with Mr. Perry?"

He shot her a surprised look. "How did you know that I went to speak with him?"

"Please. It is the obvious next step in the investigation." She practically rolled her eyes at him but was too much of a lady to actually do so. "Shall we go and see if Tacy has the keys? And you can tell me what you have learned."

* * *

Tacy did have the keys to her brother's escritoire, so Atlas and Lilliana returned the following afternoon to resume their search of Gordon Davis's things.

There were two locked drawers, and Atlas discovered a stack of letters bound together by a ribbon. He pulled at the ribbon, untying it so that the letters separated. He noted that they were written by a different hand than Davis's journal.

My dearest beloved pet, began one of them. He rifled quickly through the others and saw they also began with intimate endearments: *Dearest and beloved, I hope you are well* and *My dear sweet Gordon, I am sorry I cannot see you this week.*

Anticipation coursed through his blood. "I do believe we have found our mystery lady's letters to Mr. Davis."

Lilliana, who'd been searching the drawer on the opposite side of the escritoire, straightened, abandoning her task. "Who is she?"

He continued to go through the letters. "She hasn't signed any of them with her full name." He paused at one. "Now this is intriguing."

She came up next to him. "What is?"

He handed her the letter. "She signs it 'Mrs. Davis.'"

She studied the signature. "Do you think they married in secret?"

"Perhaps." They each took one of the hard chairs at the battered table and began to read through the letters. Each was signed either as *Your beloved wife, Mrs. Davis*, or simply, intriguingly, just with the single letter *L*.

Lilliana looked up. "Lord Merton's daughter is called Lavinia. She could be the mysterious Lady L."

"It makes sense. Davis certainly claimed an association with the young lady, to his sister at least. But then again, there are many names that begin with *L*." He smiled. "Lilliana, for instance."

She arched a brow. "Am I to be a suspect yet again?"

"I'll be certain not to make any mention of this to Endicott," he said with dark humor. He held up the letter he'd been reading. "This could be a secret code. *L* might be a private name Davis and his young lady shared only between themselves that no one else knew of."

"Do you think if we discover who Lady L is that we will have found Mr. Davis's killer?"

Atlas didn't look up from the letter in his hand. "I think she is our most likely suspect at the moment."

"Then I suppose we should keep reading and see what clues there are to be found." They read quietly for several minutes until Lilliana broke the silence.

"Oh, my." She put a hand to her chest.

Atlas glanced up from the letter he was reading. "What is it?"

She swallowed, her color high, the delicate cords in her neck sliding under porcelain skin. "Some of the letters are rather . . . amorous."

He took the missive from her, his attention going directly to the passage she pointed out to him:

> *Our intimacy is not wrong, my dear love, as I am your wife in the eyes of God—so it has been no sin our loving of each other . . . I ache for the day when we will always be together . . .*

"Well." He felt his face warming. "This seems to confirm reports of great intimacy between them, which suggests that maybe they did marry."

She was already reading another letter. "Or perhaps not." She handed it to him.

> *I am as much your wife as if we'd been wed a year . . . your visit last night was astonishing . . . how I longed for you. Only you can answer the ache in me. I can never be the wife of another after our intimacy.*

"It does not make sense for her to be the murderer." Lilliana's finely arched brows drew together. "If she loved him so, why would she kill him?"

He thought of what Mrs. Perry had said, that Davis worried his betrothed's feelings had changed. "Some love affairs cool."

Their eyes met for a moment before he rose and paced away. "These letters are ruinous to the girl, should they become public."

"Perhaps that is why she did not sign them with her true name."

He faced her. "You think she did not trust him to keep their secret?"

"I think it is possible. A woman's good reputation is all she has." Lilliana reached for another letter and focused on it. "Let's see what else there is to learn." Atlas retook his seat, and after several minutes, Lilliana found what she was looking for.

"Now this," she said, "could be a motive for murder."

Chapter Five

Atlas set aside the letter in his hands. "What have you found?"

Lilliana's eyes sparkled with excitement. "It seems Mr. Davis was keen to end the affair."

"Truly?" Atlas felt a jolt of contempt for Davis. For a man to take a young girl's innocence with the full intention of taking her to wife was one thing. To take her maidenhood and then jilt her was quite another. "If so, he was a scoundrel of the lowest sort."

"She detects that his feelings are no longer engaged." Lilliana looked to the letter and began reading Lady L's missive out loud:

> *I am truly astonished that you returned your letter to me. It will be your last opportunity to do so. Since you are displeased with my letters, our correspondence should cease immediately. You may have detected a coolness in me, and that is because my love for you has ceased.*

"It seems to have ended badly," Atlas said, stating the obvious. "On both parts."

Lilliana's eyes met his. "Even more badly than you think." She continued reading:

I trust your honor as a gentleman that you will never reveal what has passed between us. I shall be obliged if you would return all of my letters to me. Please bring them to the gate Tuesday evening at seven. I know you will comply with what I ask.

Atlas sat back in the chair, considering the implications of the letter. "It appears our mysterious Lady L was fully aware of the ruin that awaited her should these missives become public."

"Perhaps Mr. Davis intended to return them as she asked. Maybe he died before he had the chance." She turned the letter over, examining it. "There is no date on this."

"If Mr. Davis refused to return the missives, I do believe, as you have said, that the lady had a strong motive to kill him."

Skepticism filled Lilliana's refined face. "It seems a very poor plan indeed. If she were to kill him, someone else was bound to find the letters . . . as we have done."

"We are, presumably, talking about a very young girl. Perhaps an inexperienced one until her association with Davis."

"And young girls can make very foolish decisions." She shot him a wry look. "I am certainly proof of that." She no doubt referred to her unfortunate marriage at the tender age of sixteen.

"I disagree." He spoke with feeling. "You were barely more than a girl when you found yourself in a most precarious situation. Not many sheltered orphaned daughters of dukes would be enterprising enough to retain a position as a shopgirl. You knew nothing of the outside world, yet you found a respectable way to survive."

Surprise lit her eyes, perhaps because he'd spoken so vehemently in her defense. "Still my champion." She smiled softly. "As ever."

He stared at the letter in her hand. "I wonder if our mysterious Lady L has a champion. Someone who would be determined to protect her honor."

"Someone who learned she'd been ruined and was outraged, who might be driven to kill for her?" She rested her chin in her hand, her gaze far off as she contemplated. "But would such a person have left the letters behind?"

"What if this person didn't know of their existence?" He absently straightened the papers scattered on the worn table as he considered the possibilities. "What if he—or she, for that matter—believes that by killing the offender, all traces of the offense itself have been wiped out?"

"She?" Lilliana mused. "Do you truly think the killer could be a woman?"

"It was death by arsenic," he said. "Poison is said to be a woman's weapon."

"I wonder if it is men who say that," Lilliana replied, her tone as tart as a lemon pasty.

He cracked a smile. "It is more than likely."

Lilliana wasn't one to allow dubious assertions to go unchallenged. Her experience with her late husband—and the laws that had given him all right over her and their two children—seemed to have sharpened her sensitivity to the lot of women in society.

Atlas felt the need to defend himself in order to keep her good opinion. "I suppose, given the brutish nature of men, I assumed we would most naturally respond to provocation by resorting to physicality and violence, say with a good throttling or a bullet."

"And if the man is a coward who prefers not to come face-to-face with his adversary?"

He laughed out loud then, recalling how much he'd admired her keen intellect and quick wit when they'd first met. "Point taken. I stand corrected. Our killer could be a man or a woman."

★ ★ ★

Noel Archer, controlling owner of the Gunther & Archer Dye Company where Gordon Davis had worked, lived in Clapham, in the southwest part of the city. The district was perhaps best known as an enclave for social reformers—well-to-do residents who fought to abolish slavery and child labor in England.

Clapham was also favored by wealthier merchants. Over the past twenty years or so, they'd built gracious houses that fit snugly around the common. The Archer home, a large modern brick structure set behind a hedged front garden, was one of these newer additions.

Atlas alighted from the hackney, pulling his dark greatcoat more tightly around him. The unusually late spring chill had persisted, and dampness filled the air. As he approached the iron front gate, a feminine voice called out to greet him.

"Good day, sir."

He turned to find two well-dressed young women strolling toward him with their arms linked, their cheeks healthy with color brought on by the brisk weather. A black-clad maid trailed behind them.

"Have you come to call on Papa?" the shorter of the two girls asked cheerfully. He saw that a slingshot dangled from her free hand.

"If your father is Mr. Archer, then yes, I have."

"He is," the girl responded. Atlas guessed her to be around fifteen years of age. "I am Harriet, and this is my sister, Elizabeth."

"Harriet!" her sister hissed with a visible tug of the younger girl's arm. "You mustn't talk to strangers in the street." Elizabeth—clearly the older of the two—was a plainer, less vibrant version of her sister.

"Pish." The censure from her elder sibling didn't appear to bother young Harriet, an energetic pixie of a girl, who apparently had a tendency to be outspoken. "He's obviously a gentleman, and he's come to call on Papa, so he's hardly a stranger."

He drew off his hat to introduce himself. "Atlas Catesby."

Elizabeth paused for a moment, studying him. She appeared to be several years older than her sister, perhaps around twenty. The girls shared fair complexions with rosy cheeks and strawberry-blonde hair. "Catesby?"

"At your service," he affirmed.

"Are you . . . per chance . . . any relation to Silas Catesby?"

"He was my father."

Her gray eyes lit up, enlivening an otherwise unremarkable visage. "My goodness. What an honor it is to meet you."

"I'm afraid I cannot claim any credit for my father's talent. Our connection was a fortunate accident of birth." He'd become accustomed to effusive reactions at the mention of his father. Silas Catesby had been a brilliant, talented man whose poetry was among the greatest England had ever produced.

Harriet aimed her slingshot across the common. "There's Old Man Miller. I wager I could hit him right in the backside."

"Harriet!" Elizabeth exclaimed.

"What?" Harriet protested. "I'm an excellent shot, and you know it."

"That is quite beside the point," her sister admonished. "Put that thing away. Everyone will think you're an uncivilized hoyden."

Harriet lifted her chin. "I would take that as a compliment. Being ladylike is ever so tiresome."

Atlas suppressed a smile. He liked the younger girl's spirit.

Elizabeth cast him an apologetic look. "Please do come in." She sidled past him to push the gate open. "I believe Papa is at home to visitors."

Amusement danced in Harriet's eyes as she lowered her weapon. "I thought we are not supposed to talk with strangers."

Elizabeth shot her younger sister a daggered look. "This is Mr. Catesby. His father was one of England's greatest poets."

"Truly?" Harriet looked only half interested. "Are you a great poet as well, Mr. Catesby?"

"Unfortunately not." Atlas did write long letters to his sister Thea when he was abroad; he also kept a meandering journal of his travels, but he was no Silas Catesby. Few people were. "My father did not pass his talents on to his children," he said with a smile. "Though I would not have minded if he had."

They went past the gate to the curved Doric front porch. He followed the young ladies through the glazed burgundy front door, entering perhaps the newest home he'd ever visited. Elizabeth directed the servant who greeted them to bring in a tea tray and dispatched young Harriet to go and tell their father he had a caller.

Elizabeth showed Atlas to a drawing room with large sash windows, gleaming paneled flooring, and shiny new furnishings. After inviting him to sit, she asked a few questions about his father. People were generally curious about his father, and Atlas had come to repeat the answers almost by rote. He did not mind people's interest. In a way, it kept his father alive.

"Do you know Papa?" Elizabeth asked as a servant arrived with the tea tray.

"I have not had the pleasure as of yet."

She regarded him expectantly as if waiting for him to explain himself. She might be more contained than her exuberant younger sister, but Elizabeth Archer was no shrinking violet.

He saw no reason not to share his reason for visiting Mr. Archer. "I've come to speak with your father about one of his former employees, Gordon Davis."

Instead of the polite, perhaps blank stare he expected at the mention of Davis's name, some sort of comprehension lit the young woman's gaze before she guarded it. "I see. His death certainly was tragic. He was so young."

Her reaction—or rather, her obvious desire to hide it—piqued his interest. "Were you acquainted with Mr. Davis?"

Maintaining her perfectly erect posture, Elizabeth scooted forward in her chair and reached for the caddy to prepare the tea. "I had occasion to meet him when I visited the factory with my father."

He wondered if she'd come under Davis's spell in the same manner a number of other young ladies had. "And what did you think of him?"

She lifted one shoulder slightly before dropping it. "He was agreeable, I suppose. He also visited here with my brother, Trevor."

"Your brother and Gordon Davis were friends?"

"Mr. Davis came to the house just that once." She added the tea leaves to the silver pot and poured steaming water over them. "My father did not approve of the association."

Atlas wasn't surprised. By all appearances, the Archers were an upstanding well-to-do family. Elizabeth certainly exhibited the distinctive polish that wealthy young ladies acquired at expensive finishing schools. Davis, a lowly clerk, would hardly have been an appropriate association for the family's heir.

"Elizabeth?" A man in fine tailored clothing—who was far too young to be Noel Archer—stood in the aperture.

"Mr. Montgomery, do come in." She made the introductions while she poured the tea. "Mr. Catesby, this is my betrothed."

The man, who appeared to be in the vicinity of thirty years old, gave a bow. "Gregory Montgomery."

"Well met," Atlas replied.

"Mr. Catesby's father was Silas Catesby, the great poet," Elizabeth told the new arrival, her voice rich with admiration. Montgomery's eyes narrowed at her tone. His assessing gaze went from Atlas to his betrothed and back again.

"Sugar, Mr. Catesby?" Elizabeth asked.

"No, thank you."

"Are you a friend of the family, Mr. Catesby?" Montgomery inquired. An aggressive energy rolled off the man. He was apparently possessive when it came to his future wife.

Atlas stood to take his tea from Elizabeth. "No, I have just now had the pleasure of meeting the Misses Archer."

"Harriet and I were walking home when we encountered Mr. Catesby." Elizabeth poured a cup of tea for her betrothed. "He is here to visit father."

Her explanation seemed to mollify Montgomery, who turned to give the lady his full attention when she handed him his libation. "You are in excellent looks today, my dear."

She accepted the compliment with a graceful smile. As Atlas sipped the hot drink, he noted that Miss Archer did not prepare one for herself.

"Mr. Catesby?" Noel Archer, a balding man in spectacles, finally made his appearance.

Atlas put the tea aside and rose to greet his host. "I appreciate your agreeing to see me on such short notice."

"Certainly." Archer eyed him with obvious curiosity. "Have we met before, sir?"

"No, I wish to speak with you about one of your former employees, Gordon Davis."

Archer's expression didn't alter. He turned to his daughter and her betrothed. "I'm certain you young people have something far more interesting with which to occupy your time."

Montgomery put his tea aside, seeming eager to take the opportunity to steal time alone with his betrothed. "Will you come for a ride?" he asked her.

"I cannot," she said politely. "It is my afternoon to visit the Society."

"The Society?" her betrothed repeated.

"Yes, I believe I mentioned it to you previously. I volunteer one day a week at the General Annuity Society for Tradespersons Formerly Better Off."

Noel Archer chimed in. "It is for merchants who have fallen on hard times. A worthwhile and respectable charity for young ladies to visit."

Atlas understood Archer's meaning. Many charities served society's less respectable denizens, including prostitutes and former prisoners. Tradespeople who'd run out of funds were several steps above the true dregs of society.

"I myself donate to them," Archer added. "They do fine work."

Atlas found the man's interest in helping his fellow merchants to be commendable. "That is generous of you."

"I have done well for myself. There is no denying that," Archer said. "It is a small thing I do now to help those who have not been as fortunate."

Montgomery looked at Elizabeth. "May I see you there then?"

"Yes, yes," Archer said to his daughter. "Do allow Gregory to escort you to the Society."

She smiled. "Most certainly." The two made their good-byes before quitting the room.

Once they were alone, Archer turned to Atlas. "You are here about Davis? I hear he came to a sad end." Archer took the seat his daughter had vacated and reached to pour himself some refreshment. "He was an arsenic eater, you know."

"I have heard that."

"I'm afraid there isn't much else I can tell you about the young man. I am rarely at the factory."

Atlas reached for his tea. "I am curious to know why you reinstated Davis after he was caught stealing arsenic from the factory. I understand he was let go, but then you intervened."

"Did Mertin Gunther tell you that?"

"No, your partner refused to speak with me at all."

Archer quirked a smile. "Somehow that does not surprise me."

"Why did you keep Davis on? Was it because he was a friend of your son's?"

Archer balked. "The man was no friend to my Trevor. In truth, he was a bad influence."

"How so?"

"He took Trevor to some gaming hell in the less savory part of town, and they played deep, too deep. By the end of the evening, my son owed my clerk close to one hundred pounds."

Atlas let out a low whistle. "That's quite a sum."

"Yes, it is. I told Davis he could keep his job as a way of satisfying my son's debt to him."

"He accepted that?" One hundred pounds was far more than a clerk earned in a single year.

"In truth, he had little choice but to accept." Archer's expression hardened. "I am not a man to cross. Davis came to understand that." He looked meaningfully around the opulent room. "One does not acquire all this by allowing scoundrels to cheat him."

"Did it gall you to retain Davis after he'd put your son in a precarious situation?"

Archer's manner turned cool. "What is your interest in Gordon Davis?"

"His sister believes he was murdered."

"Does she?" He sipped his tea, not appearing the least bit surprised. "Her brother was a slippery one. He likely had no shortage of enemies. That still does not explain why you've associated yourself with this business."

"Davis's sister is lady's maid to Lady Roslyn, the Duke of Somerville's sister."

"Somerville." The other man's brows lifted, and he studied Atlas with renewed interest, no doubt wondering how someone like Atlas had come to be associated with someone of Somerville's wealth and rank. "Lady Roslyn, you say? Is she the one that went missing?"

"No, she was never missing." Atlas forced a mild tone. "She was living quietly in the country with her family." That wasn't quite accurate, but he intended go to his grave without revealing to anyone the full truth of how he'd become acquainted with Lilliana.

"So the Duke of Somerville wants to know how and why my clerk died."

"It would greatly relieve his sister's mind."

"I can tell you I would not kill over a bit of arsenic." He set his teacup down. "I am not a man who needs to resort to murder in order to get what I want."

Atlas suspected that was true. "What of your son?"

Archer stiffened. "What of him?"

"How friendly was he with Davis?"

"I forbade my son to have any further contact with the man. Davis was beneath Trevor in every way . . . breeding, education, and social class. As far as I know, the two did not see each other after their unfortunate gaming adventure."

Atlas wondered if the son had obeyed his father. Putting his tea aside, he got to his feet and thanked the man for his time. Archer remained seated, still finishing his libation when Atlas exited the room. As he walked through the front hall, a young voice chirped behind him.

"Are you leaving so soon, Mr. Catesby?"

He turned and bowed to Harriet Archer. "I am. Thank you for making me feel so welcome." He noted that the wooden slingshot still dangled from her left hand.

"That's a handsome sling," he remarked.

She smiled proudly. "I am quite good at it," she boasted. "I only need one rotation for a proper slinging motion, and I never miss my target."

"That's very commendable," he said, amused. Most young ladies of quality did not sling stones at targets; they generally took up archery.

As he bade Harriet farewell, Atlas's thoughts drifted back to Gordon Davis's death and the mysterious Lady L. A sudden thought of what might drive a proud man like Noel Archer to murder came to him.

"Miss Harriet, does Elizabeth go by the name Liz or Lizzie with those in her inner circle?"

Harriet made a face. "No, she doesn't. She hates both of those names."

Chapter Six

"There you go, sir." Jamie stepped back from Atlas to admire his handiwork. "Your cravat is perfect."

Atlas twisted at the waist for a glimpse of his reflection in the mirror behind him. "Is it?" The neckcloth appeared bulky and overwrought to him, almost ridiculous in fact. But he didn't have the heart to voice his concerns. Especially not after all of the effort the boy had put into painstakingly folding and knotting the white linen in a series of complicated maneuvers. "Are you certain this is the . . . erm . . . current fashion?"

"Oh, yes." Jamie nodded decisively. "Even Mr. Finch would agree that your cravat is perfectly wrought."

Atlas cast another dubious look at his reflection. "Who is Mr. Finch?"

"The Earl of Charlton's valet." Jamie scrutinized Atlas's evening attire—all black except for the shock of bright white at the neck, a new ensemble made especially for the Duke of Somerville's annual ball. Atlas would have had nothing appropriate to wear otherwise. "I'd wager my annual salary that Mr. Finch could not find a single flaw in your presentation this evening."

"Would you?" Atlas murmured doubtfully. Charlton certainly favored flamboyant tailcoats and shiny buttons, but Atlas couldn't ever recall his friend's valet outfitting the earl with such a fussy cravat.

"Yes, sir. Mr. Finch says a skilled valet who excels in knots is a great commodity to the Quality."

"I see." Atlas's brows lifted. "Commodity, hmm?" In addition to possibly perfecting the art of knotting a neckcloth, the boy certainly seemed to be improving his vocabulary.

"That means something of use or of value," Jamie said proudly, obviously pleased with himself and his newfound knowledge.

"Yes, thank you. I do know the meaning of the word 'commodity.'"

Jamie disappeared into the dressing room and returned with a brush in hand. "Do not move. I am looking for lint."

"I begin to fear that Charlton has helped create a monster."

Jamie had been a green country boy when Atlas had hired him as a particular favor to Lilliana the year before. After discovering a stack of Atlas's scorched neck ties—Jamie had been as new to ironing as he was to valeting—the earl had whisked Jamie away to his Curzon Street mansion to be trained by Charlton's own inimitable staff.

Jamie batted a few pieces of lint away. "A gentleman's valet must always assure that his master is well turned out."

Atlas decided to divert the boy's attention to more important matters. "Jamie, beginning tomorrow, I'd like you to visit a number of apothecaries."

"Certainly, sir." The boy circled Atlas, his face a frown of concentration, his brush at the ready. "What do you need me to purchase for you?"

"It's nothing I need. I want you to look in their poison books."

He raised his gaze to meet Atlas's. "Their poison books, sir?"

"Yes, every apothecary must keep a register of all the poison they sell and to whom they sell it."

Jamie's eyes widened. "Do you think you'll find this Davis fellow's killer in those poison books?"

"It's a place to start." He rattled off a list of neighborhoods he wanted Jamie to check, including all the apothecaries in the vicinity of Davis's home and work as well as those in close proximity to Viscount Merton's residence. It was a stretch to presume that a peer would purchase his own poison, but Lavinia Fenton might, especially if she were the mysterious Lady L. "Oh, and Jamie?"

"Yes, sir?"

"I want you to go out to Clapham and check the poison registries there as well." Trevor Archer had fallen into debt thanks to Gordon Davis, and his father had disdained the man for luring his son into the evils of gaming. Both father and son had reason to hate Davis. It was time to discover whether any of the people on Atlas's short list had purchased arsenic.

"Certainly, sir."

"Thank you." Atlas moved away, leaving Jamie holding the clothes brush midair. "I should be going."

Jamie followed, handing Atlas his gloves. "I'll summon the hackney."

"No need." Pulling the gloves on one at a time, Atlas headed to the front hall. "I'll walk."

Jamie handed Atlas his black silk hat. "*Walk*?"

He could not have looked more horrified if Atlas had said he planned to go out and murder a small child.

Atlas placed his hat on his head just as he reached the door. "Yes, Somerville House is barely ten minutes away on foot."

Jamie quickly sidled past him and threw open the door before Atlas could. "It is my place to see to the door for you."

Atlas clenched his jaw. "Thank you." He secretly wished the boy would get out of the way. Atlas wasn't accustomed to being fussed over. He'd never employed a valet before agreeing to take Jamie on.

"Walking just isn't done, sir," Jamie huffed. "The Quality must always arrive by carriage. You will be a laughingstock."

"I shall have to risk it." Atlas maneuvered around his valet, stepped through the door, and shut it behind him, half fearing Jamie might try to follow him down the stairs.

It did not take long for Atlas to feel vindicated in his decision to walk to the duke's ball. A traffic jam came into view as soon as he turned onto Bruton Street from New Bond Street. The coaches were lined up for blocks, no doubt carrying bejeweled and resplendently attired guests to the Duke of Somerville's fete. The ball was the most sought-after invitation of the Season, according to Charlton, who knew about such things.

As soon as Atlas reached Somerville House, easily making better time than the guests whose carriages cluttered the wide expanse of Piccadilly, it became apparent the duke had spared no expense for the evening. As enormous as the ducal abode was—it covered almost an entire Mayfair block—candlelight burned in every visible window, making Somerville House appear as bright against the night sky as fireworks at Vauxhall.

Atlas joined the throng of guests entering the mammoth dwelling and stood patiently in the reception line for his turn to be greeted by Somerville and Lilliana. In the crush of people, he could snatch only partial glimpses of his host and hostess up ahead.

Beyond them lay spacious rooms filled with dozens of elaborate floral displays, their fragrance sweetening the warm air. Light from what seemed like a thousand candles and gilded sconces reflected off the pale walls, illuminating the rooms in golden splendor. Atlas had never seen anything like it.

"Welcome, Catesby," Somerville greeted Atlas when he approached. The duke's eyes dipped to the elaborate contraption twisted around Atlas's neck. Atlas felt woefully overdone in comparison to the duke's understated sartorial perfection. Somerville's deep-blue evening tailcoat with gilt buttons was flawlessly tailored to his slender form. His snowy waistcoat, breeches, and stockings added to his impeccable appearance. Somerville relied on his particular friend, a tailor named Kirby Nash, to turn him out in the highest style.

"Your grace." He bowed. "Thank you for including me."

"My sister would not have it any other way," the duke responded before smoothly handing Atlas off to Lilliana as he turned to greet the next guest. Considering the length of the queue, Atlas suspected the man might be formally welcoming his guests for at least the next hour or so.

"Atlas." Lilliana placed both of her gloved hands in his. "How nice of you to come."

"Lady Roslyn. I wouldn't dream of missing it."

"Naturally." Amusement flashed in her amber-hued eyes because they both knew he was suffering through the evening solely for the opportunity to interrogate Merton.

"You look more lovely than ever." A gallant comment but also a sincere one. She was incandescent in a cream silk evening gown embroidered with beads that shimmered when the light caught them.

"And you are as dashing as ever." Her gaze dipped to his neckcloth.

He grimaced. "You are to blame for it."

"Whatever do you mean?"

He gestured at his cravat with an upward sweep of his hand. "Jamie is responsible for this frothy mess."

"Ah." She smothered a laugh. The green country boy had been a servant in Lilliana's house during her ill-fated marriage. "That explains much."

Although he would have liked to linger, Atlas reluctantly moved on so as to not delay the progression of the receiving line. He might not be well schooled in the ways of the ton, but Atlas knew enough about its basic tenets to acquit himself in a respectable fashion.

He strolled through the crowded rooms, looking for Jermyn Fenton, Lord Merton. The sooner he located the man, the sooner he could slip away. Although the two were not well acquainted, Atlas had seen Merton about town often enough to be able to recognize him.

Each room was as impressive as the last. The polished rock crystal chandeliers and candelabras showcased the finest lit beeswax candles, which glittered like a thousand dancing fireflies. Footmen in smart black-and-gold livery circulated with silver trays bearing cool drinks for overheated guests in spaces that had begun to grow warm.

Atlas wandered through the open glass double doors that led to the gardens. Tents had been erected outside, where more cut flowers and shrubs added ornamentation. Vast quantities of food overflowed from glass and gilded porcelain platters that had been artfully arranged atop long tables draped with deep-wine table clothes. Cold sliced meats, cheeses, and fruits—including ripe peaches, grapes, and strawberries—were heaped upon the serving dishes. Just as he reached for a strawberry, a familiar voice called out to him. Popping the fruit into his mouth, Atlas turned to greet the Earl of Charlton.

"What the devil happened to your neckcloth?" the earl asked as soon as Atlas faced him. "I do declare it appears as if the linen engaged in a violent struggle with itself."

Atlas scowled as he finished chewing the flavorful fruit and swallowed it down. "I have your man Finch to thank for it."

Charlton shook his head. "Not likely, my friend. Finch is a master at knotting a cravat."

Atlas wasn't surprised. "Unfortunately for me, he is a poor instructor." He helped himself to a drink from a passing footman. "This cravat is Jamie's creation."

"Young Jamie." Charlton's mouth trembled with suppressed laughter. "I should have known. Clearly, the boy's instruction must continue."

"Clearly." Atlas sipped from the crystal glass and was not disappointed. The lemonade—refreshingly cold and sweetly tart on his tongue—was as perfect as the strawberry. Wealth and privilege certainly had its advantages, and he expected nothing less than perfection from the Duke of Somerville.

"What a surprise to find you in attendance. Balls are not usually your sort of thing." Charlton adjusted the snowy cuffs of his white silk shirt, which were just visible beneath his claret tailcoat. "Or is it a particular lovely lady who has drawn you here this evening?"

"I'm here to talk to Merton." Atlas ignored the poorly veiled reference to Lilliana. "Have you seen him?"

"Merton?" The earl's brows rose. "Is he involved in the investigation?"

"He might be. I will not know until I speak with him." Atlas was reluctant to elaborate further when a young lady's reputation could be at stake. "The victim, Gordon Davis, worked for Merton at one time and left under rather unsavory circumstances."

"You're in luck then." Charlton looked over Atlas's shoulder. "I believe that's Merton over there helping himself to more of Somerville's champagne."

Atlas pivoted in time to see a slightly unsteady Viscount Merton reach into one of the ice coolers filled with champagne and wine that had been placed at intervals along the food tables. "Is he a drinker?"

Charlton waggled his amber eyebrows. "Is King George mad? No doubt Merton began the party at his own house hours ago."

"Excuse me for a moment."

"Certainly. A tongue loosened by champagne could be most helpful indeed."

Atlas made his way through the throng toward the man in question. He came up beside the viscount and reached over to pluck another strawberry from a silver tray piled up with the fruit.

He nodded. "Merton."

Merton blinked at Atlas, staring at him with blank eyes as if trying to place him. And then something clicked in his memory. "You're the poet's son. Catesby. The world traveler."

"At your service." Atlas popped the juicy fruit into his mouth.

"Back from your travels, I see." Sipping his champagne, Merton's red-rimmed gaze regarded Atlas over the edge of his glass. "Where were you off to this last time?"

"Jamaica."

"Partial to life among the savages, are you?"

He reached for another strawberry. "I do rather enjoy meeting people from foreign lands."

A footman bearing a tray of champagne bottles approached the long table. Merton reached for one, his action ungainly, and tipped it over. The champagne gushed out as the bottle hit the ground with a hard clunk.

Merton jumped back when the cold liquid splashed against both his and Atlas's shoes and stockings. "Clumsy idiot!"

The footman set the tray on the table while uttering a nervous stream of words of apology. The duke's butler, Hastings, appeared instantly. "I do beg your pardon, my lord."

"As you should," Merton said coldly while using the cloth Hastings handed him to brush his legs dry. Several other servants appeared out of nowhere and quickly cleaned up the mess before vanishing again.

Charlton strolled over just as the servants scurried away. "I tell you, it's deuced difficult to find good help these days."

"Charlton," Merton greeted the earl. "I can't imagine you'd have that problem. You've a reputation for employing the best-trained servants in town."

"One tries as one must." Charlton helped himself to some grapes. "But every once in a while, you get a bad one in the bunch."

Atlas took his friend's cue. "Wasn't there a footman that you had to let go not too long ago?" He made a show of searching his memory. "What was his name? Davis something or the other?"

Atlas hoped Merton was too foxed to catch the twinkle in the earl's eye. "Gordon Davis," Charlton supplied the name with an admirable show of umbrage. "I threw him out without a letter of reference. I wasn't sorry to let Gordon Davis go, I can assure you."

"Davis?" Merton's glassy gaze focused on Charlton. "Gordon Davis?"

"The very one. He left under very unsavory circumstances." Using his thumb and forefinger, Charlton carefully placed a plump purple grape into his mouth.

Merton flushed. "I had the same experience. He was in my employ for almost a year." His words were warbled. "Very pretty manners on that one. Caught plenty of female attention."

"Is that so?" Atlas said. "Why did you have to let him go?"

"Davis overstepped. Was very inappropriate in more ways than one." Anger blazed in the man's eyes. "Didn't know his place." He swallowed the last of his champagne, teetering a bit as he did so. "But I daresay he knows it now."

Atlas placed a hand at the man's elbow to steady him. "How do you mean?"

"The cur is dead."

Atlas feigned surprise. "Is he?"

"I have heard as much."

Charlton swallowed another grape. "I daresay I wouldn't have any idea if any of my former servants shoved off."

"Servants gossip like old women," Merton grumbled. "My Lavinia was inconsolable."

Atlas exchanged a look with Charlton. Merton must be beyond foxed to reveal such a thing. "Your daughter was upset to hear of Davis's demise?" Atlas asked.

"Was she very fond of him?" Charlton prompted.

A sense of self-preservation seemed to seize the viscount. His gaze grew wary, and he suddenly seemed far more sober. "My daughter is very tenderhearted," he said stiffly. "She cried when one of my hunters died as well."

"Very understandable." Charlton was all sympathy now. "It is very difficult to find a decent hunter."

Merton's distrustful gaze shifted from one man to the other. "If you'll excuse me, I need to find the pisspot." He stumbled away through the crowd, knocking into a few shoulders in his eagerness to escape Atlas and Charlton.

"Merton's daughter." Charlton plucked the last grape from the stem he held daintily in his palm. "Fascinating."

"Isn't it?" Atlas said. "I see you couldn't resist inserting yourself into the conversation."

"I did get the man to talk, did I not?" Charlton chewed his grape with a smug expression on his aristocratic face. "You are most welcome."

"Merton is as drunk as a wheelbarrow," Atlas said dryly. "The situation didn't require a great deal of finesse."

"We make an excellent team, if I do say so myself."

"On occasion." Atlas cracked a smile. He could not deny it. This was not the first time the earl had lent his assistance. When Atlas had been suspected of murdering Lilliana's late husband, Charlton had stepped in to help more than once. The earl was extraordinarily bright, far more so than his foppish appearance and manner suggested. People underestimated the man at their own peril.

Charlton plucked a glass of champagne off a tray held by a roaming footman. "Is Merton one of your suspects?"

Atlas lifted a shoulder. "It's hard to say. Clearly, he had motive, but I'm learning that our Mr. Davis was quite a bounder.

He obviously hoped to parlay his charm and handsome visage into bettering his life."

"By marrying above his station?"

"So it seems." He told Charlton about the love letters they'd found.

"Ah, I begin to comprehend," Charlton said when Atlas had finished. "You want to discover whether Merton's daughter, Lady Lavinia, is the mysterious Lady L."

"It certainly seems possible that she could be."

Charlton leaned closer. "Do you believe Lady Lavinia is also the insatiable lady who demanded multiple performances nightly from our randy Mr. Gordon?"

"Perhaps. Although I don't know how a viscount's daughter would be able to meet in secret to allow such intimacies to occur on a regular basis."

"You think our victim was courting more than one young lady."

"It wouldn't surprise me. The more associations he had, the greater the chance that one would end in matrimony."

Their discussion was interrupted by a familiar feminine voice. "Atlas, is this where you are hiding?" He turned at the sound of his sister's voice and was startled to find Thea dressed up in an opulent emerald silk gown.

As a mathematician, Atlas's sister made a habit of wearing plain black day dresses to hide the ink stains that resulted from her work. Over the years, Atlas had heard people refer to his sister's beauty, but he'd never been able to see her appeal until this evening. Against the vibrant gown, Thea's dark upswept hair, porcelain skin, and immense dark eyes were quite striking.

"Don't you look lovely," he said.

She scrunched her turned-up nose. "I can't work out if that's a compliment or a question."

Charlton cut in. "You look even more breathtaking than usual." He made a show of giving her an extravagant bow while admiration glistened in his blue gaze. "And that, my dear Mrs. Palmer, is most definitely a compliment."

Thea, who did not have much use for the earl's frivolities, gestured toward his colorful evening coat. "And I see you have reverted to your more flamboyant state."

Charlton grinned, baring gleaming white teeth. "There are times when a man's true nature cannot help but reveal itself."

"And in glorious color," she said drolly.

"But have no fear"—Charlton adjusted his tailcoat—"I still have the funereal colors you so prefer in my wardrobe as well. You'll recall I ordered a number of somber tailcoats last fall. That should please you no end."

Her brows lifted. "And whyever should that please me?"

Charlton's gaze locked with Thea's. "I ordered them for you, of course, after you made plain your disdain of my preference for vibrant colors. Pleasing you, my dear Mrs. Palmer, is one of my most fervent desires."

To Atlas's surprise, his no-nonsense sister blushed, a becoming pink curling around the apple of her cheeks. "Must you always spew such rubbish?" she said dismissively before turning to Atlas. "I understand you're involved in another investigation."

"Where did you hear that?"

"Lilliana told me while we were being dressed earlier today." She shot her brother a reproachful look. "I obviously didn't hear it from you. You've barely come around since your return from Jamaica."

"Quite right," he acknowledged, feeling chagrined. "I will make an effort to remedy that." Of all his siblings—at least those who were still living—he was closest with Thea, who was only eighteen months his senior. Yet he often felt the urge to be alone, whether it was to update his travel journal or to work on the various challenging puzzles he spent hours with.

Charlton poured himself another glass of champagne. "You dressed for the ball with Lady Roslyn?"

"Not that it is any of your concern"—she favored the earl with a withering look—"but yes. Lilliana thought it would be much less tiresome if we readied for the ball together."

"Ahh." Eyes bright with interest, Charlton scrutinized her appearance. "That explains much."

It did. Thea normally paid little attention to her appearance. That she was so well turned out that evening was clearly due to Lilliana's deft touch.

Atlas regarded his sister thoughtfully. "I was not aware that you and Lilli—er—Lady Roslyn had renewed your acquaintance."

"Renewed it?" she responded with a dismissive motion of her hand. "You may have removed yourself, but I have not. Lilliana and I have become great friends."

"You have?" Lilliana had not mentioned her closeness to his sister. However, it made sense, he supposed, given that Thea had once offered Lilliana shelter when she'd had no place to go.

Thea canted her head. "Why do you appear so surprised?"

"Oh, I don't know. I suppose I hadn't given it much thought." When he'd put Lilliana out of his life, he'd naturally assumed that his sister had as well. "The Catesbys hardly move in the same circles as the Dukes of Somerville and their ilk."

"Lilliana isn't like that, as you well know."

A new feminine voice chimed in. "Isn't like what?"

Lilliana approached, and as Atlas and Charlton bowed to her, Thea responded. "I was questioning Atlas about the new investigation."

Lilliana smiled, resplendent in her embroidered gown, her eyes sparkling. "You must continue your conversation later because I've come to claim Mr. Catesby for myself."

"That sounds positively scandalous," Charlton said.

Lilliana exchanged an amused smile with the earl. "Mr. Catesby has the next dance." She held her arm out, displaying an unusual silver and mother-of-pearl accessory dangling from her wrist by a decorative cord. "The waltz."

"Really, Atlas," Charlton admonished, "a lady should not have to seek you out in order for you to claim your place on her dance card."

Atlas blinked. "Dance card?" He had no idea what they were talking about.

"I'd never heard of it either until Lilliana introduced me to the concept," Thea reassured him. "For some reason, the ton is entranced with dance cards."

"It's rather new, something to keep us entertained," Charlton explained. "A dance card is actually a booklet. You write your name down next to whichever dance you'd like to claim."

"Precisely." Lilliana dangled her dance card. "And the next one is yours."

It dawned on Atlas that he'd seen other women at the ball wearing dance cards such as Lilliana's but hadn't given them any thought. "Forgive me." He offered his arm, trying to recover himself. "Shall we?"

Charlton shifted closer to Thea and offered his arm as well. "I do believe your waltz is mine, Mrs. Palmer."

Thea stepped back. “I don’t recall your writing your name down on my dance card.”

Lilliana took Atlas’s arm. “You haven’t paid any attention at all to your dance card, Thea. I added you myself of adding the earl’s name.”

Charlton beamed. “At my request, of course.”

Chapter Seven

"Not that I am complaining," Atlas said as he escorted Lilliana to the ballroom, "but I do not recall writing my name down on your dance card."

"I took the liberty of adding you myself," she said smoothly, looking straight ahead as they conversed. "Gentlemen are supposed to keep pencils with them in order to write their names on ladies' dance cards. I presumed you would not have a pencil."

He was flattered. But then she added, "Besides, this gives us an opportunity to speak in private."

They passed through elaborately gilded doors and into as opulent a room as Atlas had ever seen. The space was mammoth, its walls hung with red damask, the windows and paintings all encased in gilded frames. The vaulted blue-and-white compartmentalized ceiling was adorned with gold medallions. As they waited at the side for the present dance to end, Atlas filled Lilliana in on his conversation with Merton.

"I have taken it upon myself to befriend the girl," Lilliana said when he had finished. "It seems my maid's younger brother had prurient interests."

"Lady Lavinia told you this?"

Lilliana dipped her chin in affirmation. "I called upon her earlier this week, and we spoke again this evening. She was most forthcoming."

Atlas didn't hide his shock. "Lady Lavinia told you of these lewd interests of his?"

A corner of her small mouth hitched up. Her smile had always intrigued him. Her lips were slightly crooked so that, when she smiled, she seemed to smirk, lending her a certain haughty smugness. "She has proof of it."

He inhaled sharply. "I beg your pardon." Maybe he'd been mistaken. Perhaps Lavinia was the lustful lady Davis had bedded many times over. "What sort of proof?"

"She wouldn't say. But Lady Lavinia has promised to call on me on the morrow and bring this evidence with her."

The current dance ended, and their conversation ceased while they made their way onto the dance floor. There was quite a crush, but everyone made way for their hostess, sister to the venerable Duke of Somerville. The duke's guests also pretended not to stare, but more than a few eyes followed Atlas and Lilliana.

They came to a stop at the center of the dance floor. Atlas put his right hand around Lilliana's trim waist and held her gloved hand. He had never danced with her before. Even though he was a large man, well over six feet with the strapping form of an athlete, she was statuesque enough to easily rest her left hand on his shoulder as they glided into a waltz. He concentrated on the steps—he was not one who waltzed often—conscious of the curious eyes closely monitoring their movements. He felt big and awkward next to Lilliana, whose posture was sublime as she waltzed with such grace that it seemed as though dancing came as naturally to her as breathing.

"I begin to see how the rhinoceros at the Exeter Exchange must feel," he remarked, referring to the royal menagerie on the north side of the Strand, which also included a tiger, a lion, a camel, monkeys, a hyena, and a hippopotamus. "I am unused to being on display."

"Rhinoceros? Surely not." Her topaz eyes twinkled. "At the very least, you should count yourself as one of the big cats. You can be rather fierce at times."

"You are teasing me, which is most uncharitable." He led her in a circle, trying his best to avoid entangling them with another dancing couple. "I am far more accustomed to the role of inconspicuous observer."

"You could never go unnoticed." He assumed she referred to his size, but then she added, "I have caught more than one lady taking your measure this evening."

"They are no doubt wondering the identity of the man to whom the lovely Lady Roslyn has deigned to grant a waltz."

"Some of them, perhaps," she allowed. "But that is not why the young marriage-minded maidens are watching you with such unabashed curiosity."

He brushed off the notion. "Once they learn I have neither a fortune nor a title, they will turn their attentions elsewhere."

"I would not be so certain of that if I were you." They took another smooth turn. "In any case, the reason we are drawing more than our share of attention is because this is my first major entertainment since leaving off my mourning."

"I hadn't realized."

They glided past Thea, who was dancing with Charlton. She was rigid in the earl's arms, her lips pressed into a hard line, the rest of her face stamped with the exasperated expression she often wore in the earl's company.

Lilliana noticed them as well. "I see Charlton has finally persuaded Thea to take a turn with him."

"I wonder why he bothers. She treats him abominably."

She regarded him with surprise. "Surely you've noticed Charlton has a *tendre* for your sister."

"What?" Atlas scoffed. "That's absurd."

She shook her head. "For an observant man, you can be remarkably obtuse at times."

He gave a huff of skepticism. "Thea is hardly the sort of woman to interest Charlton. For one thing, she is married, and he is drawn toward—" He stopped short, not wishing to discuss with Lilliana the earl's sexual exploits.

"Actresses and opera singers," she said tartly. "Yes, I am aware."

"And Thea is a prickly mathematician who pays little attention to her appearance and even less to the social graces." His sister couldn't be more different than Charlton's usual painted beauties, who excelled in the art of conversation, flirtation, and, well, sexual congress.

"Men." She shook her head. "At times you cannot see what is right before your eyes."

He scanned the crowded dance floor until he found his sister and friend again. The earl was certainly staring at his sister with keen appreciative interest. He frowned, considering the possibility that Lilliana might be correct. "Charlton is holding her rather closer than he should."

"Nonsense. There's a perfectly respectable distance between them."

"How long has this been going on?" The thought crossed Atlas's mind that perhaps his travels had put him too out of touch with important happenings in his own family.

She looked heavenward. "Nothing is 'going on,' as you put it. Thea is a married woman."

"True, but her husband is rarely in residence." Charles Palmer spent most of his time in the country. It was unfashionable for married couples to appear too fond of each other, but Atlas had always sensed that Palmer would prefer to spend more time with his wife. "Is Charlton the reason she doesn't want Palmer around?"

"Now you're being ridiculous." They executed a one-two-three promenade. "While it is true that Charlton carries a torch for your sister, I'm fairly certain she'll douse that flame with a bucket of ice water should he ever find the courage to declare himself."

"Oh." A strange sort of relief filtered through him. "So I'm not completely mistaken. She does find him tiresome?"

Lilliana lifted one elegant shoulder. "It would appear so."

It took him a moment to realize the music had stopped, bringing their dance to an end. As he escorted her off the floor, Atlas's thoughts returned to the investigation. "When did you say Lady Lavinia plans to call upon you, with the . . . erm . . . proof of Davis's prurient nature?"

"On the morrow. At two o'clock."

He frowned, filtering the possibilities through his mind. "I still cannot imagine what form this evidence might take."

"Come and see me tomorrow at three o'clock if you'd like to find out," she said as they reached the side of the ballroom—just before her next dance partner whisked her away.

⋆ ⋆ ⋆

The following day, when Atlas called upon Lilliana at the prescribed time, he expected to be shown to the same tasteful sitting room as when he'd last visited, but she received him instead in one of the duke's numerous formal drawing rooms.

The space was elegantly ornamented with flowers, plants, sculptures, and engravings, artfully arranged on various mahogany and marble tabletops. Gilded mirrors adorned the walls, reflecting the daylight filtering through the drawing room's sizable windows, which gave the room a light and airy feel. Atlas suspected the value of the artifacts in that room alone far exceeded that of everything he would own in his lifetime.

As soon as he joined Lilliana, Atlas saw she was not alone. While Lady Lavinia was nowhere in evidence, a well-dressed gentleman Atlas had never seen before was ensconced in the stuffed chair opposite Lilliana.

"Atlas," she said after Hastings, the butler, announced him. "Do you know Roxbury?"

The name sounded vaguely familiar, yet Atlas felt fairly certain he'd never met the pleasant-faced man taking tea with Lilliana. "I'm afraid I have not had the pleasure."

The man rose to his feet. He was of medium height and cut a fine figure in his expensive tailored clothing. "Jonathan Bradford, Marquess of Roxbury."

Atlas bowed. "I believe I am acquainted with your brother, Adam. We were at Harrow together. I hope he fares well."

In that moment, Atlas recalled why the name sounded familiar. Charlton had mentioned that Roxbury was courting Lilliana.

At the lady's invitation, Atlas took a seat, discreetly examining the man with more interest. Roxbury had an agreeable demeanor, and while not overtly handsome, the marquess's features were neat and even. Atlas judged him to be in his late thirties, about a decade older than Lilliana.

"I understand you were most recently in Jamaica." The marquess exuded an easy confidence. "Lady Roslyn has told me as much."

Lilliana had discussed him with the marquess? At his surprised look, she interjected, "Roxbury was present when your sister last visited. Mrs. Palmer was kind enough to share the contents of your letters with us."

Not that there was anything particularly intimate in his rambling missives, but it had never occurred to Atlas that Thea might share their contents with others. "I do beg your pardon if she bored you with the details of my journey."

Lilliana regarded him over the rim of her porcelain teacup. "I was anything but bored."

"Your descriptions of the sugarcane fields were most vivid," the marquess said. "How will the island fare, I wonder, now that the slave trade has been abolished?"

"The slave trade is banned. However, slavery itself is still firmly entrenched in Jamaica." He accepted a cup of tea that the butler brought in for him.

"Your abhorrence of slavery is quite apparent in your letters," Lilliana remarked. "You were most passionate."

His face warmed. As a rule, he did not guard his emotions in letters to his sister in the way he might to others, but they'd touched upon a subject that Atlas felt strongly about. "Until the very institution of slavery is banned, I suspect the island will continue on its current course, at its own peril. It is inevitable that an economy based on enslaved people will eventually fail."

"An interesting point." Interest flicked in the marquess's eyes as they continued the conversation about Atlas's time in Jamaica. Thirty minutes later, both men had finished their tea, but neither showed any sign of departing. As a rule, morning calls were not long, and Roxbury had far exceeded the acceptable duration of a visit. Perhaps Lilliana regularly allowed the marquess this particular liberty. However, Atlas noted with satisfaction, she had not invited her suitor into her private sitting room as she had Atlas.

"More tea?" Lilliana finally asked. "Shall I ring for Hastings to bring in a fresh pot?"

Roxbury stood, no doubt because he'd stretched the rules of protocol almost to the breaking point. Lords were expected to set an example by adhering to etiquette rather than flouting it. "No, thank you, my dear. I really should be leaving." He paused, casting an inquiring glance at Atlas.

Atlas did not take the other man's unsubtle hint. He felt no compunction to abide by the ton's rigid strictures. After all, Lilliana had invited him to call upon her at three o'clock, a time when morning calls normally ended. Besides, he had no intention of going anywhere until he saw the evidence Lady Lavinia had dropped off.

Lilliana answered for him. "It was good of you to come, Roxbury." She rose and rang the bell. "Hastings will see you out."

If Roxbury was surprised by her less-than-subtle dismissal, he gave no sign of it. He made his farewell with grace and followed the butler out the door. Once the door closed behind them, Lilliana exhaled.

"Thank goodness he's gone."

Her candor took Atlas by surprise. "Roxbury seems like an amiable enough fellow."

"Oh, he is. Most amiable and very charming." She whisked over to a settee by the window and knelt beside it. "But I am keen to see what proofs Lavinia Fenton has of Gordon Davis's lesser nature."

She pulled a small box out from under the settee and tossed the top off. Her face fell.

"Why, it's just a book." She lifted the tome out and flipped through a couple of pages, and her dubious expression transformed into one of complete shock. "Oh, my."

Chapter Eight

Alarmed by Lilliana's reaction, Atlas strode to her side. "What is it?"

She'd become so engrossed in the book that she seemed to have forgotten his presence. "I had no idea," she murmured, turning the pages far more slowly now, studying some of them rather closely. "Surely not . . ."

When he drew near, she slammed the book shut and lobbed it back into the box as though it were one of the deadly scorpions he'd once seen in Carthage. She stood and scooted away, putting distance between them, her cheeks flushed as she avoided his gaze. It was the first time he'd ever seen her flustered.

Curious as to what had shattered Lilliana's crystalline reserve, Atlas squatted down on his haunches and reached for the book. He flipped it open and inhaled sharply, shock coursing through his veins. Aghast, he paged through it.

The book was full of indecent illustrations, one page after another showing graphic portrayals of men and women engaging in sexual congress or performing various sex acts upon one another. Some involved more than two people; others depicted men in explicit situations with other men or two women enjoying each other. More than indecent, the drawings were outright obscene, so detailed that they left nothing to the reader's imagination.

He closed the book with a sharp thud and remained staring down at it for a moment as he regained his composure. Exhaling long and steady through his nostrils, he put the book aside and straightened to his full height, appalled that Lilliana had been subjected to the base drawings, which no doubt introduced to her a litany of sex acts she couldn't have even imagined before now. He forced himself to look at her and found the lady watching him with undisguised curiosity.

"What is that?" she asked.

He didn't quite know how to answer her question. A rising anger heated his words. "Gordon Davis was a vile, repugnant man to show such things to an innocent, gently bred woman such as Lavinia Fenton."

"Is that the sort of thing men . . . read . . . erm . . . regularly?"

His cheeks were hot. "No, most decidedly not."

"But you have seen the like before."

Of course he had. "At Harrow, the boys secretly passed dirty books around."

"Oh, I see." She swallowed, her composure returning. "And is this common?"

He hardly understood what she asked. "Is what common?"

"These sorts of books."

"They can be." Inwardly, he breathed a sigh of relief. He had feared she wanted to know whether the explicit acts portrayed on the book's pages were common. "There is a street, Holywell, off the Strand, where these types of materials can be found for a certain price."

"Holywell?" Her forehead wrinkled. "But isn't that where radicals sell their books and pamphlets?"

"You will find both. Recently, authorities have cracked down on dissenters, prompting many on Holywell Street to turn to alternate ways to make a profit."

She remained silent for a few moments, seeming to consider his answer. "And two men, together in that way . . ." She hesitated. "Is that done?"

He wondered if she inquired for the reason he suspected. Something about the grave manner in which she asked, the seriousness of purpose in her eyes, told him her interest wasn't of a prurient nature.

"Not by most men, no." He spoke with care. "But there are some whose tastes deviate from the norm."

He abruptly turned the conversation back to the investigation. It was, after all, why he'd come. Besides, he wasn't about to discuss buggery with Lilliana. "About Lavinia Fenton. What did she tell you about this book? Aside from the fact that Davis gave it to her?"

"Very little. Roxbury arrived before we had an opportunity to talk about the contents of her package and her acquaintance with Mr. Davis."

"This book suggests their acquaintance might have been of an intimate nature."

Interest gleamed in her eyes. "You think Lavinia is the mysterious Lady L."

"The book certainly makes it seem very possible, but we need to learn more about how well they might have known each other. I also have not told you about my visit to Clapham." He went on to share the details of his encounter with the Archers.

"Is the elder Miss Archer a candidate for the unknown Lady L?"

"It is hard to tell. We do know she was acquainted with Davis, but on the surface, it appears that they barely knew each other." He leaned forward and helped himself to a biscuit from the tea tray. "And she is betrothed. It is difficult to imagine Miss Archer carrying on a torrid affair with a footman-turned-clerk while promised to another man."

"What do we know about her intended?"

"His name is Gregory Montgomery. He appears to be besotted with Miss Archer, and she seems to enjoy his regard."

Lilliana contemplated the possibilities. "It would be exceedingly difficult for a well-bred young woman to carry on an illicit liaison. It is difficult for maidens to go anywhere without a chaperone."

"Quite right. But Davis did manage to get those books to Lady Lavinia."

"We must talk with her." Lilliana tapped a tapered finger against her pale cheek. "When Lavinia departed today, she mentioned she walks in the park every morning at eleven."

"An unsubtle hint of where to find the girl in the event you wish to speak with her again?"

"I believe so. She is anything but shy."

He wondered exactly what Lilliana meant by that, but he supposed he'd find out soon enough. "I gather you plan to take a walk tomorrow morning?"

"Yes," she said with that lopsided smile of hers, "and you can just happen upon us after I accidentally run into Lavinia."

★ ★ ★

Although Atlas had never met Lavinia Fenton and knew almost nothing about her, he realized the moment Lilliana introduced them that the girl was trouble.

He'd pretended to accidentally encounter the two ladies in the park late the following morning, just as he and Lilliana had arranged. Lady Lavinia was very young, blonde, fair, and somewhat buxom, but what left the deepest impression on him was the mischief sparkling in her vivacious blue eyes.

"How delightful to make your acquaintance, Mr. Catesby." The girl batted her eyelashes and, to his surprise, thoroughly perused his form with unabashed inquisitiveness—all the way from the tip of his black beaver-skin top hat down to the pointy toes of his polished boots.

Startled by her boldness, he exchanged a look with Lilliana before greeting them both with a bow. "Lady Lavinia, a pleasure."

Lilliana's eyes twinkled. "Mr. Catesby, what a surprise it is to run into you here."

"A very pleasant one," Lavinia added with a saucy grin. That this cheeky girl might have a penchant for trouble would not surprise Atlas in the least.

The three of them strolled along the path, exchanging the usual polite pleasantries, with Lavinia's maid strolling at a distance behind them. It was not the fashionable hour to be seen in Hyde Park—that would come much later in the afternoon—so the atmosphere was sedate. The weather had held; the air was damp and thickly humid, but it wasn't raining.

After a few minutes, Lilliana paused and addressed the young lady in a more serious manner. "As I mentioned to you previously, Mr. Catesby is looking into Mr. Davis's death."

The girl lost some of her pluck. "It's so very sad. Gordon was the most agreeable footman we've ever had."

"Anything you share with me will be held in the strictest confidence," Atlas reassured her. "I care only about finding out how Davis died."

She leaned closer, totally enrapt. "Do you think someone killed him?"

"We cannot be certain," he answered, "but I do believe it's a possibility."

"I shall be pleased to tell you anything I know."

He decided Lavinia was a young lady who would appreciate directness. "Why did Davis give you those books?"

"Because I asked him to."

He and Lilliana exchanged a startled look. "Were the two of you very close?"

She lifted a shoulder. "Not particularly, no."

"Then why would you ask for books of that nature from your footman?"

"I wanted to show them to my friends."

"Friends?" Lilliana echoed.

"Yes," she said pertly. "You see, I found similar books hidden in my brother Wade's bedchamber. They were ever so enlightening, and I wanted to share them with my friends, but Wade removed them before I had a chance to show them to anyone."

If Atlas had initially worried about getting the girl to disclose what she knew about Davis, he needn't have concerned himself. Lavinia Fenton was a bold piece who spoke plainly.

"Is that why you asked Davis to procure similar material for you?"

"Yes, because Adora and Frances didn't believe dirty books like the one I'd seen in Wade's chamber existed. So I asked Davis to help me prove that they do."

"Adora and Frances?" Lilliana's brows drew together. "Adora Bradford?"

"Yes, do you know her?"

Lilliana blinked. "Somewhat."

Atlas wondered what it was about this Adora Bradford that prompted Lilliana's obvious consternation. He directed his attention back to Lavinia. "You asked Davis to buy the . . . erm . . . books to show to your friends."

"Exactly." She smiled smugly. "And then Adora and Frances had to believe me, didn't they now? I had the proof right there."

"What made you feel so comfortable asking Davis to procure these books for you?" he asked. "What kind of relationship did you have with him?"

She wrinkled her pert little nose. "What do you mean?"

He was grateful when Lilliana interjected. "Were you perhaps drawn to him," she prompted, "in the way men and women are sometimes drawn to each other?"

Lavinia's eyes widened. "Of course not! I'm a viscount's daughter. I expect to marry no lower than an earl." She cast an appreciative look in Atlas's direction. "Unless it is a love match and the man is of noble blood. In that event, titles are unnecessary."

Ignoring the way Lilliana's mouth trembled with suppressed laughter, Atlas resisted the urge to loosen his cravat, which suddenly felt uncomfortably tight. "Did Davis ever behave inappropriately with you?"

"He was a flirt and very handsome. But I would never become enamored of a footman. Imagine that." Lavinia laughed as if truly amused. "Besides, he was engaged in a liaison with a married lady."

Atlas blinked. "I beg your pardon? Did Davis tell you that himself?"

She shook her head, her artful curls bouncing. "No, I heard it from my lady's maid. She said all of the servants were gossiping about it. No one knew who it was, but they say she was a grand lady in Mayfair and that theirs was a long-standing affair that preceded the lady's marriage."

Her words made Atlas recall that Henry Buller, the clerk at the dye factory, had told him Davis had claimed to be betrothed to a wealthy young lady who'd jilted him to marry a title. He wondered if it was the same lady.

"I would never have run away with a *footman*," Lavinia was saying, "but Davis was convenient to have about. For a little bit of coin, he would do or get whatever I wanted."

Atlas still wasn't certain he believed Lavinia's relationship with Davis had solely been that of mistress and servant. "Why did your father let Davis go without so much as a letter of recommendation?"

He saw the moment she decided to lie to him. Her gaze slipped away before coming back to meet his. "I'm afraid I have no idea."

"Can you think of any reason?" he prompted.

"No." She gave him a bold look. "Is there a Mrs. Catesby?"

Atlas's eyes widened. He hadn't spent a great deal of time in the company of gently bred young women, but he never imagined one could be as forward as the dark-eyed prostitutes he'd encountered upon arrival at Constantinople's Galata docks. "There is not."

Lilliana decided to rescue him. "Mr. Catesby is wed to the world. Travel is his passion. Affairs of the heart will never compare to the romantic embrace of foreign lands."

Lavinia's eyes lit up. "The stories Mr. Catesby must have to tell." She fluttered her long lashes in Atlas's direction. "Perhaps you will call upon me one day soon and share tales of your exotic adventures."

Atlas remained silent. A gallant reply was in order, but he had no intention of giving this child even the slightest hope that he might consider courting her. Yet his tepid reaction did not seem to deter the girl.

With a brazen *we-shall-see-about-that* smile, she said, "I really must go. I promised Papa I'd have the carriage back by midday."

He watched the girl waltz away with her maid scurrying in her wake.

"You could do worse." Lilliana fought a smile. "I'm told she has a sizable dowry."

"That child doesn't need a husband," he grumbled. "She needs to be sent to bed without supper. She cannot possibly be a day over seventeen."

"She is eighteen. Surely you haven't forgotten that I was two years *younger* than Lavinia when I wed."

And she had certainly suffered for it. "Those were extraordinary circumstances."

"Indeed," she said mildly as she turned back on the path to continue strolling. "Do you think Lavinia could be our mysterious Lady L?"

He fell in step beside her. "Before meeting her, I would have said no. I could not have imagined a sheltered viscount's daughter being so brazen as to take a lover." He exhaled through his mouth. "However, with Davis employed as a footman in Merton's household, engaging in a liaison would not have been difficult. A minx as forward and artless as Lady Lavinia might be capable of anything."

She cast him a sidelong glance. "Even murder?"

His mouth twisted as he considered the possibility. "We've no proof that the mysterious Lady L is the killer."

"But we cannot rule Lavinia out as Lady L."

"True. Nor can we rule her out as our killer." He paused, filtering through what they'd learned so far. "Then there is the matter of the married lady Davis was supposedly involved with."

"How do we find her?"

"I'm not certain. But perhaps you might be able to ferret something out from the ladies of Mayfair at these many social functions you attend during the Season."

She seemed skeptical. "I suppose I could try, but I have formed no close associations since my return." She shot him a wry look. "However, perhaps it is time I started."

He did not doubt she would succeed at anything she attempted. "If she is well born and they were acquainted before her marriage, perhaps she was a daughter of the house where Davis was in service before he joined Merton's household."

She nodded. "I'll ask Tacy about her brother's past employers." She paused as if ready to turn back. "Now I really must get back to join the children for their midday meal."

"May I escort you home?"

"Of course."

"Excellent," he said briskly, offering his arm to accompany her back to near Stanhope Gate, where one of Somerville's coaches awaited to return her to the duke's residence. "I'd like to get that book Lavinia gave you, if I may."

Her eyebrows lifted. "Should I ask why?"

His cheeks warmed. "So that I may see if it offers any clues, such as where the book was purchased."

"What would that signify?"

He twisted his lips. "We won't know until we explore this particular avenue."

A few minutes later, as they settled into the ornate chariot's cerulean-blue tufted seats with a lush patterned carpet under their feet, he asked about her children. "How are Peter and Robin?"

"They are very well." Sitting opposite her, he could easily see Lilliana's face soften at the mention of her sons. "You should come and see them."

"I would very much like to." The invitation pleased him. In the aftermath of their father's untimely death—and before he'd learned who she really was—Lilliana had insisted Atlas maintain his distance in order to keep the boys from forming an attachment to him.

"You cannot imagine how well they bowl hoops now." She referred to the game he had taught the boys shortly after meeting them. "I daresay they might be able to best you."

He laughed, thinking of the two energetic boys he'd run with in the park. "I do not doubt it." He slid a hand along the smooth damask wall of the carriage, over the gold-and-red silk embroidery of the Somerville family crest. "The duke says you plan to send Peter to Eton in the fall."

Her smile faltered. "Somerville is most determined that the boys be given every opportunity to succeed in society despite their sire's low birth."

"That's commendable of him." Godfrey Warwick hadn't exactly been common, but he had been a minor member of the gentry, far below where a duke's daughter would normally marry. But Lilliana's circumstances had been unique. She'd needed protection, and wedding the detestable Warwick had provided it. "How do you feel about sending the boy away?"

She looked away, out the window, which was only partially covered by the silk shade. "He is only eight."

He knew her to be very attached to her children. She had not relegated them to a nursery during her marriage. They had not been looked after by nursemaids and only presented to their noble parents for an hour or so before bedtime. "Is Somerville firm in his decision?"

"He can be dissuaded." She turned from the window, her gaze troubled. "But I must do what is right for the boys' future."

"Perhaps it is best for young children to be with a loving mother. You certainly fought hard enough for them." Before his death, Lilliana's husband had kept the boys from her.

She exhaled, and he sensed how heavily the decision weighed on her. "Yes, but I mustn't be selfish. I must think of the boys first, above all else."

"I've never known you to do otherwise." The carriage came to a stop, and the footman opened the door and laid out the step. Atlas alighted and turned to help Lilliana down.

She placed her gloved hand in his. "Will you stay and have luncheon with me and the boys?"

He closed his large hand around her delicate fingers. "I would be delighted."

Chapter Nine

Even without its questionable reputation, Holywell could barely be considered a proper street. It was a narrow rambling lane, a dark alley beset by foul smells emanating from shadowy corners along the way. Grimy, timber-framed houses teetered over the stone street, blocking any daylight that might otherwise illuminate the crooked buildings, with their high gables and overhanging eaves perched over the lane.

Shops selling used books abounded in this shabby stretch of London, which ran parallel to the Strand. The tomes were crowded into filmy shop windows and piled up on trestles in front of the shops.

The hackney let Atlas off in front of one of these dilapidated buildings. Pain arrowed through his left foot when he alighted. Atlas suppressed a grimace and shifted the weight to his right foot. The discomfort was the price to be paid for having spent the previous afternoon bowling hoops with Lilliana's young sons. Both boys had grown a great deal since he'd last seen them, and he'd foolishly acquiesced when they'd begged him to race.

He began to walk, taking care not to limp. The injury from the accident, which had occurred well over a year ago when he'd jumped clear of an overturning hackney, continued to plague him. He hadn't realized that a single foot contained so many bones. Surely the occasional distress he still experienced signaled that at least one of those bones had not healed properly.

He surveyed his surroundings as he walked. He'd been let off opposite the bookshops, on the side of the street dominated by secondhand clothes sellers, mostly Jewish immigrants. The cries of these merchants—"Old clothes!"—resonated through the crowded lane, which was also known as Rag Street. A gray-bearded man in flowing robes sat on a hard chair watching the happenings on the street.

"Good day," Atlas said to the ragman when he drew near enough.

The man responded with a polite nod and waited for Atlas to state his business.

"I am looking for a bookseller by the name of Saunders. I was hoping you could direct me to his place of business." He'd found a stamp bearing the name *Saunders* in the back of Lavinia Fenton's dirty book.

The merchant looked almost apologetic. "A man minds his own business on this street."

Atlas understood the man's reticence. Aside from being the place to procure low publications, Holywell was a hotbed of radical activity where government spies abounded. The merchant knew to be cautious when speaking out of turn about one of his neighbors.

Atlas attempted to reassure the man. "I am not interested in causing Mr. Saunders any trouble."

The man shrugged both shoulders. "I'm afraid I cannot help you."

A portly, wrinkle-faced woman in black bustled up, carrying baskets overflowing with fruits and vegetables. Atlas acknowledged her with the tip of his hat. She spoke a few rapid-fire utterances to the older man. Atlas recognized some of the Yiddish words. He'd met a Russian Jewish scholar on one of his journeys and had passed the long ship voyage amusing himself by learning some Yiddish words and phrases.

Appearing satisfied with Gray Beard's response, the woman rushed into the shop. Atlas missed most of the old man's answer, but he picked up enough to make out something about "the neighbor beside the moon." Having no idea what that could mean, Atlas thanked the man and continued on his way.

A few minutes later, as he stepped around a man unloading used books from a horse-drawn cart, the old clothes seller's words suddenly made sense. Up ahead, on the bookseller side of the street, a carved crescent moon sign hung above a shop. The ragman had mentioned one of the neighbors by the moon. Perhaps he'd referred to Saunders. Atlas headed first to the nearside shop to the right of the crescent sign.

He entered a dark cluttered space that smelled of dust and old books. The merchandise was piled up in the window and on wooden lean-to shelves stacked against the walls. He paused by a table littered with books and saw most of the titles were old used tomes. Nothing scandalous.

"May I help you?" A bespectacled man—tall, slender, and serious looking despite his shaggy brown hair and rumpled clothing—emerged from the back carrying a crate of books.

Atlas decided to be direct. "I'm looking for a publisher named Saunders."

"You found him. I'm Isaac Saunders."

"You're Saunders?" This man in no way fit Atlas's idea of what a purveyor of low publications might look like. He'd expected someone tawdry, a person far less respectable in appearance than this mild-mannered man, who brought to mind some of the more eccentric professors he'd studied with at Cambridge.

"In the flesh." The bookseller set the box on the scarred counter with a loud thud. "What can I do for you?"

Atlas introduced himself. "I . . . erm . . . a friend of mine purchased some books here." Saunders began unpacking the box, stacking the books on the counter. "Books of a certain nature," Atlas added.

Saunders paused, shifting his attention from his task to settle a probing look on his visitor. "And you are interested in procuring such a book for yourself?"

"Not exactly. I'd like to learn a little bit more about the man who purchased the book." He shifted subtly, so that his right foot bore most of his body weight. "I was wondering if he might have had a long-term association with you, either as a friend or as a patron."

Saunders rested an elbow on the edge of the crate. "I thought you said this man was a friend."

"He wasn't exactly. His name was Gordon Davis, and I am looking into the circumstances surrounding his death."

Saunders ran an assessing gaze over Atlas. "You don't look like a runner."

"Nor am I." Considering the illegal political activity that abounded on this narrow lane, no runner would be welcome on Holywell Street. "I don't work for Bow Street. I am here because Davis's sister is naturally distraught about his suspicious passing and is eager to know the truth regarding how he died."

"Never heard of a Gordon Davis." Saunders resumed unpacking the crate. "But that doesn't mean he didn't buy books from me. I don't know the names of all the people who patronize my establishment. And those who procure the sorts of publications I believe you are referring to don't necessarily wish for me to know their names."

Atlas glanced over at a nearby lean-to where a familiar name caught his attention. It was emblazoned on the faded cover of a well-worn book. He reached for the tome and paged through it, momentarily caught up in a wave of nostalgia.

"An admirer of Silas Catesby, are you?" Saunders asked.

"You could say so. He was my father."

"Was he now?" Saunders set the empty crate on the dusty floor. Atlas could not tell what impression, if any, his affiliation with the great English poet had on the bookseller. "What makes you think this Davis fellow patronized my shop?"

"Davis worked as a footman, and he—"

"Footman?" Saunders rested both elbows on the counter and leaned his weight into them. "This Davis fellow of yours was a footman?"

"Yes." Atlas closed the book in his hands. "Why? Do you remember him?"

"There was a fellow in livery who came about a year ago. He escorted some young ladies."

"Do you recall what color he wore?" Atlas had no idea what the Merton servant uniforms looked like, but he intended to find out.

"Brown, maybe, with gold buttons, if I recall correctly."

"And he came in with some young ladies, you say?"

"Yes. He wanted to show them an assortment of low publications, which was unusual." Saunders carried a load of books over to the window and began stacking them. "Holywell hasn't completely lost all respectability. Even so, the highborn don't make a habit of coming this way, especially not noble young ladies."

"They were gentlewomen?" The back of Atlas's neck prickled. "Do you recall what these young ladies looked like?"

"There were two of them, and they were wise enough to wear overlarge bonnets that kept their faces hidden. But one of them was as bold as brass, I can tell you that."

Atlas had an inkling who Miss Bold-as-Brass might have been. "In what way?"

"She let me see her face. Those big blue eyes were asking for indecent things from a man, but at the same time, I doubted she comprehended what she was about."

That sounded about right. "Did you sell them some dirty books? Do you sell those here?" Atlas wanted to clarify because this shop was not obvious in the way of others on Holywell that brazenly displayed their illicit wares in the window.

"To certain people."

"I see."

Saunders was unapologetic. "Lifting the curtain on the mysteries of Venus is an important form of free expression and, in some cases, can be regarded as art." He paused to look at Atlas. "It is not for me, or my king or regent, to decide what we can and cannot read."

Even before Saunders's impassioned speech, Atlas had suspected the bookseller was favorably inclined toward the dissenters. He wouldn't be surprised to find a radical press hidden somewhere in the bowels of this musty building. However, Saunders's candor did surprise him. Sedition was a dangerous offense. Perhaps knowledge of Atlas's paternity had loosened Saunders's tongue on the matter. Silas Catesby had not believed in a division of the classes.

"So you sold them the book?" Atlas asked.

"I never got the chance," Saunders responded with a shake of his head. "Before I knew it, some toff storms in here, darkens the footman's daylights, and ushers the girls out."

"A toff? A nobleman? You're certain?"

"Father to one of the fair maidens."

"How can you be sure?"

"One of the ewes called him 'Papa,' although I cannot say which girl."

"Did the man, this father, say anything?"

"He told Davis he'd have his head. Thrashed him pretty good. The toff broke the footman's nozzle. There was blood everywhere."

Atlas wondered if it was Merton who had broken Davis's nose. "Was he a large man?" The viscount was on the diminutive side.

"Not as tall as you but not short, mind you." Saunders tilted his head back as he assessed Atlas. "And not as bulky as you. He was slender and a man of obvious stature. Carried himself like he knew his worth."

That definitely sounded like a titled gentleman. But if not Merton, then who? "Was there an insignia on his carriage?"

Saunders gave him a look. "If you were fetching your daughter from the wanton clutches of Holywell Street, would you arrive in a carriage bearing the family crest? It's hardly an outing someone of that ilk would care to advertise."

Atlas saw the man's point. "So this gentleman pounded Davis before ushering the young ladies out. Is there anything else you remember about him?"

"He apologized for the mess and gave me a couple of pounds for my trouble." Saunders bent to pick up the now-empty crate on the dusty floor. "Now if there is nothing else, I do have work to do."

"One more thing." Atlas set his father's book on the counter. "I'll take this."

★ ★ ★

On his way home from Holywell Street, Atlas went by Thea's in search of ice to soothe his aching foot.

Charles Palmer, his sister's perennially absent husband, had built an icehouse for the specific purpose of indulging his wife's sweet tooth and love of frozen desserts. Yet Palmer's thoughtfulness hadn't stopped Thea from practically banishing the man to the country . . . if she had indeed exiled Palmer. In truth, Atlas had no idea why his sister's husband spent so much time away from his wife.

When he arrived at the house on Russell Street, Atlas was surprised to learn from Fletcher, Thea's ancient butler, that his sister was working in the Great Room, which was most unusual. Thea could normally be found scrawling her equations in the sunny breakfast room where she'd turned the circular dining table into a desk piled high with notebooks, papers, and mathematical implements.

Thea made little use of her Great Room, which had likely hosted many routs in its time, well before the Palmers had acquired the home. The room was spacious—long and wide, with high molded ceilings and wooden floors that had probably gleamed at one time but had long since lost their shine. A few pieces of forlorn furniture leftover from those glory days were carelessly shunted to the perimeters of the space.

The first thing Atlas spotted when he entered the cavernous room was the Earl of Charlton standing with both arms extended from his sides, holding a rope in each hand. The ropes each had little red ribbons tied around them at what looked like foot intervals. Following the twin twines down the length of the room, Atlas caught sight of Lilliana, looking particularly fine in an elegant gown of violet silk, holding the opposite ends at the far end of the chamber. Thea moved between the cables, her face a study in concentration, her lips moving quietly as she calculated something.

Atlas sidled up alongside the earl. "Dare I ask what is going on here?"

Charlton shushed him. "Thea is counting," he whispered. "We mustn't break her concentration."

Atlas took a moment to study his friend, who was practically beaming. "What precisely is she counting?"

"Damned if I know, but I'm always happy to be of use to Mrs. Palmer."

Thea finished whatever it was she'd been calculating, wrote something down in her notebook, and then looked up to greet her brother. "Atlas, this is a surprise."

"What are you doing?"

She pointed her pencil in the direction of the earl. "Charlton is always underfoot, so I decided to put him to work."

"And precisely what kind of work is that?" Atlas glanced back at his friend. "Noble scarecrow?"

"You wouldn't understand," she said dismissively before resuming her counting.

"You're probably right," Atlas agreed, making his way down to Lilliana.

"How did it go?" she asked when he reached her, speaking quietly so as not to interrupt Thea's deliberations. Lilliana allowed him to relieve her of one of the ropes she held but kept a grip on the other. "Did you learn anything of interest?"

"You could say so." Not wishing to incur his sister's wrath, Atlas kept the rope taut, holding it just as Lilliana had, while they spoke. "Lady Lavinia is definitely one to court scandal. She and a friend made a visit to Holywell Street."

Lilliana's eyes widened. She looked both amused and scandalized. "No!"

"I'm afraid so. Davis escorted them there, but the plan went awry. They were caught by the angry papa of one of the hellions, who thrashed the footman before bundling the young ladies into his carriage and carrying them away."

"My goodness." Lilliana's hold on the rope slackened. "Who was the father, do you think?"

"Atlas!" Thea's shrill voice cut into their conversation. "Pray do no distract Lilliana. I am almost done here."

Lilliana startled and immediately pulled the twine tight again. "So sorry, Thea."

While Thea returned to her work down near Charlton, Atlas answered Lilliana's question. "Not Merton. The viscount isn't tall, and Angry Papa is. The bookseller who witnessed the interaction described the man as shorter than I am."

"Almost everyone is," she put in.

"But he also did not describe him as short. The bookseller characterized Angry Papa as a man of stature."

"Hmm." She fell silent, and he could see her mind working.

"What is it?"

She paused. "Not Merton then. Angry Papa is the father of the other girl."

Her reaction the other day at the mention of one of Lavinia's friend came back to him. "Who is this Adora that Lavinia spoke of?"

She hesitated. "She's Roxbury's daughter."

"Adora Bradford." This time he was the one to almost drop the rope, but he caught himself before drawing his sister's ire. "I should have put it together myself."

"I didn't think it signified before now." Her tone was almost apologetic.

"You thought to protect your suitor's good name." He kept his tone neutral, even though a distinct sense of betrayal cut through him. She'd withheld pertinent information in order to protect the man who was courting her. "It's natural you wouldn't care to have scandal attached to a family you might wish to join."

"Roxbury is a powerful peer who hardly needs me to look after his interests," she said pointedly. "However, when it comes to young innocent girls getting in over their heads, I naturally have a great deal of empathy toward them."

"Roxbury fits the bookseller's description."

She nodded. "He is not short, and although he is not as tall as you, he is a man of stature."

"If word got out that these supposedly innocent maidens were procuring low publications from a footman, it could ruin their reputations."

Lilliana finished the thought for him. "And their chances of marrying well."

"That could be a motive for murder," Atlas pondered aloud. "Davis had information that could damage the reputations of two noble houses."

"Roxbury does not strike me as the murderous type." She paused. "But then, neither did my husband's killer."

"Precisely. It seems there are many people who are capable of killing another human being . . . particularly if they have a great deal to lose."

"You must speak with Roxbury."

He wondered if that worried her. "Yes, I plan to call upon him on the morrow."

"That won't be necessary." The words were brisk. "He is hosting a garden party in four days' time. Merton and his daughter are likely to be in attendance." She gave him a sly smile. "I don't suppose you'd care to escort me?"

"I can imagine how much Roxbury will appreciate my turning up as your escort," he said dryly.

"So you'll attend?"

"Most certainly."

"Excellent." She adjusted her hold on the rope. "I spoke to Tacy about her brother's previous employers."

"And?"

"I'm afraid I have nothing of use to report. The only other household where Davis was employed was a bachelor home on South Audley Street. The master was the grandson of a marquess. Davis was in service for several years until his employer passed. Then he moved on to work for Merton's household."

"There was no young lady of the house for Davis to seduce," Atlas said. "I suppose there is nothing more to be gained by pursuing that course of investigation."

"It would appear not," she agreed.

"That's it," Thea called out. "I am finished here."

"Which is most convenient"—Lilliana released the rope—"for I must go if I am to be home in time to have supper in the nursery with the boys." She gathered her things and walked toward the door with Atlas following.

"I will go out with you, Lady Roslyn." Charlton dropped both ropes and shook out his arms. "I have an engagement this evening." He settled his azure gaze on Thea. "Unless you have further need of me."

"Not at all." Scribbling in her notebook, Thea did not bother to look up. "I have no reason to keep you."

"I am crestfallen," Charlton said. "First, the lady has her way with me, and then she tosses me into the street."

Lilliana laughed and took his arm. "I will attempt to console you as we walk out."

Atlas stood looking after them until his sister's voice cut into his thoughts. "Woolgathering?"

He turned to face her. "How well acquainted are you with Roxbury?"

A knowing expression settled over his sister's face. "He is wealthy, titled, and very well regarded."

"I know that much," he said impatiently. "Tell me something I do not know."

"He seems quite taken with Lilliana."

"Any idiot with eyes could discern that much. Does he have a temper?"

"I cannot say. But one does get the distinct sense that Roxbury is not a man to be trifled with." She put down her notebook and started rolling the rope.

He moved to assist her before heading to her icehouse in search of relief for his aching foot. "I had the same impression."

Curiosity glimmered in her dark eyes. "Does your sudden interest in the Marquess of Roxbury have to do with the investigation? Or is this about Roxbury's association with Lilliana?"

He decided to be truthful. "Perhaps both."

Chapter Ten

The following day, late in the afternoon, Atlas took a hackney to Spitalfields and stood in the driving rain across from the Gunther & Archer Dye Company until a slender young man exited the gateposts flanking the main entrance of the brick-front property. Sheets of water pouring off his black wood-frame umbrella, Atlas made his way across the mud-slogged street, drenching his boots in inky black filth.

"Buller," he called out loudly enough to be heard over the deluge. The skies had opened up after he'd departed Bond Street, but the dark clouds had appeared ominous enough for him to have brought an umbrella.

The clerk paused and regarded Atlas with a guarded gaze. "Mr. Catesby."

"Do you have a moment?" When the young man hesitated, Atlas decided to sweeten his offer. "Time enough for a cup of ale perhaps? And a bite to eat, of course."

If the youth lived alone, the offer would tempt him. Hot food and ale on a rainy evening—at someone else's expense—would be difficult for a struggling clerk to resist.

"The Seven Crowns is around the corner," Buller said.

They hurried along in the downpour until they reached the tavern, which was tucked down a narrow alley. A crush of working-class people filled the tight space, the air crowded with boisterous conversation and a silvery haze of smoke. But the alehouse was also warm and dry, for which Atlas was grateful. The owner behind the wood-paneled bar spotted them and led the two men through the crowd to a corner table.

Generous servings of beefsteak and cabbage followed, and when Buller also showed interest in pie, Atlas ordered that as well. He watched the younger man dig into his meal, his full attention on the hot food before him. Meat was a luxury for someone surviving on a clerk's wages.

Atlas took a long draw on his ale. "Was Davis extorting Viscount Merton or anyone else?"

Swallowing a big lump of food, the clerk dragged his attention away from beefsteak. "How'd you know about that?"

"Not from you, obviously."

Buller blinked, his eyes wide. "You didn't ask."

Atlas swallowed down his impatience. "I'm asking now."

"Gordon was paid off by the Quality." Buller gulped his ale. "But he never mentioned names."

"Do you know why they were paying him?"

Buller popped another large piece of meat into his mouth. It bulged in his right cheek as he answered Atlas's question. "To keep him quiet."

Anticipation pounded through Atlas's veins. "What did they want him to keep quiet about?"

Buller grinned, a string of beef stuck between his two front teeth. "Gordon took two chits to buy dirty books. The 'young ladies of quality'"—sarcasm twisted his words—"had a taste for common fucking."

Shocked, Atlas set his ale down with a clunk. "Davis told you he bedded the young ladies?"

"Nah." Buller spoke around a mouthful of cabbage. "They wanted to see the drawings. Insisted Gordon take them to Holywell so they could pick out their own dirty books."

"Why did he agree? He risked losing his situation."

"He was a gambler, was Gordon. And the ladies paid him well. He insisted that each one pay him a fee."

"I presume you know he got caught."

Buller nodded. "Gordon said the nob popped his cork and threw him out of the house. But it was of no account to Gordon." Buller took a long swig of his ale. "He said he was going to make their fathers pay to keep him quiet, or else he'd tell all Mayfair where he'd taken their precious daughters."

"Did they pay him?"

"Yes, both of them did."

Atlas shook his head. Davis had clearly been a sharper of the lowest sort, running a game anywhere he could find one, always in search of the big score. The question was, had one of those games proved deadly for him?

Buller bottomed out his drink and set it down. Atlas motioned for the barkeeper to bring another. A well-fed and well-hydrated Buller was apparently a fount of information. "What do you know about Trevor Archer?"

The question made Buller stop eating for the first time since the food appeared. "Mr. Archer's son?"

"The very same."

Both men were quiet while the barkeeper came over to refill their ale.

"What about him?" Buller asked once the man was gone.

"Did Davis tell you the boy played deep?"

Buller grinned. "He said Trevor Archer had more money than brains." He paused as if trying to recall something. "Gordon took him to Mrs. Leach's gaming hell on Bennett Street."

"Mrs. Leach's?" Atlas wanted to make certain he had the correct name.

Buller nodded. "It seemed to me that Davis got paid to take pigeons there. Can I have more beefsteak?"

Clearly, a visit to Mrs. Leach's gaming hell on Bennett Street was in order. Atlas rose and dropped several coins on the table. "By all means."

Hopeful that the deluge outside had eased at least a little, he said his farewells, grabbed his dripping umbrella, and headed for the exit.

⋆ ⋆ ⋆

Later, at home in his sitting room, warm, dry, and wrapped in his well-worn dressing gown with a fire blazing in the hearth, Atlas sat at his game table working on a puzzle.

It was his most challenging one to date. Most puzzles were too rudimentary for his tastes, so he had them made to order. He might have gone too far with this latest one, though—Hogarth's depiction of the Jacobite rebellion, featuring a crowd of people and dozens of small faces—which was proving to be quite a challenge. He'd already assembled the frame on all four sides and turned his focus to the sky. As he pushed two pieces of gray-white cloud together, his mind sorted through the facts of the investigation.

At the moment, the most likely suspects included Merton, Roxbury, and the still mysterious Lady L. The dead man had been a threat to all three of their reputations, something the ton tended to take most seriously. Few things were worse than losing face in society. Atlas intended to speak with both the viscount and the marquess soon, but the identity of Lady L remained a mystery.

He also needed to learn whether Trevor Archer had become indebted to Davis again. What if the younger Archer had been too afraid to admit as much to his father? As the owner's son, Trevor likely would have had access to the arsenic at the factory. Atlas needed to speak with the young man before he could fully form an impression of how involved he might be.

Tomorrow evening, he'd stop in at Mrs. Leach's on the off chance Trevor Archer might also decide to visit his favorite hell. Having settled that particular matter, he turned his full attention to the puzzle before him, letting his mind take him off to a particularly relaxing state of blankness, a time when he tended to do his best thinking.

And this case certainly required plenty of that.

⋆ ⋆ ⋆

"Tell me again why we're visiting this establishment." Wrinkling his nose, Charlton surveyed the smoky interior of Mrs. Leach's gaming hell. "We must be the only people above the age of thirty here."

"Then we are very likely in the right place," Atlas said.

The earl had followed him down narrow stairs to reach the unobtrusive off-street entrance. Inside, decorated in red velvets and dark woods, the hell was surprisingly sumptuous despite the low ceilings and belowstairs location.

"We've come because a little bird told me I'd find Trevor Archer here this evening." Atlas scanned the crowded floor, where much of the attention was centered around the primary hazard table. The patrons, mostly young wealthy men about town, were focused on the action at the table. A loud cheer went up, followed by excited murmurs.

"Ah, the factory owner's wayward son," Charlton said. "This certainly looks like a place where a lamb could be fleeced."

It was Atlas's second visit to the hell. The first time, two nights before, he'd come away empty-handed, but he had managed to enlist one of the girls who worked the floor to send word if she spotted the young man. He surveyed the room searching for her, but Nellie surprised him when she suddenly appeared and sidled up next to him.

"Guv, I see you got my note." She wore the same cheap gown as when they'd first met, with front lacing very loosely done up, providing a generous view of her ample assets.

"A small bird, hmm?" On Atlas's other side, Charlton murmured in his ear. "More like a ladybird."

"Which one is he?" Atlas asked her.

Nellie pointed toward the hazard table. "The cove in the brown jacket." The husky form she pointed out as Trevor Archer sat with his back to them. "He's a pigeon."

"Whose pigeon?" Atlas expected Nellie to confirm what Buller had told him.

"Some cove named Davis brought 'im a few weeks back. Mrs. Leach pays well for those who brings in fresh 'uns."

Charlton watched the action at the table with interest. "I suppose the fresh ones you speak of possess plenty of blunt but a limited supply of sense and experience at the gaming tables."

She winked at the earl. "Exactly as you say, my lord." She shot a look over at Archer. "That 'un over there weren't happy when he learned Davis got paid for bringing 'im here."

Atlas gave her his full attention. "How do you know Archer was angry with Davis?"

"It was hard to miss. Archer challenged 'im on it right here. They shoved each other until Mrs. Leach's men put a stop to it." She shook her head. "Not too smart, that Archer. He owed a small fortune to both the gaming house and Davis."

"How much did he owe the house?"

"Can't say, guv. But I do know he managed to pay his debts. That's the only way Mrs. Leach would let him back in to play."

Atlas dropped a couple of coins into her open palm. "Thank you, Nellie, you've been most helpful."

She slipped the payment somewhere into the folds of her skirt. "That's right generous of you." She nudged up against him so that he could feel the insistent press of her breast against his arm. "How about a quick tumble? A big 'un like you would be a lot of man."

He caught her straying hand as it slid down his belly. "That's most generous, Nellie, but unfortunately, I must see to matters pertaining to Mr. Archer."

Undeterred, she shrugged and ambled over to Charlton. "What about you, milord?"

"As tempting as your offer is"—Charlton drew back—"I must unfortunately stay and assist my friend here." As he spoke, the earl dropped another few coins into Nellie's hand to send her away. With a jaunty smile, she went off in search of new game.

Atlas took in the exchange with amusement. "Most men pay for women to come to them, not to go away."

"She seems like a lovely woman. But when I think of how many others have already had the pleasure . . ." He shuddered as if a cockroach had run up his spine. "I'd be sure to catch the pox."

Atlas moved closer to the action to get a better look at Archer, who held the dice in his hands.

"What's the main, Archer?" someone called out.

"Five!" Trevor Archer grinned. He shared his sisters' pale complexion and rosy cheeks. Trevor blew on the dice and tossed them across the table, coming up with eleven.

"Archer throws out!" The setter, a gaming hell worker, leaned forward to scoop up the money on the table. The boy barely seemed to notice and quickly placed another bet. Atlas and Charlton watched Archer lose several rolls in a row.

"He doesn't know when to stop." The words were murmured by a young man who'd come up next to Atlas. His expensive tailored clothing and cut-glass tones spoke of wealth and breeding. Distaste rippled through Atlas. This lordling was likely the scion of some indolent peer with an inflated sense of self-worth, someone like Vessey, the man responsible for his sister Phoebe's death.

"Do you know him?" Atlas asked the lordling, seeing if he might garner any useful information about Archer.

"Not terribly well. His name is Trevor Archer," the young man replied. "A fortnight ago, I intervened and sent him on his way before he could get in any deeper."

"You intervened on Archer's behalf?" Atlas regarded the lordling with surprise. "Why?"

The young man shrugged. "Mrs. Leach has bled him dry. Archer's desperation that evening was especially painful to watch. And it is wrong to prey upon men's weaknesses. Especially those of young men."

Atlas gave the lordling a second look. If the young man was to be believed, he'd done a good turn for someone he barely knew simply because it was the right thing to do. And Atlas had to admit the lordling's manner was amiable enough. In addition, there was something very familiar about him, even though Atlas was certain they'd never met. The lordling's hair was a golden brown, his eyes a warm hazel. Atlas attempted to place the boy, trying to puzzle out why he didn't feel like a stranger. "It was good of you to stand up for him," Atlas said to him.

"Someone had to." The lordling smiled wryly. "There are times when rank has its privileges. One might as well make some use of it."

Atlas nodded approvingly. "Indeed."

"Lennox. There you are." A friend of the young man's appeared. He too wore fine attire and exuded the ennui common to so many members of the nobility. "Let's go. There's a rout in Kensington that's supposed to be all the crack."

The lordling shook his head. "I'm afraid I cannot. I'm meeting my father for a late supper."

The friend let out an exaggerated groan. "Surely Vessey won't mind."

"I think he might. Another time, Miles." He turned to Atlas. "Good evening then." With a friendly smile, he disappeared in the crowd.

Atlas felt as though the breath had been knocked out of him. *It couldn't be.* Pain twisted in his chest, and he pressed a hand over his heart. His ears buzzed; the noise in the gaming hell seeming to recede.

"Atlas? Are you well?" Charlton's concerned voice seemed to come from a great distance. "You've gone gray."

Atlas gasped, struggling to suck air into his depleted lungs.

"Atlas? What is it?" Charlton put a hand on his arm. "Come and sit down."

Atlas allowed the earl to lead him to a seat and push him down into it.

"You stay here." Charlton ordered. "I'll get you a drink." He turned to go. "Make way. Make way," he commanded imperiously, vanishing into the throng of gaming hell denizens. Closing his eyes, Atlas tilted his head back and tried to calm his racing heart.

Nicholas Lennox. The memories rushed back, flooding his senses and resurrecting emotions he'd buried for more than twenty years. In his mind, he still pictured Nicholas as a young child, not the well-spoken young gentleman he'd encountered that evening.

"Here." Charlton was back, pushing a cool libation into his hand. "Drink."

Atlas obeyed his friend's command. Taking the glass, he upended all of its contents into his mouth. He swallowed in a few large gulps and waited for the fiery heat to scald his chest, hoping it would numb a fraction of the pain wedged there.

"What the devil is it?" Concern shadowing his gaze, Charlton took the seat across from him. "You look like you've seen a ghost."

Atlas finally managed to draw a lungful of air. Relief coursed through him as he exhaled long and loud, relishing the sensation of being able to breathe again. "In a way, I have. Seen a ghost, I mean."

Charlton's amber brows furrowed. "Care to explain?"

"That boy"—he could hardly say the words out loud—"is Nicholas Lennox."

"So? Who the bloody hell is Nicholas Lennox?"

Atlas almost spat the name of the man he hated more than anyone on earth. "Vessey's son."

"What has that got to do with you?"

"My late sister, Phoebe, was his mother."

The confusion on the earl's face gave way to pure shock. "That boy is your nephew?"

Atlas nodded. He tapped the bottom of his empty glass on the tabletop. "More," he croaked.

Charlton turned and gestured for someone to refill Atlas's drink before facing his friend again. "You never told me your sister had a child."

He swallowed hard against the knot of fury and sorrow barreling up his chest and into his throat. All these years, it had been easier to forget the boy, to pretend Nicholas didn't exist, to act as if a part of his sister did not still roam the earth. "He was an infant when Phoebe died. Barely three months old."

"He didn't know you just now," Charlton said, half to himself. "Why doesn't he know who you are?"

Someone appeared and refilled Atlas's glass. As soon as he was done, Atlas took a large gulp. "Vessey wouldn't allow us to see him. The bastard said he didn't want us tainting the boy with lies."

"Or with the truth, rather, of how his mother died."

"Exactly."

"How ghastly." Charlton made a tsking sound. "How old is the boy now?"

"One-and-twenty." The same number of years Nicholas's mother had been dead. He looked blindly at the table next to them where he caught sight of Nellie perched on a rowdy young buck's lap as he drank with a group of boisterous friends.

Charlton searched Atlas's face. "Young Lennox is old enough to do as he pleases. He could seek you out."

Atlas dragged his gaze back to the earl. "Yes, but he hasn't, has he? That says it all, don't you think?"

"To the contrary. I believe it tells us nothing at all. Who knows what manner of lies Vessey has fed the boy about your family."

At the next table, Nellie pulled away from her young buck and came over. "Guv, your chicken is about to leave."

Atlas blinked, momentarily confused by her words, before comprehending her meaning. Trevor Archer—the reason he'd come this evening—was departing before Atlas had had a chance to talk to him. Scanning the establishment for his quarry, he came to his feet.

"Perhaps this is best left to another time," Charlton said.

"Nonsense." Atlas spotted Archer near the entrance, preparing to make his exit. He started in that direction, grateful to have something besides Phoebe's son to focus on.

Archer was reaching for his greatcoat when Atlas caught up with him. "Trevor Archer?"

"Yes?" Trevor met his approach with polite disinterest. "And you are?"

"Atlas Catesby. I'm looking into the death of Gordon Davis."

"What is there to investigate?" Trevor drew his coat on. "I heard he did himself in."

"His sister believes otherwise."

"I'm not sure how I can be of any help."

"As I understand it, you two were friendly at one point."

Trevor accepted his beaver hat from an attendant. "He was more of an acquaintance."

"Why did you argue with Davis here on the gaming floor?"

Trevor flushed. "Who told you that?"

"It's not exactly a secret. The confrontation occurred in full view of the entire hell."

"I learned he'd brought me here for the distinct purpose of being fleeced by the house." He huffed his indignation. "As if I'm some green boy waiting to be taken advantage of."

Atlas suspected that that was exactly what Trevor Archer was but decided it was prudent to keep that particular opinion to himself. "Did you owe Davis money at the time of his death?"

"Most assuredly not."

Yet someone had paid off Archer's gaming house debt. If not Davis, then who? Trevor's father perhaps? "How did you meet your obligations?"

Archer appeared affronted. "You overstep, sir. That is certainly none of your concern."

Atlas's patience with this insolent child was close to running out. "Perhaps I should ask your father."

Archer paled. "You wouldn't."

"I most certainly would. I intend to get to the bottom of this matter—one way or the other."

Archer fairly simmered with resentment at being trapped into answering Atlas's question. "A generous friend intervened and paid off all the debts I owed the gaming hell."

"Why would someone do that?"

"Perhaps he is a Good Samaritan."

"What is this friend's name?"

Archer paused, his reluctance obvious, before answering, "Nicholas Lennox. If you don't believe me, you can ask him yourself."

Chapter Eleven

"I thought you said this was a garden party," Atlas said to Lilliana.

"And so it is." They entered the Marquess of Roxbury's rather immense garden, where strains of a lively tune floated over to greet them. "Although this affair is slightly more lavish than the garden parties I used to attend in Slough," she said, referring to the cozy village she'd called home during her ill-fated marriage.

He shot her a dubious look. "*Slightly* more lavish?" The Marquess of Roxbury's garden party was almost as excessive as the Duke of Somerville's ball. Despite being held outdoors, almost every indoor comfort was provided for the guests. Colorful carpets were laid out on the damp grass, protecting slippers, boots, and hems from the muddy mess beneath the floor covering. Stuffed sofas and chairs were arranged on the rugs, creating sitting areas for guests to lounge in.

Beyond the seated guests, couples danced on a wooden platform, and a quartet of musicians nearby proved to be the source of the merry music filling the air. The entire tableau, with the ladies in their white-and-pastel gowns and the men smartly attired in light-colored suits, was rather idyllic.

"I didn't realize there were gardens this enormous in the city," Atlas said.

"These grounds are likely the largest in Town, next to Somerville's, of course." Lilliana gave a regal nod to an older couple that paused to greet her. Curious gazes followed Lilliana and Atlas as they strolled on. "The Roxbury marquisate is one of England's oldest and most prosperous."

And the current marquess was courting Lilliana, no doubt hoping to make her his marchioness. Atlas could easily envision Lilliana—with her natural elegance and impeccable breeding—as mistress here. She would, no doubt, assume the role with ease and grace.

"My dear Roslyn." Roxbury approached with a welcoming smile. "As always, you are a vision for the eyes."

"No doubt you say that to all of the ladies," she responded airily.

Admiration glimmered in Roxbury's keen gaze. "But with you, my lady"—he bent over her gloved hand—"it is always meant most sincerely."

"Mr. Catesby was kind enough to escort me," Lilliana said. "I do hope you don't mind."

"Of course not. Any friend of yours is most welcome here." Roxbury turned to greet Atlas with gracious amiability. "Catesby. Delighted to see you again."

"Roxbury. Your garden is to be admired."

They exchanged a few more pleasantries before moving on to allow Roxbury to greet his other guests. They strolled past young men and women playing at archery.

"Look," Lilliana said. "There is Lavinia Fenton." The young lady in question aimed and fired, her arrow landing slightly right of the center of the target.

"She's a good shot," he observed.

"You'd better have a care. She's likely to aim Cupid's arrow at you."

Atlas scoffed. "She's a child."

"A comely child of marital age."

"And I am a man without a title or a fortune."

"You have other attributes." She withdrew her hand from where it rested on his arm. "I shall leave you to it."

"Where are you off to?"

"I will mingle while you question Lavinia."

"Why don't we speak with her together?"

He did not look forward to being alone with the cheeky girl. Especially if she truly had designs on him. The last thing he needed was to be leg-shackled to an infant.

"She seems remarkably eager to please you." She tapped him lightly on the arm. "Use some of that considerable charm of yours to coax the necessary information out of her."

He frowned after Lilliana as she glided away. She'd no doubt find herself in Roxbury's company before too long. The marquess made little secret of his esteem for the lady.

"Mr. Catesby." Lavinia appeared before him. She looked quite fetching in a becoming white gown and jaunty bonnet. "Are you perchance looking for me?"

"Lady Lavinia." He made her a bow as she curtseyed. "You're quite skilled at archery."

"Yes," she replied with a meaningful look. "When I put my mind to it, I always hit my target."

He resisted the urge to loosen his cravat. Although light flirtatious banter would be appropriate at this juncture, he judged it more prudent to stick entirely to the matter of the investigation.

"I visited Holywell Street and learned something of great interest."

"Is that so?" She took his arm. "Shall we walk?"

They began a circuitous route around the garden as he posed his question. "You went there, did you not, with Davis to buy inappropriate materials?"

"You have caught me." The side of her body brushed up against his. He did not believe the contact was accidental. "Yes, I did go. I was very interested to learn more about what passes between a man and a woman."

He distanced his body from hers. "A man and a woman who are wed."

She shot him a naughty look. "Are you suggesting all of those pictures depicted married couples?"

He stifled a sigh. This girl was trouble in every way. If her father were wise, he'd have her married off before she caused a scandal and brought the entire family to ruin. "Roxbury found you there—you and his daughter—didn't he?"

"Yes." Her eyes sparkled as if she thought it was all good fun. "The marquess was livid. He thrashed Davis and ushered me and Adora out to his carriage."

"You'd paid Davis to take you both there."

"Yes." She pouted. "All we wanted was to have a bit of fun. I never realized the marquess had such a temper. He is usually so agreeable." They passed a group of young people laughingly engaged in a competitive game of croquet.

"I gather the visit to Holywell Street is the reason your father released Davis from his position without references."

She nodded as they stepped around a ball being chased after by a young gentleman. "He was most infuriated."

"I suppose you had a motive for not telling me this earlier?"

"Certainly. I wanted you to have a reason to come back and see me." She batted her lengthy lashes. "Without Lady Lilliana present."

"This is a very serious business." He punctuated each word with a sharp edge. "A man is dead, and his sister is in mourning. Gordon Davis's demise is not child's play."

"She is very old, you know."

"What? Who?"

"Lady Roslyn. I know you admire her. But she's probably almost thirty. That's practically ancient."

He drew a deep breath, struggling to keep his temper in check. "Is your father here?" He hadn't seen Merton during their walk through the garden. Now that he'd confirmed the Holywell visit with Lavinia, he intended to take the opportunity this rout presented to speak with both Merton and Roxbury about Davis's alleged extortion scheme.

"My father? No, he's gone out to the country for a few days. Why?" Her smile was sultry and beckoning. "Do you wish to speak with him about your intentions?"

Had she completely taken leave of her senses? "Absolutely not." He lost all courtesy and regarded her with open incredulity. "I am far too old for you."

"Papa is twenty years older than Mama."

"I have no intention of wedding." *Least of all to such a saucy baggage of trouble.* He deliberately changed the subject. "Is there anything else you've neglected to tell me about Gordon Davis and your interactions with him?"

"Not that I can think of." She squeezed his arm. "Now since I've answered your questions, I think you should reward me by escorting me to the dining room for some refreshment."

He was trying to think of a gracious way to refuse when one of Roxbury's footmen appeared. "Mr. Catesby?"

"Yes?"

"The marquess requests you attend him in his study. If you could please follow me."

"I'd be delighted to." Not only did Atlas want to speak with Roxbury about the incident on Holywell Street, but the marquess's summons provided the perfect reason to excuse himself from Lavinia's presence, which he did happily before following the footman into the house.

★ ★ ★

"Ah, Catesby, there you are." Roxbury was ensconced in a velvet armchair with his legs elegantly crossed, a silvery haze engulfing him while he sucked on a smoking cheroot. "Do join me."

The footman closed the door, leaving them alone. It took Atlas a moment for his eyes to adjust to the dark room after coming in from out of doors. The space was everything one would expect of a wealthy marquess—large and well appointed with sumptuous furnishings and dark, shiny surfaces. He took a seat opposite Lilliana's suitor. "What can I do for you, Roxbury?"

"You can tell me what your intentions are toward Roslyn."

The man certainly was direct. "I fail to see how that is any of your concern."

Roxbury stared at him. "It is very much my concern because I intend to wed her."

"Are you betrothed?"

"Not as of yet."

"Then I cannot fathom why we are having this discussion."

"We are speaking because I hope that, as a gentleman, you will not take advantage of Roslyn's gratitude."

"I'm afraid I don't follow."

"She has told me what occurred in Slough."

Atlas remained silent. He had pledged never to speak of the abomination Lilliana's late husband had subjected her to.

Exhaling a lungful of smoke, Roxbury examined his cheroot. "She assures me you behaved in a most gentlemanly manner after coming to her rescue. I do hope that you will continue to do so."

Again Atlas declined to respond. He felt no compunction at all to defend his character to this man.

Roxbury continued. "It is natural that Roslyn would feel beholden to you. I gather that is why she continues to receive you and appears intent on introducing you into society."

Atlas let out a startled laugh. "I assure you, I have no interest in society."

"I gather you would not say the same of the duke's sister." Atlas's grip on the chair's armrests tightened. When he remained silent, Roxbury went on. "I have everything to offer her. Wealth, position, and rank." He paused. "If I may be frank?"

As if Atlas could stop him. "Please."

"It is not my intention to offend you, but as the fourth son of a baron, you have nothing to offer the daughter and sister of the Dukes of Somerville."

"And yet, you felt the need to summon me here."

Roxbury's lip curled. "As my marchioness, Roslyn would be protected if what occurred in Slough were to become public. I could shield her with my name and rank."

Atlas forced himself to ease his grip on the chair's armrests. "It is up to Lady Roslyn to decide whether she will have you." He pushed out his next words. "If she does, you both will have my sincere felicitations."

"Thank you." Roxbury took a long inhale of the cheroot, which had burned down to almost nothing. "I am confident that she will accept me—in time. You should know that I always protect what is mine."

Atlas held the other man's gaze. "I wonder how far you would go to protect what is yours."

"As far as necessary, I'd expect."

"Would you kill for your daughter?"

Roxbury straightened, his glare menacing. "What are you about?" he growled. "Do you dare to threaten Adora?"

"Me? Of course not. But you seemed to think Gordon Davis posed a threat."

Roxbury's expression steeled. This time he was the one to remain silent as Atlas continued speaking.

"I know you found him on Holywell Street with your daughter and Lavinia Fenton, Merton's daughter. I also understand you paid him for his silence on the matter."

Roxbury calmly took another long draw on his cheroot before responding. "And your reason for revisiting this unfortunate incident is?"

"Davis is dead. From arsenic poisoning. His sister believes he was murdered."

That prompted an incredulous laugh out of Roxbury. "And you think I killed the man?"

"I don't know what to think as of yet, but I must follow all leads."

"And this is not personal?" Roxbury asked tightly. "Does Roslyn know you are pursuing this matter?"

"She does. As a matter of fact, it was Lady Roslyn who asked me to look into Davis's death. Her maid is the victim's sister." He could not resist adding, "I had not been in contact with her for almost a year when she reached out recently to request my assistance."

Roxbury quickly masked his surprise. "I see."

"Did you pay Davis for his silence?"

Roxbury hesitated. "Do I have your word that this goes no further?"

"You do."

"Then yes. Merton and I each paid a handsome sum to keep the footman quiet." He stubbed out his cheroot. "However, we also made certain he wouldn't work in Mayfair again. We were loath to inflict him upon any unsuspecting household with impressionable young ladies in residence."

"That's very understandable. When was the last time you saw him?"

"About a year ago, shortly after the Holywell incident. We met here. I paid him and sent him on his way."

"Did you not worry that he would return and ask for more once he ran out of funds?"

The marquess's face darkened. "I saw to it that he would not dare."

"And how did you manage that?"

"I told Davis that if he came back, I would see him brought up on theft charges."

"Theft?" Atlas blinked. "For what?"

"For stealing the money he extorted from me."

"You're referring to the blunt you gave him to keep him quiet."

Roxbury dipped his chin. "Davis understood that, given my position in society, a charge like that would see him transported."

"Whether or not it was true."

"Exactly. That's the only approach that type of filth understands."

Atlas couldn't disagree. "Did Davis ever come back and ask for more?"

"He did not. He knew better than to cross me again." The marquess came to his feet. "I do have guests I must see to."

Atlas rose as well. As he followed the marquess to the door, Roxbury paused.

"As to your question earlier, about whether I'd kill for someone I loved."

"Yes?"

"I believe I would." Roxbury pulled the massive door open. "Given the opportunity, I would like nothing more than to call Roslyn's husband out for what he did to her. The scoundrel certainly deserved it."

Atlas followed Lilliana's suitor out the door. "On that, at least, we can agree."

Chapter Twelve

"There really is no need to visit faraway lands when the fruits of those lands can come to you." Charlton turned to Atlas. "Don't you agree?"

"I do not," Atlas returned. "A museum is hardly the same as seeing foreign provinces with one's own eyes."

They entered Mr. Bullock's Museum in Piccadilly, which was quite the sensation in London if the crowds were any indication. The exotic animal exhibits in the center of the rooms seemed to draw the most visitors. The beasts—elephants, zebras, and various creatures from other continents—had been preserved, stuffed, and mounted, still incredibly lifelike long after their deaths. Curiosities from Africa and the Americas—fish, shells, minerals, and botanicals—filled the glass display cabinets lining the walls.

Charlton paused before the enormous stuffed pachyderm. "I say, in those lands you visit, are many animals running around?"

"Yes, they are ambling down the streets." Atlas did not hide the sarcasm in his words. "One of my hosts had a pet donkey that joined us for meals."

"Ah, you jest." Charlton wandered over to a glass case to examine the rocks and minerals within. "But here in London, I have certainly broken bread with a number of asses in my time."

"As have I." Atlas chuckled. "Your point is well taken."

"Where will you go next?" Charlton asked. "Have you decided?"

"I'm thinking of India." He'd received a note on the matter just that morning from Edward Hughes, an acquaintance at the East India Company. "There's a spot for me aboard a ship leaving London in a matter of weeks."

"India?" Charlton grimaced. "How long would that journey take?"

"I'm told it is a voyage of about five months, possibly six."

Charlton shuddered theatrically. "Why you would choose to leave the comfort and civilization of England for heathen lands truly escapes me."

"Nothing is for certain at the moment. The investigation keeps me here for now."

"Is it the investigation that draws you to Town?" Charlton smirked. "Or perhaps a certain lady?"

Atlas chose to ignore the blatant insinuation. "I gave Lilliana my word that I would find Davis's killer, and so I shall. I cannot leave London until that obligation is met."

Charlton made a skeptical humming sound in his throat as they wandered into the next room and stopped before a floor-length cloak made of red, black, and yellow feathers, a cape of honor worn by a tribal chief in the South Pacific.

"I've no engagements for this evening," Charlton said as they studied the garment. "Care to join me for supper at my club?"

"Why not." Atlas had no plans beyond staying in and working on his puzzle. "What time?"

"I'll come around for you at nine, shall we say?"

A vaguely familiar voice remarked behind them, "How many birds had to die, do you think, to produce this rather magnificent garment?" Atlas turned, and the beat of his heart lost its steady pace.

Charlton reacted first. "Lord Nicholas. A pleasure to see you again."

Nicholas Lennox bowed. "We meet again."

Atlas tried not to stare at his sister's son, but it took effort. Although Nicholas looked more like his father, a man Atlas hated more than any being on the planet, a trace of Phoebe was evident in the young man's guileless smile.

Atlas swallowed, his throat tight. "Indeed we do." He had a hundred questions for the boy. But also none. Where did one begin after twenty-one years with so much left unspoken between them? The boy didn't even know who Atlas was.

Atlas grappled for a way to fill the silence and quickly found one. He had wanted to speak with the young man about Trevor Archer, to confirm that Nicholas had indeed paid Archer's debts, but had not seen a way to approach the son of his greatest enemy.

He decided to grab this unexpected opportunity. Putting the puzzle together, filling the holes in the investigation into something orderly, would also calm his mind—and the riotous emotions assaulting him. Atlas had never truly learned how to cope with the extreme reactions his sister's death had ignited within him. "I am pleased to have happened upon you, Lord Nicholas."

The young man smiled. "How may I be of service?"

"Trevor Archer told me something interesting the other evening at Mrs. Leach's."

"Is that so?" Nicholas inquired politely. His manner, gentle and agreeable, was so like this mother's that it took Atlas's breath away. "And what was that?"

Atlas forced an even tone. "He said you paid off his gaming house debt."

Color bloomed on Nicholas's cheeks. "It was nothing."

It was hardly nothing. "Did Archer speak the truth?" Atlas asked. "Did you pay all his debts?"

"Yes, he was in very deep, and I am fortunate to have more than ample funds. My father is most generous with me."

Atlas gritted his teeth at the mention of the boy's bastard of a father. Did Nicholas know Vessey had killed his mother?

Charlton quickly stepped in. "What brings you here?" he asked Nicholas. "Are you an admirer of the exotic?"

"I admit to being curious about the world outside of England," Nicholas answered. "Unfortunately, due to the war on the continent, my grand tour was canceled. I had so looked forward to it."

"Then you will be interested in speaking with our friend here." Charlton flashed a look at Atlas before returning his attention to the young man. "Mr. Catesby is an adventurer who has traveled the world."

"How fascinating." Interest lit the young man's gaze. "Where have you visited?" Then it seemed to hit him. He frowned. "Catesby, did you say?"

Atlas's heartbeat was chaotic. "Atlas Catesby." He waited for a reaction.

All agreeability drained from Nicholas's face. "Are you by chance related to the poet?" he asked uncertainly.

"Yes." Atlas heard the strain in his own voice. "Silas Catesby was my father." *And your grandfather.*

Nicholas's face paled. "I see." He stepped back. "If you'll excuse me, gentlemen. Good day." He spun on his heel and was swiftly lost in the crowd. Atlas and Charlton stared after Nicholas as he made his escape into the throng.

"Well," Atlas said grimly, his heart a burdensome weight in his chest. "That went well."

⋆ ⋆ ⋆

Atlas arrived home to find the front door ajar and Jamie running a finger over the fireplace mantle in the front hall.

Bess, the middle-aged woman who came in twice weekly to clean Atlas's bachelor's quarters, stood by the door with her wrap on, apparently ready to depart. She glared at Jamie's back. "I cleaned it as I always do."

"Hmm." Jamie held his finger up to the light to examine it. "This surface could be dusted a bit more thoroughly."

Outrage stamped the cleaning woman's face. "There is nothing wrong with my dusting. I've been scrubbing floors since before you were even a glimmer in your da's eye."

"I must see to my master's every comfort." Jamie looked down his nose at her. "It is my duty as valet to ensure that you sweep and dust properly."

Bess flushed. "And it just might be my duty to take you over my knee like the insolent boy you are and teach you some manners," she snapped.

Jamie lost his assumed air of superiority. "I should like to see you try!" he exclaimed, looking genuinely affronted.

Atlas closed the door behind him with a decisive click. Jamie and Bess both turned in his direction with a startled look.

Bess recovered first. "Good afternoon, sir. I was just leaving."

"Thank you, Bess. I'll see you later this week as usual?"

"Indeed, sir." She tossed a malevolent look in Jamie's direction as she sailed out the door. "Good day to you," she said pointedly to Atlas.

Jamie stomped over to slam the door behind her. "Wretched old woman doesn't know her place."

Atlas suppressed a sigh. "Someone doesn't. That's for certain," he murmured mostly to himself.

"Clearly Bess doesn't understand that a valet is at the highest rung of the servant chain."

"And because we have no servants for you to lord it over, you decided to exert yourself on poor Bess?"

Jamie's full cheeks flushed. "I was just making certain she did her duty."

"I appreciate that." Atlas handed Jamie his hat and shrugged off his coat. "But please leave Bess alone to do her job. I have seen no fault with her cleaning." He paused. "And, Jamie."

"Yes, sir?"

"You would do well to remember that respect is earned. You cannot force it. Conduct yourself in the manner of a man who deserves respect, and it will come to you."

While a still-disgruntled Jamie tramped into the bedchamber to put away the coat and hat, Atlas settled before his puzzle and tried to push Nicholas Lennox from his mind. Pondering a puzzle piece depicting half a face, he called out to the boy, "How are you coming along with the poison books? Did you find any familiar names?"

Jamie reappeared from the bedchamber. "There is no sign of Gordon Davis buying poison at any of the apothecaries near his work or business. No Henry Buller either."

Not looking up from the puzzle, Atlas slid a piece into place, uniting two sides of the same face. "What about the Mayfair apothecaries?"

"No sign of Lord Merton or his daughter, Lady Lavinia, purchasing arsenic. Nor any of their house servants."

Atlas looked up. "How can you know whether their servants purchased anything?"

"I stopped by the Earl of Charlton's to take tea with the staff. They still consider me part of the staff over there, seeing as how I'll go back there when you go traveling again—"

Atlas interrupted. "Perhaps you could favor me with the abridged version of the story."

Jamie's face scrunched up. "Abridged? I didn't mention a bridge."

"A shorter version of the story," he clarified.

"Oh, yes, sir," Jamie continued eagerly. "As I was saying, while I was at the earl's, I managed to get the names of Lady Lavinia's lady's maid, Lord Merton's valet, and their footmen. You see, all the downstairs folk know each other in Mayfair. For example, when the Duke of Caraway's butler made improper advances to his grace's housekeeper—"

"Jamie," Atlas interrupted before the boy could share all of Mayfair's belowstairs scandals. "Let us not digress. You were saying that you learned the names of Merton's servants and . . . ?"

"Yes, sir. And none of those servants' names appear in any of the poison books I checked."

Atlas considered. "That was very enterprising of you, thinking of checking the servants' names." He'd known before that moment that the boy was eager to learn and better himself, but he hadn't credited Jamie with cleverness as well. "I must tell you that I am very impressed."

Jamie grinned, tilting his head in a jaunty fashion. "Thank you, sir."

"What of Clapham? Have you checked those poison books yet?"

"Yes, sir. But there is no sign of either a Noel or a Trevor Archer purchasing any arsenic."

Atlas pushed another puzzle piece into place. "I suppose this avenue of investigation has led us to a dead end."

Jamie paused. "Not exactly."

Atlas tapped a finger on a puzzle piece while trying to make out where it belonged. "What do you mean?"

"I didn't find the elder nor the younger Archer gentlemen's names, but I did find another name. I don't know if it signifies."

Atlas glanced up. "Which name is that?"

"Elizabeth Archer."

"Elizabeth Archer?" Recalling the proper young woman who'd served him tea when he'd gone to call on her father, Atlas lost all interest in the half-assembled Hogarth painting on the table before him. "Are you certain?"

"Yes, sir. Is she related to Noel and Trevor Archer?"

"She's a daughter of the house. Noel is her father, and Trevor is her brother. When did she purchase the arsenic?"

"March sixteenth."

Atlas did a quick calculation. "That's three weeks before Davis died."

"But the name 'Elizabeth' doesn't start with an *L*."

"True, but it might be a term of endearment known only between the two of them." In truth, Atlas did find it difficult to envision the prim Miss Archer as the libidinous Lady L.

But he'd been surprised before. If his first investigation had taught him anything, it was that—when pushed to the limit—almost anyone was capable of murder.

Chapter Thirteen

Calling hours were long over in polite society, but Atlas was so enthused about his first genuine lead that he disregarded the late hour and immediately walked over to see Lilliana.

Before leaving for Somerville House, he dashed off a quick note to Charlton, informing him that he was meeting with Lilliana about the investigation and thus had to regretfully decline the earl's invitation to dine at his club.

Striding at a brisk pace, he pulled his greatcoat tight around him to ward off the damp early evening chill. The streets were muddy, and the wind howled past his ears during the short walk. Winter still held London firmly in its grip, even though May was almost upon them. Ahead, despite the darkening skies and relentless fog, Somerville House still managed to loom large over Piccadilly, dwarfing anything around it. Atlas bounded up the front stairs, eager to share his news with Lilliana.

A footman opened the massive carved door straightaway. If Hastings, the butler, who appeared immediately, was surprised to find a guest—who was neither invited nor expected—standing on the ducal doorstep, he was far too well trained to show any sign of displeasure.

"Good evening, sir." Hastings ushered him in out of the cold. Atlas stepped into the welcoming warmth of the mammoth front hall, where a huge marble statue greeted all who entered Somerville House. "If you will wait here, I will see if my lady is at home to visitors."

The butler returned quickly and led Atlas up the stairs. Behind them in the front hall, a footman appeared with a pristine cloth and briskly wiped away any mud and dirt Atlas had tracked in from outside.

Atlas adjusted his cravat as he was shown to Lilliana's private sitting room. She was standing by the window and turned to face him when he entered. She wore a white lace dressing gown beneath a sheer robe of the same color. Almost immediately, Atlas regretted his impulsiveness. The ton lived by certain rules, and he had most certainly violated one of those strictures by calling upon Lilliana at this hour. That she received him in a state of undress confirmed his misstep.

"I apologize for the intrusion," he said immediately. "If you are indisposed, I shall be happy to call upon you on the morrow when you are receiving."

"Nonsense." She came toward him, a welcoming expression on her face. "If I were indisposed, I would not have received you." She turned to Hastings. "Do bring in a cheese and fruit tray."

Hastings nodded. "Very well, my lady." He bowed out of the chamber, leaving the door slightly ajar.

"There is no need to feed me," Atlas protested.

"Whyever not?" Lilliana arched a brow in that imperious way of hers. "Have you eaten?"

"Yes," he lied, not wanting to impose himself any more than he already had.

"Well, I have not." She lowered herself on the peach stuffed silk sofa in a graceful motion. "And as long as you are here, you might as well keep me company." She gestured with a sweep of her delicate hand. "Do sit."

He eyed the cream silk bergère he'd wedged himself into the last time she'd received him here in her private sanctuary, uncertain of whether the delicate tapered legs could bear his strapping form.

Lilliana chuckled. "Come to the sofa. You will be more comfortable." He did as she bade, settling himself at the opposite end from where she sat. "Now tell me why you have come."

"I have news. I believe I may have discovered the identity of Lady L."

"And?" She regarded him expectantly. "Who is she?"

"Elizabeth Archer. She purchased arsenic three weeks before Davis died."

Lilliana's autumn-hued eyes widened. "The factory owner's daughter?"

"The very one."

"How do you know this?"

"It's thanks to Jamie, really. I had him check the poison books."

She flashed that enchanting, crooked smile that was so uniquely hers. "One hopes young Jamie is more adept at reading poison registers than he is at tying cravats for evening entertainments."

"Indeed," Atlas said wryly. But she was barely listening. He could see her mind working. "What is it?"

"You must talk to Miss Archer again. How will you manage it?"

He'd wondered that himself on the walk over. "I doubt her father will welcome another visit from me, particularly if my purpose is to accuse his daughter of murder."

"And is that your purpose? Do you think she killed Davis?"

"I cannot say. But I need to know why she purchased the arsenic."

"We also need to know what the letter *L* stands for, if it is not the given name of the letter writer."

He tried to think of words that began with *L*. "It could be Lady Love or Lady Lovely."

Wickedness flashed in Lilliana's eyes. "Or Lady Libidinous, if her letters are anything to go by."

He cleared his throat. "Indeed."

"Even if she did purchase the arsenic, her brother or father could have taken it and found a way to slip it into Davis's food or drink."

Atlas nodded. "That is entirely possible."

A tap at the door was followed by a footman, who brought in the food tray—cheese, grapes, bread, and wine. He set it on the table before Lilliana and Atlas and departed.

Lilliana handed Atlas a glass of wine and then took a sip from her own. "There is no way to know what to think of Miss Archer until we speak with her."

"We?" he inquired before bringing the crystal to his lips to taste the wine. He was not at all surprised to find that it was excellent—probably a much finer vintage than he'd ever had before that evening.

"Yes, given my position, I might have more luck persuading Miss Archer to call on me."

"But you are not acquainted with Miss Archer. What reason will you give for reaching out to her?"

"I shall have to find one." She plucked a grape off the stem from the tray before them. "Tell me everything you know about the young lady."

"In truth, I know very little." He searched his memory, recounting for Lilliana everything he remembered of Elizabeth Archer. "And she is betrothed," he said in conclusion.

"Hmmm." Lilliana rested her chin in her hand as she pondered what he'd told her. "That is not much to work with."

"No, it isn't," he agreed, but then something else came to him. "Also, Miss Archer volunteers once a week at a charity."

Interest lit Lilliana's gaze. "Which one?"

"One that helps tradespersons who have fallen on hard times." He tried to remember the exact name. "Ah, yes. 'The General Society for Tradespersons Formerly Better Off,' or some such thing."

"Very good," Lilliana said. "I shall have Somerville's secretary look into it for me."

Atlas drank more wine, savoring its full fruity taste. "For what purpose?"

"I am in a particularly charitable mood." She reached for a piece of cheese. "I feel the need to be generous."

He smiled knowingly. "And I suppose indigent tradesmen are your latest interest?"

"However did you guess?" She bit into the cheese. "At least you have made progress, while I have learned nothing."

"How do you mean?"

"I have tried to encourage gossip about the married lady of quality who took up with a footman but have come up with nothing about the lady Davis was seeing."

"Perhaps I shall enlist Charlton's assistance in the matter. Gentlemen might be more inclined to discuss such things." Concerned about overstaying his welcome, Atlas was about to bid Lilliana good evening when Hastings appeared.

"My lady has another gentleman caller."

Atlas flushed. He should have surmised the moment he'd caught sight of Lilliana in an alluring dressing gown that she was expecting someone—most likely Roxbury. Instead, Atlas had charged into her inner sanctum without giving any thought whatsoever to Lilliana's privacy.

"Really?" Lilliana appeared as surprised as Atlas. "Who is it?"

"The Earl of Charlton, my lady."

"Charlton?" Atlas echoed the butler. What the devil was the earl doing calling on Lilliana at this late hour?

"Shall I show him up?" Hastings asked.

"By all means," Lilliana said. She turned to Atlas. "Do you know what this is about?"

Atlas shrugged. "I've no idea."

Charlton rushed in wearing evening clothes, looking as harried as Atlas had ever seen him. "Is Mrs. Palmer here?" he asked urgently after greeting them both.

"No," Lilliana answered. "And I do not expect her."

Charlton's attention shifted to Atlas. "I'm sorry, old boy, I had no idea."

"Sorry about what?" Atlas asked. "Is something amiss?"

Before Charlton could elaborate, Hastings reappeared, followed closely by Thea. "It's quite all right," an obviously irritated Thea was saying to the butler. "I'm certain Lady Roslyn is at home to me."

"Yes, indeed." Lilliana waved the butler away. "Thank you, Hastings. You may leave us."

Thea too wore evening clothes. She scanned the room before her furious gaze landed firmly on her brother. The anger radiating off her almost prompted Atlas to take a step back. "How dare you!" she exclaimed.

"Am I to know to what you are referring?" Atlas shot a confused look at Charlton, who studiously avoided his gaze. "What has upset you so?"

Thea advanced on him, her hands planted on her hips, her face flushed. She looked like a fishwife about to take her cheating husband to task. "Why didn't you tell me?"

"About?"

"Nicholas. How could you keep something like that from me?"

A sickened feeling slid through Atlas's gut. The last thing he wanted to do was to discuss his sister's lost son with anyone. "I saw no point in telling you."

Her eyes widened. "No point? No point?" Her agitation notched up. "He is our sister's son. I should think the point would be obvious. We've neither seen nor heard anything about the boy for twenty years. And Charlton here tells me you've seen him twice. Twice! And you never mentioned it."

Charlton interjected, his tone apologetic. "I should never have said anything. I naturally assumed you'd told Thea."

"Yes." Thea glared at Atlas. "Charlton assumed that precisely because telling me would be the natural thing to do. Instead, Atlas prefers to run away from things he'd rather not face. Have you booked your next passage yet?" she added sarcastically.

"*I'm* running away?" Anger and frustration boiled up inside of Atlas. "Me? You are the one who escapes her perfectly nice husband every chance she gets. I'm hardly the person in this family who runs away from things. I pity Charles Palmer for having to put up with you."

Lilliana, appearing concerned about the malevolent turn in the conversation, hurried to Thea's side. "Why don't we all sit down and have a glass of wine and discuss this rationally?"

Ignoring Lilliana, Thea kept her irate focus on Atlas. "Do not try to obfuscate. This has nothing to do with my marriage, which, by the way, is none of your concern." Her voice became tremulous. "Did you not think I would want to know what Nicholas looks like, what he said, what his voice sounds like, if he resembles Phoebe? All these years I have wondered. Haven't you?"

"He wants nothing to do with us." It hurt Atlas's lungs to breathe. "I did not tell you," he continued in a tight voice, "because there is no point. Nicholas is forever lost to us. His father has seen to that. Telling you about our late sister's son would have been cruel because it rips open a wound that can never heal."

Thea's eyes glistened with emotion. "Is he like her?" she whispered.

"He has her smile."

"Oh." Thea put a hand to her chest. "Phoebe did have a rather marvelous smile."

"Yes, she did," he agreed, his voice gentle now.

They stood for a moment, neither of them saying anything until Thea turned to Lilliana. "I do beg your pardon for intruding like this."

"No apology is necessary," Lilliana reassured her. "Come and sit. Have a glass of wine."

"Thank you, but I do believe I have discomposed you quite enough for one evening." She looked to Charlton. "May I trouble you to see me home?"

"It would be my pleasure." The earl stepped toward her and offered his arm.

Thea took it and, for the first time, seemed grateful to have Charlton's strength and support by her side. They said their farewells, and Charlton solicitously escorted Thea out, the expression on his face both gentle and protective.

Atlas watched them go before turning to Lilliana. "I am sorry you had to witness that disagreeable exchange. As you might have noticed, Thea and I can be quite sharp with each other when we have words."

Lilliana brushed his mea culpa aside. "It is no wonder. You are both passionate people."

He stared at the door his sister and his friend had just departed through. "What the devil were Thea and Charlton doing together?" he wondered aloud. "Did you notice they were both in evening clothes?"

"I have no idea what they were up to." She paused. "Atlas, Somerville is acquainted with Vessey. I could see if he is willing to arrange a meeting. Perhaps you two could come to an understanding that would make it more comfortable for young Nicholas to call upon his mother's family."

"No." The word came out more harshly than he intended. Atlas made an effort to soften his tone. "If I see Vessey at close quarters, I'm likely to kill him."

Her expression softened. "I cannot say that I blame you."

"I'm no longer a child." He had been only a boy when Vessey had killed Phoebe, his much-beloved elder sister, and as such, had not been in a position to make the bastard pay for what he had done.

"If I see Vessey now, as a grown man, I will call him out. And I will kill him." He gave her a grim look. "And that would not endear me to my nephew."

Chapter Fourteen

Few people would decline an invitation from the sister of the Duke of Somerville—most certainly not a merchant's daughter, no matter how well-to-do her family might be. A young woman of Elizabeth Archer's social status had little hope of being received by someone of Lilliana's superior class and breeding, so it came as no surprise when she appeared at Somerville House at the precise date and time of Lilliana's choosing.

What might have taken Elizabeth aback more than Lilliana's summons, based on her expression when Hastings showed the girl into the one of the duke's gleaming formal drawing rooms, was Atlas's presence by Lilliana's side. He stood when she entered. Lilliana remained seated.

"Miss Archer," he greeted her. "A pleasure to see you again. May I present Lady Roslyn?"

The girl dipped a careful curtsey. "My lady."

"Do take a seat, Miss Archer." Lilliana was at her supercilious best—posture perfect, chin angled upward, arrogance tingeing every syllable. She'd apparently determined that a certain level of hauteur would be most effective in this particular situation. Hers was a performance to behold. At the moment, even Atlas himself was a bit daunted by the force of Lilliana's masterful display.

"I've already called for tea," Lilliana announced.

"Thank you, my lady." The girl slipped self-consciously into the nearest gilded chair with carved tapered legs. "In your note, you indicated an interest in the General Society?"

"Yes indeed. Mr. Catesby mentioned his acquaintance with a young lady who volunteered at the Society."

"Yes, my lady. What is it you would like to know?"

Lilliana asked a few general questions about the charity for tradesmen until the tea tray came in. "Sugar, Miss Archer?" Lilliana perched on the edge of the sofa to serve the tea.

"No, thank you," Elizabeth answered. "Just cream, if you please." Miss Archer apparently didn't care for sweets, because she passed on the tray of cakes while making two selections from the sandwich tray.

Once they were all settled with their tea, Lilliana said, "I do believe my brother, the duke, should very much like to contribute."

"His generosity will no doubt be greatly appreciated, my lady," Elizabeth replied.

"Then it is settled." Lilliana sipped her tea while continuing in a conversational tone. "Elizabeth is such a lovely name. I have a cousin named Elizabeth. We call her Lillibet."

"How charming," Elizabeth said. "My family calls me Libby."

Libby. Lady L. Triumph gleamed in Lilliana's eyes, but she lowered her gaze before the young woman could register her reaction. "I understand you were acquainted with Gordon Davis."

Elizabeth's porcelain cup landed in the saucer with a little clatter. "Yes, my lady."

"He was the brother of my maid. She is understandably distraught at his passing. Were you well acquainted with him?"

"I was not, my lady." Her expression politely bland, Elizabeth set her tea on the marble table beside her with care. "He was a particular friend of my brother."

"I see," Lilliana said. "I have asked Mr. Catesby to look into Mr. Davis's death. His sister, my maid, believes he was murdered."

"How ghastly," Elizabeth murmured.

"Indeed." Lilliana nibbled on a dainty lemon cake. "Mr. Catesby has a talent for solving riddles and puzzles of any sort. He has kindly agreed to investigate Mr. Davis's death as a personal favor to me."

Taking Lilliana's cue, Atlas finally stepped into the conversation. "Mr. Davis died by arsenic poisoning."

"Did he?" Elizabeth listened politely, as if she had no idea whatsoever what any of this had to do with her.

Atlas decided the time had come to shake her out of her complacency. "It has come to our attention that you purchased arsenic shortly before Mr. Davis perished."

Wariness immediately shadowed the young woman's face. "Has it?"

"Yes, all poison sales are registered, and your name was written in the register."

"My private purchases are my own affair."

"Yes, they are," he allowed. "Unless, of course, the arsenic you purchased was used to kill Mr. Davis."

Elizabeth paled. "That's absurd."

Lilliana set her tea down. "Perhaps you might be so kind as to tell us why you bought arsenic."

This time Elizabeth flushed. "It was for personal reasons."

She was clearly embarrassed, but Atlas doubted Elizabeth's reasons for purchasing arsenic were the same as Davis's. "We've no wish to cause you discomfort, Miss Archer, and please be assured that nothing you share with us will leave this room."

She looked from Atlas to Lilliana and back again. "It was a beauty treatment. A friend suggested I try it to improve my complexion."

"You used it yourself?" Atlas asked.

She nodded. "I have freckles, which some find unattractive. Arsenic washes also help with blemishes."

"Are you still using it?" Lilliana wanted to know.

"No, I did not see any improvement, so I stopped washing with it after five or six times."

"Do you still have the unused arsenic in your possession?" Atlas said.

"No, my mother does not approve of arsenic. I threw the remainder of it away before she could discover I had made use of it."

Atlas decided to take the most direct approach possible. "Did Gordon Davis ever call you Lady L?"

Elizabeth's brow furrowed. "Certainly not."

"Did you exchange letters with him?" he pressed. "We have letters of an intimate nature in our possession that Mr. Davis exchanged with a young woman who signed the missives with a single letter *L*."

"I know nothing about that," she said stubbornly.

Atlas pressed on. "Were you hoping to marry Mr. Davis?"

"Most certainly not." She seemed affronted. "I am betrothed to Mr. Montgomery, as you well know."

"Please do not take offense." Lilliana smiled reassuringly. "Mr. Catesby does not mean to question your reputation. He is simply attempting to be thorough in his investigation."

"Yes, my lady." Despite her words, Elizabeth held herself very still, tension emanating from her slender form. She rose. "My father will expect me home soon. I really must go."

"Thank you for coming, Miss Archer." Lilliana rang for Hastings to escort the young woman out. "I'll see to it that a check is sent directly to the General Society."

Once Elizabeth was gone, Lilliana turned to Atlas. "What do you make of it?"

"I think she could very well be Lady L."

Lilliana appeared doubtful. "It is rather difficult to envision that young lady as the amorous Lady L. I don't mean to be unkind, but she is rather"—she searched for the correct word—"colorless somchow."

"She is rather ordinary of face and tempered of demeanor," he acknowledged, "but we must consider that her true private self might be at odds with the personage she shows polite society."

"You think there is a vixen deep down beneath all of that reserve?"

"There is one way that I can think of to find out."

She regarded him with interest. "You have a plan involving Miss Archer."

"I do." He couldn't help the smugness that leaked into his words. "We will soon know for certain whether Elizabeth Archer is our Lady L."

⋆ ⋆ ⋆

"It's deuced cold," Walter Perry complained. "How long have we got to wait out here?"

"Hopefully not too much longer." Atlas held tight to his beaver hat as the wind whipped around them. He'd brought Gordon Davis's former neighbor to the home that temporarily housed tradespersons who had fallen on hard times, the home where Elizabeth Archer volunteered once a week on Tuesdays.

At least, Atlas hoped she came on Tuesdays. When he'd visited the family in Clapham, Elizabeth had remarked that she volunteered at the home once a week. He could only hope she visited on the same day each week. He did not relish the idea of standing outside the society's old-fashioned, somewhat ramshackle house on the edge of town for an entire week.

Not that he was concerned about Perry's continuing cooperation. He felt confident the man would continue to meet Atlas here as long as he was paid for his time. Since Atlas's pockets were not bottomless, he certainly hoped Elizabeth would present herself soon. Although Lilliana would happily assume the investigation's expenses, Atlas would never ask her to.

He straightened when a coach pulled in front of the home. A young lady alighted. Elizabeth Archer. Atlas breathed a sigh of relief. Now he would know for certain whether Elizabeth was Lady L.

"Well?" he prompted Perry.

Perry stared so long and hard that Atlas's stomach began to sink. It seemed Perry did not recognize Elizabeth as the young lady he'd seen with Gordon Davis near the Strand.

"That's her," he finally said with total surety.

"What?"

"I said that's her." Perry's gaze remained on Elizabeth as she walked up to the house, followed by her lady's maid.

Atlas watched the young lady disappear through the front door. "Are you certain?"

"Like I told you, I never forget a face. That's the gel I saw with that popinjay." Perry's disdain for the dead man didn't appear to have diminished at all. "She made a close escape, if you ask me. It's lucky for her that he went and cocked up his toes."

Atlas remained silent, considering the implications of what he'd just learned. Not only was Elizabeth Archer very likely the elusive Lady L, but the revelation pointed more directly to certain suspects—not only Elizabeth herself but also her father and brother, who might have discovered Elizabeth's scandalous indiscretion, or possibly her jealous fiancé, who'd made no effort to hide his possessiveness of Elizabeth in Atlas's presence. Any of them might have been angry enough, or fearful enough of scandal and ruination, to silence Gordon Davis forever.

"Is that all?" Perry asked him. "My missus will be waiting on me."

"Yes, we're done here." Atlas dropped a few shillings into the man's open palm. "You've been most helpful."

Perry tipped his hat and went on his way. Eager to escape the cold, Atlas crossed over to the home with his guaranteed admittance pass—the Duke of Somerville's generous check—folded neatly in his pocket.

Once Atlas invoked the Duke of Somerville's name, he was shown to a private parlor with threadbare carpets and worn upholstery to await Elizabeth Archer.

"Mr. Catesby." She came in after keeping him waiting just a few minutes. She was expensively yet modestly dressed in an unremarkable gown. There was nothing flamboyant about Miss Archer.

"Miss Archer. Allow me to apologize for interrupting your good works."

"I was reading to the children, but they are outside playing." She closed the door behind her. He noted that she did not leave the door ajar to protect her virtuous reputation, as most young women of good family would be inclined to do. "The fresh air will do them well, but it is cold. I'll rejoin them in a trice to continue our lesson."

He registered the subtle warning on her part that she did not intend to spare him much of her time. He pulled the check from his pocket. "I have brought his grace's contribution."

"You needn't have troubled yourself." She took the proffered check and folded it away somewhere in her skirts without observing the generous sum the duke had bestowed upon her favored charity. "We could have sent someone for it."

"It was no trouble at all. I volunteered to bring it because I hoped to speak with you again." If his words discomfited her, she did not show it. Folding her hands serenely in front of her, Elizabeth Archer waited for him to continue.

"Gordon Davis had a neighbor who once saw Davis on the Strand with a well-dressed young woman of obvious good breeding."

She betrayed nothing. Her calm reserve remained firmly in place. "I'm afraid I fail to understand what any of this has to do with me."

"That neighbor, Mr. Perry, accompanied me here today and saw you arrive. He identified you as the young woman he saw accompanying Mr. Davis."

"He is mistaken."

"Mr. Perry was very certain."

"I do not know your Mr. Perry, and I was just barely acquainted with the late Mr. Davis." Indignation laced her words. Atlas had succeeded in ruffling her reserve. Was it because he had come too close to the truth—that she was indeed Lady L? Or was it simply that, by accusing her of walking near the Strand with Mr. Davis, he had questioned her virtue?

"I am betrothed and will marry in the fall," she said pointedly. "Now if you will excuse me, I must see to the children."

She did not wait for his response before departing the room without sparing him another look. After she'd gone, Atlas saw himself out. Passing through the front hall, he went by a black-clad young maid. After a moment, Atlas recognized her as the maid who'd accompanied Elizabeth Archer to the Society.

"Good afternoon," he said pleasantly.

Her brown eyes went wide, and she dipped a nervous curtsey. It was not customary for a gentleman to greet a servant unless he had a need to be taken care of. "Sir."

"Are you waiting for your mistress, Miss Archer?"

She licked her lips. "That I am, sir."

"I believe she is still conducting the children's lesson."

"Could be, sir. I don't expect her for another hour or so."

"Is that so? I wonder if you would be so kind as to answer a question." He paused to draw a few shillings from his pocket.

Her eyes followed the movement. "Yes, sir?"

"I wonder if you ever saw Miss Archer out with a particular friend of mine, a Mr. Gordon Davis."

A mulish look came over the girl's thin face. "I'm sure I cannot say, sir."

Rather than being discouraged, Atlas took the girl's initial reluctance as a positive sign. A servant unwilling to tell tales about her mistress would also be less likely to lie about said mistress. "I assure you, I wish her no harm."

"Please do not ask me to speak against my mistress, sir. I have only recently gone into service for the Archer family."

"You're new? When did you begin your employment with the Archers?"

"Just a few weeks ago. After they let Sara Lloyd go. I replaced her."

"What happened to this Sara you speak of?"

"She was accused of stealing, sir. Sara agreed to leave quietly."

A theft accusation was ruinous for someone in service. "Do you know where she went?"

"She still works in Clapham, sir. She's employed by an abolitionist family now."

It made perfect sense that a family of abolitionists, who were natural do-gooders, would take in a maid who had nowhere else to turn. "Do you happen to know the name of the family?"

The girl's pointed look went to the money in his hands. He placed it into her ready palm.

"Sara works for the Price family," the servant said promptly. "They have a home on the common."

CHAPTER FIFTEEN

The following morning, before venturing out to Clapham in search of the disgraced lady's maid, Atlas joined Charlton for a late morning meal at a new establishment in Pall Mall known as the Voyager's Club.

Unlike other gentlemen's clubs, Voyager's kept early hours, opening in the morning to serve breakfast and closing by eleven in the evening, hours ahead of other gentlemen's clubs where gaming continued well into the early morning.

"I thought you might enjoy Voyager's," Charlton said as they took their seats in the Eating Room. The morning light poured in through floor-to-ceiling windows, spotlighting paneled walls painted in shades of mustard and gray. "This club draws travelers and diplomats. You might find the library of particular interest, and there is a map room."

Atlas knew Charlton normally preferred Boodles, a gentleman's club just down the street. "I gather this is your way of apologizing for your loose tongue," he remarked after the coffee had been poured.

Charlton winced. "I do beg your pardon. I would never want to cause a rift between you and your sister."

"Put your mind at ease." Atlas sipped the hot, bitter libation and was pleased to discover the club brewed a particularly flavorful cup of coffee. "There is no chasm between Thea and me."

"That relieves my mind. The heated exchange the two of you had the other evening was very concerning."

"Disagreements between Thea and me are not for the faint of heart." Atlas blew softly on the steaming cup before taking another sip. "However, we forget about them the following day."

Distaste marred the earl's aristocratic visage. "I barely speak with my sister, and when I do, we are most cordial. I do believe a stiff British upper lip is preferable to all of that drama."

Atlas suppressed a smile. Charlton valued order and courtesy, states of being that were in short supply within the Catesby family. "Relationships between me and my siblings can certainly be untidy," he acknowledged with a wry smile. "Speaking of my sister, what exactly were you doing with Thea that evening?"

"Which evening?"

"The evening Thea confronted me, when you and she came to Somerville House. You were both attired in evening clothes."

"Oh, that." Charlton partook of his coffee with his pinkie elegantly extended. "I happened to run into Thea at a gathering of the London Mathematical Society."

"The Mathematical Society?" Atlas shot him a skeptical look. "I know why Thea was there, but what exactly is your interest in mathematics?"

"I'm not certain whether you are acquainted with my cousin, Beresford, but he is a member of the society. I found myself at loose ends that particular evening after you declined my supper invitation, so when my cousin invited me along to the monthly meeting, I went to see what all the fuss was about."

"And what did you learn?"

Charlton grimaced. "It boggles the mind that someone would voluntarily—and, indeed, eagerly—attend mathematical functions."

"I daresay it's a highlight of Thea's month."

"Naturally, I saw Mrs. Palmer there, and during a break, I happened to mention meeting your young nephew."

"And she came directly to Lilliana's to have it out with me."

"Unfortunately."

"I wondered how Thea knew where to find me. It is not as though I make a habit of visiting Lilliana at all hours."

"As much as you'd like to," Charlton returned drolly. "Yes, I did mention that you'd gone to Lady Roslyn's to discuss the investigation."

Their conversation was interrupted by the arrival of beef-steak with onions. Atlas's stomach growled as the heaping plates of freshly cooked food were placed before them. As they ate, the conversation turned to the investigation.

Atlas gave Charlton some of the particulars, although he declined to mention the latest about Elizabeth Archer. He didn't care to tarnish a young woman's reputation without proof of any wrongdoing. He also did not specifically mention that Merton and Roxbury's daughters had visited Holywell Street, but he did reveal that Davis had information about the young ladies that could prove damaging to their standing in society.

Charlton smirked as he chewed his beef. "It would be dashed convenient for you if Roxbury did turn out to be the killer. With the marquess out of the way, you'd have Lady Roslyn all to yourself."

Atlas sliced off a piece of steak. "He did warn me to stay away from her."

Charlton's amber eyebrows drew together. "Did he now?" His mouth twitched with barely suppressed amusement. "Knowing how much you enjoy being told what to do, I'm certain you appreciated that."

"Wedding the marquess would ensure Lilliana's return to respectability." Atlas washed the tender, succulent beef down with a sizable draught of coffee. "If the events of last year were ever to be revealed, she would be protected by his name."

"Very gallant of you to stand down. But she would also be afforded the same protection as your wife."

Atlas shot him a skeptical look. "We both comprehend that is not true."

"I know nothing of the kind." Charlton pointed at Atlas with his fork. "Yours is an old and distinguished family. Few members of the peerage, myself included, can claim to be a descendant of King Edward III, as the Catesbys can."

"I'm a man of no title and modest fortune. Roxbury can offer her far more than I."

"For someone who generally cares nothing for titles or fortune, you do seem oddly fixated with both when it comes to the fair Lilliana."

Atlas changed the subject. "I need your help with the investigation."

"My help? Is this your artless way of attempting to divert me from discussing your pursuit of the lovely Lilliana?"

Atlas bristled. "There is no pursuit." He learned forward. "I am quite serious about needing your assistance. Gordon Davis was having an affair with a married titled lady who lived in Mayfair."

"Was he?" Charlton shook his head. "The scoundrel."

"Lilliana has been attempting to learn the woman's identity through the ladies of Mayfair but has had little luck."

"And you want me to inquire among the gentlemen of Mayfair."

Atlas nodded. "The gentlemen . . . as well as the ladies you might know particularly well."

"Ah, you are referring to pillow talk." Charlton no longer kept a regular mistress, as far as Atlas knew. The earl had dismissed his most recent ladybird shortly after Atlas's carriage accident the previous year. Since then, the earl had taken to engaging in very discreet liaisons among the Mayfair set. "Very well. I'll see what I can learn. What do you know about this Davis's lady love?"

"Very little. Apparently they met before the lady married and continued their affair after she wed."

"Hmm. Not much to go on, but I shall try." Charlton was distracted by something behind Atlas's shoulder. "Oh, look, there's Merton."

Atlas shifted in his seat to find the viscount standing on the threshold surveying the Eating Room. "It appears that he's alone."

"Didn't you say you wished to speak with him?"

Atlas nodded. "Merton had as much of a motive to kill Gordon Davis as Roxbury."

"So you say. Both of their daughters face ruin for some mysterious reason you refuse to reveal." Charlton stood up and waved to get Merton's attention. "I understand you are being discreet, but your moral rectitude can be tiresome at times. It definitely gets in the way of an interesting conversation."

Atlas watched him. "What are you doing?"

"You need to speak with Merton. There's no time like the present, I say." Charlton caught Merton's eye and gestured for the viscount to come and join them.

As Merton weaved his way through the busy diners, Atlas said, "I can hardly ask him delicate questions about his daughter with you present."

"No worries. I'll make myself scarce." He turned to greet the viscount. "Merton, good day. Are you alone? Do join us."

Merton cast a wary glance at Atlas, who nodded in greeting. "Thank you, but no. I am meeting Harrington here." He gestured toward the plates on the table. "I wouldn't want to interrupt your meal."

"You are not intruding," Charlton said amiably. "We'd welcome the company, wouldn't we, Catesby?"

"Absolutely." Atlas swallowed his last bite of beef, his hunger thoroughly sated. Now he had a craving to satisfy his curiosity as well. "Do join us, my lord."

Charlton beamed. "There, it's settled. Have a coffee with us while you wait for Harrington to appear. The man does have a tendency to run late."

Left with no graceful way to refuse, Merton took a seat. Charlton did the same while gesturing for the server to bring coffee for Merton.

"Oh, look." Charlton popped up again before his arse hit the seat. "I believe I saw my cousin Beresford heading to the library. Excuse me for a moment, gentlemen. I need a word with him."

He was gone before either man could react. When the server appeared with the coffee, Merton stopped him. "I'll have ale."

Even though the man was having spirits at breakfast, Atlas knew he couldn't count on the viscount being foxed so early in the day, so he decided to be direct. "I am investigating Gordon Davis's death."

"Why would you bother?" Merton sniffed. "The man was a plague."

"His sister works for the Duke of Somerville."

Merton's eyes widened. "Somerville asked you to look into Davis's death?"

"Davis's sister believes her brother was murdered." He paused while Merton's ale was set down before him.

"I fail to see what any of this has to do with me."

"I know Davis took Lady Lavinia and Lady Adora Bradford to Holywell Street."

Merton's face flushed with anger. "I should call you out for impugning my daughter's reputation."

"I have no wish to harm your daughter—or Roxbury's, for that matter—and no one will hear of their visit from me."

Merton took a long drink of his ale, his cheeks still red. "What is it that you want?"

"I understand Davis demanded money to keep quiet."

Merton exhaled. "He did. We paid him, and that was the end of it."

"When was the last time you saw Gordon Davis?"

"That same afternoon when he took our daughters to . . . that place." Merton's face contorted with disgust. "Naturally, Roxbury informed me of what happened, and when Davis returned to the house, I met with him in my study and relieved him of his duties."

"Did he ask you to pay him to keep quiet at that time?"

Merton shook his head. "No, I never saw him again after that. Roxbury dealt with him. I paid my share to Roxbury, and he gave it to Davis." He stood abruptly, almost upending his chair. "Harrington is here. Excuse me."

As Atlas watched Merton go, he heard someone call out his name.

"Atlas Catesby." The voice came from behind him. "I thought that was you."

Atlas stood to greet Edward Hughes, the acquaintance who worked at the East India Company. "Hughes, it is good to see you."

Hughes smiled as he shook Atlas's hand. "There's still a spot for you aboard one of our cargo ships, should you care to take it."

"The thought of seeing India is most tempting," Atlas said, "but I have matters that keep me in London for the moment."

"Do send a note if you change your mind. Although, I cannot guarantee the spot will remain open."

"I understand." The two men chatted briefly before exchanging farewells.

Charlton reappeared, passing a departing Hughes on his way back to the table where Atlas sat. "I have another puzzle for you to solve," Charlton said as he drew near.

"Oh?"

"There's been a robbery."

"A robbery?" Atlas asked. "Where?"

"Here at the club."

"When?" He straightened, his interest piqued. "What was taken?"

"I'm not certain exactly when, but the thieves got away with a bundle of silver. Will you come and speak with the butler?"

Never one to resist a good puzzle, Atlas followed Charlton through the back corridor to where the butler, a trim and tidy older man, awaited them with a grim expression on his face.

"Hurley," Charlton said to the man. "This is Mr. Catesby, who is quite clever at solving puzzles."

"What exactly was taken?" Atlas asked the man.

"Silver candlesticks. When I went to retrieve them from the plate closet this morning, they were all gone."

"Who else has a key?"

"No one, sir. Just myself."

Charlton asked, "May we have a look?"

"Certainly, my lord." The butler led the way to the plate closet, where the lock on the massive double doors had been forced. Atlas examined the interior, which was stacked with porcelain plates and saucers.

"When did you notice the candlesticks were missing?" Atlas asked.

"This morning, sir, when the breakfast tables were being put in readiness. I came to get the candlesticks and found this."

"When did you last see the silver?"

"Last evening at eleven."

Atlas considered the possibilities. "I would like to examine all of the back and side doors, the windows, roof, and gutters."

The butler, who was not familiar with Atlas, looked askance at Charlton.

"Mr. Catesby is an excellent investigator," the earl reassured him.

The butler inclined his head. "We'd be most pleased to have your assistance, sir."

Accompanied by the butler and Charlton, Atlas spent the next several minutes checking all of the club's possible points of entry and found no evidence of a break-in.

"It seems," Atlas said, once he'd completed his search, "that the thieves came in through the front door and left the same way."

The butler's eyes went wide. "We have a hall porter, sir, who is here all evening. He would surely have seen any intruders."

Charlton exchanged a look with Atlas. "I imagine Mr. Catesby would like to speak with this porter."

They went in search of the hall porter, who'd been on duty since the previous evening. Bernard Mullins, a grizzled older man with ruddy cheeks and twinkling eyes, seemed eager to be of assistance.

"I stayed behind once the theft was discovered," Mullins told them. "I presumed Bow Street would be along."

"You heard nothing all evening?" Atlas asked. "No one came or left after the club closed last night?"

"No one," Mullins said. "Except for the sweeps."

"The chimney sweeps?" Atlas asked. "When did they come?"

"At around five o'clock this morning."

The butler's face reddened. "Why did you not mention this earlier?"

"I did not think it signified," Mullins said.

"Who let them in?" Atlas asked.

"I did," Mullins answered. "They banged on the door, and I opened it for them as I always do."

Atlas turned to the butler. "Was the chimney due to be swept?"

The butler shook his head. "Not until next week."

Atlas turned back to Mullins. "How did you know they were the sweeps?"

"They said it, didn't they?" Mullins said. "Said they were from Pope's on Argyll Street and that they were to sweep the chimney in the pantry."

Atlas looked to the butler. "Are you familiar with that service?"

The butler nodded. "We do use that service, sir."

Atlas turned back to the night porter. "Did you recognize the particular men who came? Have they been here previously?"

"Can't say that I did." He shrugged. "They send different people all of the time."

Atlas studied the man. "How long were they here?"

"Well over an hour," Mullins answered. "They said it took a while because the chimney was very foul."

"Did they take much soot with them?" Atlas asked.

Mullins nodded. "About half a sack full."

Atlas turned to the butler. "You might want to check with Mr. Pope to see if he sent sweeps this morning."

"Yes, sir." The butler appeared agitated. "You may be certain that I will."

A familiar voice called from behind them. "Mr. Catesby. I might have known I'd find you in the midst of my latest investigation."

Atlas turned to find Ambrose Endicott, the Bow Street runner, lumbering toward them. "Hello, Endicott. I presume you remember the Earl of Charlton."

"I do indeed." Endicott tipped his hat. "How do you do, my lord?"

"Very well," Charlton said, "as long as you do not implicate Mr. Catesby in this investigation."

Endicott chuckled at the earl's reference to the last time the three men had all been together the previous year. "I do believe in this case Mr. Catesby is safe from suspicion, my lord."

Charlton, who had an appointment to keep, took his leave, while Atlas remained to relay to Endicott what he'd learned so far. "And so," he said in conclusion, "I suppose it is time for your men to visit the fences in St. Giles, Seven Dials, Westminster, and White Chapel."

"Yes, indeed." Endicott scribbled notes in his worn notebook. "First, we will stop by Pope's to see if he sent his men to sweep the chimney in the pantry."

Satisfied that Endicott had the burglary investigation well under control, Atlas prepared to take his leave. As he waited for his coat and hat to be brought to him, Endicott paused and scratched his chin with thick fingers.

"I say, are you still looking into that Davis fellow's death?"

"Gordon Davis? Yes, I am."

"Have you had any luck?"

"I'm making progress. I'm off to Clapham now to speak with a maid who used to work for Noel Archer, the man who owns the factory where Davis worked."

"I've heard of the man. You think Archer is involved with Davis's death?"

"I cannot say." The servant arrived with Atlas's greatcoat and hat. Atlas swung the wool garment onto his shoulders. "Davis lost his situation after he was caught stealing arsenic from the factory, but Archer forced the manager to give Davis his job back."

Interest lit the runner's small ebony eyes, which looked like glowing currants among the fleshy folds of his face. "Now why would he do that?"

"That's what I am attempting to ascertain." He placed his hat on his head. "Now if you will excuse me, I do have my own investigating to accomplish this day."

* * *

When Atlas reached Clapham in the early afternoon and inquired about the Price house, he was directed to a stately structure that fronted the commons. It wasn't as large or obvious as the much newer Archer dwelling on the opposite side of the green, but the Price abode was a substantial home nonetheless.

Having no desire to inconvenience the Prices—and having no need to speak with them—Atlas made his way around back to the servants' entrance to inquire after Sara Lloyd. He stepped carefully to avoid the muddy spots as an icy burst of wind swept by. The air remained uncommonly brisk for early May; Atlas was relieved he'd worn his greatcoat.

When he reached the servants' entrance, a delivery boy departing with his empty basket stepped past Atlas. Behind the lad, a tiny, trim woman in a white apron with streaks of gray in her curly hair issued instructions.

"And we'll be needing sugar," she called to the boy. "Don't forget."

"Yes, Mrs. McNab." The boy tipped his cap. "I'll remember."

"And say hello to your ma."

As the boy departed, Mrs. McNab turned her attention to Atlas. Her eyes widened as she took in his appearance, including the beaver hat, fine wool coat, and polished boots that distinguished him as a gentleman, or at least as someone of high enough stature not to use the entrance reserved for servants and deliveries. "Good afternoon, sir. The main entrance is around front."

"Thank you. Mrs. McNab, is it?" he asked, recalling the name the delivery boy had used.

"Yes, sir." She stood in the aperture, a stance that effectively denied him entry.

"I am here to speak with Sara Lloyd. Is she perchance available?"

Curiosity flitted across the older woman's face. "You want Sara?"

"Yes, I hoped for a word with her."

"She's in the scullery. She has much work to finish."

"I understand." His tone was politely sympathetic. "I won't keep her long."

Mrs. McNab gave him another assessing gaze. "Very well." She moved aside. "Follow me."

She led him through a narrow corridor, past the servants' hall, where a couple of footmen were taking their tea, and another small room where shoes were being cleaned and shined. Curious looks followed their progress. It wasn't every day that a gentleman traversed the servants' domain.

Mrs. McNab stopped at the landing atop four steps that appeared to lead to the scullery. "Through there." She pointed in the direction he was to go.

Atlas thanked her and trotted down the stairs. He found a dark-haired, broad-faced woman, who appeared to be in her midthirties, hard at work in the hot, humid room where clothes were being cleaned in a large copper pot over a fire. He stepped past an ironing board stacked with clothes to where the woman was hard at work at the wringer.

"Sara?" he inquired. "Are you Sara Lloyd?"

She looked up from her task, her face flushed from her exertions, appearing to notice him for the first time. "Yes?"

"My name is Atlas Catesby."

She looked him over. "I recognize you. You paid a call at the Archer house a few weeks ago."

"Yes," he said with surprise. "How do you know that?"

"I saw you. You were talking to Miss Elizabeth and Miss Harriet out in front of the house."

"I was indeed." He drew off his hat and set it on the ironing board. "I was hoping you could answer a few questions."

"About Gordon Davis?"

Sara Lloyd was full of surprises. He wondered how much she knew about Gordon Davis. "Did you have occasion to meet Mr. Davis?"

"Aye." She turned the crank to wring out what looked like someone's chemise. "I did."

"When he was with Trevor Archer?"

"No, with Miss Elizabeth." She pulled the garment out of the wringer and set it aside. "The first time she pointed him out to me, he was in the street, and we saw him from the drawing room window."

"And what did she say when she pointed him out?"

"That he was a friend. She did not tell me his name."

Anticipation danced along Atlas's nerve endings. Elizabeth had strongly denied any sort of friendship with Davis. "Did Gordon Davis ever visit Miss Elizabeth Archer?"

She nodded. "I told her it would come to no good, but she wouldn't listen to me. She kept seeing him."

He struggled to keep his tone neutral. "Are you saying Davis visited Miss Elizabeth more than once?"

"Yes." Blowing a loose tendril of hair out of her perspiring face, Sara pulled another soaking garment out of the large tub by the wringer. Watching her labor, it occurred to him that she had come down in the world since leaving the Archers' employ. To go from upstairs maid, who served the young ladies of the house, to the scullery was a precipitous fall for someone in service.

"How is it possible that Davis visited Miss Elizabeth?" He grew more skeptical. If Sara was bitter about her fallout with the Archer family, she might be inclined to slander their good name. "Davis could hardly visit her at the Archer house, given

Mr. Archer's disdain for the man. And the young ladies of the household appear to be well chaperoned whenever they venture out."

Her half smile was cynical. "Determined young ladies know how to get what they want."

He thought of Lavinia Fenton and her scandalous visit to Holywell Street. "Well, yes, I see what you mean. So how did Miss Elizabeth manage it?"

"Davis came to the house. Miss Elizabeth instructed me to open the back gate for him."

"Where was the rest of the family?"

"That first time, it was a Sunday. They were all at church. Miss Elizabeth stayed behind because she pretended to be ill."

"What happened then? She visited with Davis by the back gate?"

Sara shook her head. "He went into the laundry. She showed him in and shut the door. They were in there together for about half an hour."

Half an hour. So Elizabeth had not only befriended Davis, she'd also been alone with him on at least one occasion. "He visited more than once?"

"He did. It was always the same. I would leave the back gate open, and she would go out to him."

"Did they always go into the laundry?"

"I cannot say. After that first time, he only came at night, after the family had retired for the evening." Her distaste was apparent. "I would leave the back gate open, and then I would go to my room."

"So you cannot say whether or not he came into the house again after that first time."

"I cannot." The dispassionate way in which Sara spoke seemed to suggest she did not particularly care whether Atlas believed her story or not.

"I wonder how Miss Elizabeth managed to go out to the back gate and visit with Davis without anyone in her family hearing her."

"Miss Elizabeth's chamber was on the ground floor, while the rest of the family was abovestairs. The family would not have heard anything once they were abed."

Atlas absently watched the maid thread a dark garment into the wringer. If Sara was to be believed, Davis and Elizabeth had enough time and privacy to engage in the types of intimacies described in Lady L's letters.

"Do you know if Miss Elizabeth wrote letters to Davis?" he asked.

"She did."

"And the reason you know this is . . . ?" he prompted.

"She gave me letters addressed to Davis and asked me to post them."

"I presume he wrote her back?"

"Yes, only he would address the letters to me. When I received them, I would give them to her."

"How many letters were there?"

"A good many. I cannot say exactly how many."

He paused. "Forgive the intrusion, but I am interested to know why you left the Archers' employment."

She stopped her work to look him full in the face. "Once she became betrothed to Mr. Montgomery, I refused to send or receive any letters for her, but Davis kept walking by the house and delivering letters to her through the window."

"Which window?"

"The window in Miss Elizabeth's bedchamber. He would visit her there late in the evening."

He tried to picture the windows on the ground floor of the Archer home. "Those windows are barred, are they not?"

"Yes, but Davis could still pass items through the bars." Her lips twisted in distaste. "He could hold her hand."

"I'm surprised Miss Elizabeth kept up the friendship with Davis even after she became betrothed to Mr. Montgomery."

"She told me she was trying to end it, but Davis kept coming around. I threatened to tell her father." She fairly spat the words. "Davis was up to no good. Miss Elizabeth had a respectable man who wanted to wed her, but for some reason she allowed Davis to keep visiting her. It wasn't right."

It dawned on him that Sara had attempted to do right by her young mistress. "You tried to protect her."

"Yes. But she feared I would carry out my threat to tell her father everything."

The pieces clicked into place in his mind. "That's why she accused you of stealing from her. That way, if you told Mr. Archer anything about Davis, he would be disinclined to believe you."

"Yes," she said resignedly. "And who will hire a lady's maid accused of theft? I am fortunate Mr. Price offered me a place here."

Sara Lloyd had paid a heavy price indeed for trying to save Elizabeth Archer from Gordon Davis's machinations. Atlas thanked her for her time and readied to take his leave. As he picked up his hat from atop the ironing board, he discreetly slipped a few shillings in its place before seeing himself out.

Chapter Sixteen

"I am astonished," Lilliana said. "Lady Lavinia seemed a much more likely choice to be Lady L."

Atlas did not disagree. "A person's true private nature can certainly surprise."

They strolled in Kensington Gardens, falling well behind Lilliana's sons, Peter and Robin, who ran and shouted up ahead as they rolled their hoops over the damp grass. The gardens were lush and elegant, a place where people of fashion mingled with well-dressed city dwellers of various ranks. Atlas and Lilliana had not come at the fashionable hour; consequently, the crowds had yet to descend, which gave the boys plenty of room to frolic.

When Atlas had sent Lilliana a note indicating he had news, she'd asked him to join her and the children at Kensington Gardens. It was the second time she'd invited him to spend time with her children. Now that she and the boys were comfortably settled with her brother and Somerville was firmly ensconced as the boys' guardian and paternal figure, Atlas supposed Lilliana no longer worried about her children becoming too attached to Atlas.

Lilliana righted her straw bonnet, adjusting the satin bow, which matched the blossom pink of her walking dress. The shade brought out the color in her cheeks and enhanced the luminous quality of her skin. She looked as fresh and appealing as any of the vibrant flowers lining their path.

"You believe this maid?" Lilliana asked.

"I have no reason not to. But to be certain, I'd like to compare the writing on Lady L's letters to Elizabeth Archer's to see if they were composed by the same hand."

"Consider it done," she said airily. "I shall send Miss Archer a note—one that naturally requires a reply—and then we shall be able to compare her handwriting against Lady L's."

"A clever plan."

"Well, I can be rather nimble-minded at times."

"More often than not, in my experience."

She tapped him with her closed parasol. "Flatterer."

It was not false praise. Lilliana was probably one of the most adroit women of his acquaintance. But he did not say so. Instead, he turned the conversation back to Elizabeth Archer. "If what the maid says it true, it is interesting that Miss Archer maintained her connection to Davis even after her betrothal."

"Indeed. There are two possible reasons that I can think of. Either she still had feelings for him . . ."

"Or she feared he would use the letters to disgrace her," Atlas finished the thought.

Robin came running up to them, his cheeks flushed from exertion. "Come and play with us, Mr. Catesby. I've been practicing."

His older brother came up behind him. "Yes, please do."

"Not now, my darlings," their mother said, her tone tender. The cut-glass edges of her precise diction always softened around her children. "Mr. Catesby and I are having an important conversation."

Peter looked expectantly at Atlas. "What about after? Will you race us after?" He shot a disdainful sidelong glance at his brother. "Robin's too little, but I think I can best you."

"I am not too little," Robin said indignantly.

Peter's only response to his younger brother was to roll his eyes before asking Atlas, "Will you play? Will you?"

"I am not too little," Robin repeated.

"Boys," Lilliana interjected. "You must not impose on Mr. Catesby. He is not dressed for sport."

"It is no imposition," Atlas reassured her before directing his next words to her children. "I will race you both if you give your mama and me a few minutes to finish our discussion."

Seemingly satisfied with his answer, both boys ran off, using their sticks to roll their hoops along the graveled path.

Lilliana watched after them, but her thoughts were clearly on the investigation. "What if Miss Archer and Mr. Davis were truly married? She did sign some letters as Mrs. Davis."

He considered the possibility. "If that were the case, in order to wed Montgomery, the man she is betrothed to, she would need to rid herself of her secret husband."

A visible shiver ran through Lilliana. "How desperate a person must be to feel pushed to commit murder."

"I doubt Miss Archer and Davis were married. As I recall, the letters seemed to indicate that she considered herself to be his wife because of the . . . erm . . . intimacies they'd shared."

She nodded. "Yes, I agree it is unlikely she was his wife in truth. Although if she was, she'd certainly be free to marry now."

"Davis did return at least one of her letters unopened, and she admonished him for it. Perhaps he did jilt her and she poisoned him out of spite."

One of Lilliana's autumn-hued eyes narrowed as she considered that scenario. He'd noticed she had a tendency to do that—squinting just the left eye, not both—when she was deep in thought. "She implored him to return the letters. We found them in his room, so obviously he never gave them back."

"There are certainly many possibilities."

"We have to speak with Miss Archer again."

"I agree, but where?" He considered their options. "I suppose I could go back to where she volunteers, to the home for tradespersons."

"*We* can speak with her at the upcoming benefit."

"What benefit?"

"Now that Somerville is an extremely generous patron of the charity, we receive information about their activities."

"And there's a benefit?"

"Indeed. It's being held at the arcade."

"A shopping area seems like an odd place for a benefit."

"Ah, but it's an event to raise funds for tradespersons who have fallen on hard times. Their fellow tradesmen are assisting them by organizing the benefit. A portion of the proceeds, including any shopping that is done, will go to help fund the home."

"So it seems we are to go shopping for a good cause?"

"Yes. And it just so happens that I am in need of an escort."

He doubted that. "I'm surprised Roxbury hasn't already offered to accompany you."

"I don't believe that he is aware of the event."

He paused. "Roxbury won't be pleased if he learns I've escorted you." He thought to warn her of her suitor's likely negative reaction. If Lilliana had hopes in that direction, Atlas did not want to stand in her way.

Her tone was dismissive. "He has no claim on me."

"He thinks he does." Atlas found himself watching closely for her reaction. "Roxbury warned me off of you."

"Did he?" She seemed both surprised and intrigued. "When was that?"

"At his garden party. It's clear he hopes to make you his marchioness."

"And?" Her eyes were alight with interest. "What did you say?"

There hadn't been much to say. He admired Lilliana greatly, but given their disparate social standing, he harbored no hopes in that direction. "Very little."

She lifted her delicate chin and favored him with a haughty look he was coming to know quite well. "You don't strike me as a man who warns off easily."

"I am not."

Her mouth curved upward in that off-kilter, insolent way of hers. "I am glad."

Her last response threw Atlas off. They seemed to have reached some sort of understanding, but he wasn't quite certain what it was. Before he had time to fully contemplate their exchange, the boys were upon them again like a swarm of determined bees, this time pulling and tugging at Atlas, imploring him to come along.

"We've been patient," little Robin said. "Haven't we, Mama?"

Lilliana laughed, a throaty genuine sound. "Yes, indeed." Her face was open, her expression guileless and carefree. It was only on the rarest occasions that she allowed herself to be seen in an unguarded moment, and he felt privileged to witness it.

With an admiring smile in her direction, Atlas reluctantly permitted himself to be pulled away and went off to bowl hoops with Lilliana's children.

Chapter Seventeen

"Perhaps I should just purchase a new watch," Charlton said to Atlas as they exited the watchmaker's shop off Berkeley Square. The earl had just left his fob to be repaired for the second time in as many months.

"Surely you own more than one," Atlas remarked.

"Yes, but that's hardly the point."

Atlas wasn't certain what the point was but did not particularly care to be enlightened. He was just grateful to be out stretching his legs. They'd opted to walk over from the earl's Curzon Street mansion because the watchmaker's shop wasn't far, and it was a rare sunny day, although a relentless spring chill still held the metropolis in its stubborn grip.

They approached Gunter's Tea Shop, which always made Atlas think of Thea. No one loved lemon ices more than his sister. It was her particular fondness for the icy treat that had prompted her husband, Charles Palmer, to build that icehouse for her.

"I say," Charlton observed, "isn't that Mrs. Palmer's conveyance?"

Atlas looked over at the outdated old carriage parked in the shade under the maple trees across from the tea shop. "Yes, it is."

"It's positively archaic," Charlton said indignantly. "Why doesn't Mr. Palmer buy something more suitable for his wife?"

"He has tried. Thea won't hear of it."

Charlton stared at him. "Whyever not?"

"She views a new carriage as a waste of funds when her current carriage is perfectly serviceable."

"Ridiculous," Charlton harrumphed. "As her husband, he should insist she be in the newest and safest of conveyances."

Atlas shot him a sidelong glance. "Having met my sister, I'm sure you can imagine how much she appreciates being told what to do."

A smile cracked Charlton's frown. "About as much as you do." They came to the front entrance of the tea shop. "Shall we go in and say hello?"

They stepped inside, where the mouth-watering scents of vanilla, orange, chocolate, and cinnamon perfumed the air and ornate towering wedding cakes were on display under vast glass domes. Atlas spotted Thea in one of the shop's more private corners, engaged in a lively conversation with a well-dressed, auburn-haired gentleman with a strong jaw and twinkling green eyes.

"Who the devil is that with your sister?" Charlton stared at the couple. "Do you know him?"

Atlas smiled. "I most certainly do."

Thea's companion grinned widely when he spotted Atlas. "This is a surprise." He rose to greet Atlas, heartily shaking his hand. "I thought you might be off on another of your adventures."

"I am just returned . . . a few weeks ago. What of you?" Atlas asked. "What brings you to town?"

"I'm here to visit my lovely wife. Only a foolish man would stay away from Thea a moment longer than he has to."

"Your wife?" Charlton blinked. "You're Charles Palmer?"

"At your service." Palmer regarded Charlton with polite friendliness. "I'm afraid you have me at a disadvantage, sir. And you are?"

"This is Lord Charlton." Thea made the introduction from her seat at the small round table. "He's a great friend of Atlas's."

"Is that so?" Palmer extended his hand. "Any friend of Atlas's is most welcome. *Lord* Charlton, you say?"

"Yes, Gabriel Young." After a moment's pause, Charlton reached out to shake Palmer's extended hand, a gesture usually reserved for men who were well acquainted, but Palmer was a friendly sort. "Earl of Charlton."

"You two should sit," Thea said. "My ice is melting."

"We cannot have that." Palmer shot an amused look at the other two men. "I've brought my wife to Gunter's for a special treat, and she must be allowed to enjoy it."

Thea favored her husband with a soft smile. "You are always very thoughtful."

"How goes the farming, Palmer?" Atlas asked when they were all settled.

"Very well. We've enjoyed a good season." Palmer spent a few minutes speaking about the crops and an improved method of tilling the soil. Palmer was as passionate about farming as Thea was about mathematics.

"You look well," Atlas said, referring to Palmer's strong, toned physique. "I gather you still get out in the fields and assist the tenant farmers?"

"A man needs to get his daily constitutional." Palmer grinned. "I like to keep the blood pumping. And I don't believe my wife would appreciate it if I ran to fat."

"Looking at you, one can see there is little chance of that." Thea swallowed her final spoonful of ice. "But if you insist on continually indulging my partiality to lemon ices, the same cannot be said of your wife."

Palmer's eyes glittered with admiration. "Nothing could dim your considerable beauty, my love."

Charlton, who'd been uncharacteristically subdued up until this point, watched the exchange with a pained expression. "I say, Palmer," he said in an unusually abrupt manner, "how long will you be in Town?"

Palmer pulled his fond gaze from his wife to give Charlton his attention. "It's hard to say. I suppose as long as my wife tolerates my presence."

"Oh, please." Thea looked skyward. "As if you don't come and go exactly as you see fit."

Palmer raised an auburn brow. "I'd like to go home with my wife now and enjoy her company."

"Well, I'm all through here," Thea said in her no-nonsense way, "so that can easily be arranged."

They lingered for a few more minutes before the entire party rose to take its leave. "Atlas," Palmer said as they exited the shop. "I presume we'll see you later?"

"Indeed." Atlas closed the shop door behind them. "Thea has invited me to dine with you this evening."

"Capital." Palmer turned to Charlton and gave him a slight bow. "A pleasure, Lord Charlton."

"Palmer," Charlton said stiffly. "I do hope you enjoy your stay in London."

"My thanks," Palmer said amiably. "I always treasure time spent with my wife." He offered his arm to Thea. "Good day."

The farewells were said all around, and Palmer escorted his wife across the road to their waiting carriage. Charlton's gaze lingered after the couple for a few moments before he and Atlas resumed their walk to the earl's Curzon Street address.

"You are unusually quiet," Atlas observed after they'd gone a fair distance in silence.

Charlton's manner was subdued. "It's the surprise of meeting Mr. Palmer, I suppose."

"Why? You've known since you first became acquainted with Thea that she is married."

"Yes, of course. But Mr. Palmer in the flesh is most unexpected."

"How so?"

"He's so vigorous. And young." He looked at Atlas as they walked. "How old is he?"

"A few years older than you and me. I believe he is seven-and-thirty."

"I envisioned him to be much older. Bald. Rotund. Perspiring profusely."

"Why would you think that?" Mindful of his friend's subdued mood, Atlas suppressed the urge to snort. "My sister is widely acknowledged to be a beauty. It is no surprise she would wed an equally handsome man."

"It's just that he stays apart from her most of the time, minding that farm of his. It's dashed unusual."

"I agree." Atlas shrugged. "But they seem happy with the arrangement and appear to enjoy each other when they are in company, so who are we to judge?"

"Who indeed?" Charlton agreed, lapsing into silence for the remainder of the short walk home.

* * *

Atlas borrowed Charlton's shiny lacquered post chaise to escort Lilliana to the benefit for merchants who'd fallen on hard times. He owned no conveyances of his own, while the earl, who was something of a collector, possessed several. When Atlas requested use of his barouche, Charlton had pressed him to take his newest vehicle, an even more opulent chaise, insisting it would better guard against the stubborn chill than the barouche, which offered less protection from the elements.

Atlas arrived at Somerville House to find the duke himself, impeccably attired in evening clothing, in the marbled front hall preparing to depart. A liveried footman stood at the ready with the ducal outerwear folded over his arm.

"Catesby." The duke pulled on a pristine white evening glove. "How goes the investigation?"

"Your grace." Atlas bowed. "We are making progress."

"It pleases me to hear it, especially considering that this endeavor has cost me more than a few pounds."

"Your donation to assist the struggling merchants was most generous."

"Lady Roslyn certainly saw to that," Somerville said sardonically, tugging on a matching snowy glove, "thus demonstrating that a man does not have to acquire a wife in order for his purse to dwindle significantly."

"But at least it is for a worthy cause," Atlas said with humor.

"Indeed," the duke agreed with a haughty wave of his gloved hand. "It has come to my attention that I stand to lose quite a few more shillings this evening."

"It seems likely." Atlas suppressed a smile. "I am escorting Lady Roslyn to a benefit for the merchants."

"To be held at the arcade, I hear." He stood perfectly erect as the footman set a billowing black cape, lined with a cream satin, on his ducal shoulders. "Will the murderer be among the guests?"

Atlas thought of Elizabeth Archer, her intimate letters to Davis, and her purchase of arsenic. "It's very possible."

"Is it?" Somerville's brows lifted, his dark gaze intent. "I trust you will keep Lady Roslyn safe from any danger."

It was a warning. Not that Atlas required one. He would never allow any harm to come to Lilliana. "I will do everything in my power to protect her."

Somerville donned his ebony silk top hat. "See that you do," he commanded. Without another word, he swept toward the door, which was hastily thrown open by the attending footman.

"Mr. Catesby?" As the door closed behind the duke, Atlas turned to find the butler at the foot of the grand staircase. "Lady Roslyn asks that you join her in her sitting room. If you will follow me."

Atlas assumed Lilliana was not yet ready, but he found the lady standing at the center of her sitting room—fully attired for their evening out—anxiously awaiting his arrival. She looked enchanting in a pale-pink gown with a daring décolletage, adorned with beads that shimmered when the light caught them.

As soon as Hastings left them, her eyes lit up. "Come and see." She hurried to her escritoire, the frothy layers of her dress floating around her lithe form as she moved.

She bent over, smoothing two letters laid on the shiny satinwood surface with a pale fine-boned hand. Atlas came to stand by her side. The subtle fleeting scent of jasmine and cloves drifted over to him.

She pointed to the missive on the left. "This is the note I received from Miss Archer today. I pretended to have some questions about this evening's benefit, and she responded promptly this afternoon." Her hand shifted to the letter on the right. "And this is Lady L's letter."

He leaned in, his gaze darting back and forth to compare the handwriting. Excitement surged through his veins. "There can be no doubt."

"Exactly my feeling." She exhaled in a quick rush. "They were written by the same hand."

"We have discovered the letter writer's identity." Satisfaction settled deep in his core at having slipped this piece of the puzzle into its proper place. "Elizabeth Archer is Lady L."

Chapter Eighteen

"We did it." Excitement filled Lilliana's voice. "We discovered the identity of Lady L."

They straightened at the same time, and Atlas suddenly became very aware of how close to her he was standing. Lilliana's eyes glistened as they met his. "We make a good team, you and I."

"Yes." He could not look away. "I suppose we do."

She released a breath, a soft exhalation. Her color heightened as she inched closer until they were almost touching.

He soaked in the pleasure of being so near to her, drinking in the fine-boned loveliness of her face and the unique shade of her eyes—dark, certainly, but touched with a rich jewel tone that reminded him of leaves in the fall. His attention lingered on a faint beauty mark sprinkled just above the delicate arch of her left brow; he'd never noted it before.

Without stopping to think, he touched the dark dot, feathering his finger over her warm skin. His heart beating hard, it seemed the most natural thing in the world to lower his face until his lips touched hers.

Her mouth was stiff and untutored against his. Well aware that she had not had an easy time of it with her late husband,

Atlas showed a restraint he did not feel, kissing her gently, even as a conflagration of desire burned through his veins.

Her lips softened, tentative yet eager, and when they parted, allowing him certain liberties, exhilaration shot through him. He tasted her with tender care, relishing the privilege, suspecting how difficult it must be for Lilliana to share intimacy with a man after what her husband had put her through.

He indulged for several moments before forcing himself to end the kiss. Pulling back, he set his forehead against hers. "Well," he said, his voice husky.

"Indeed." Her voice was thready. It pleased him to know she was not unaffected by what had passed between them.

He cleared his throat and straightened. "Perhaps we should go."

She nodded, her eyes bright. "Yes, we wouldn't want to be late."

* * *

The benefit was held at the Eastern Bazaar, Mayfair's fashionable new shopping emporium, a stucco-fronted, gold-lettered extravaganza on Oxford Street. Inside, it was one spacious hall with high ceilings, skylights, and a gallery level where paintings were on exhibit.

"I never realized that shopping could involve such pretension," Atlas remarked.

"Almost everything about the ton involves some degree of ostentation and conceit," Lilliana said. "Surely you will have noticed by now."

They strolled among the stalls and open counters, which were organized with precise military-like precision on the main floor. Lilliana paused here and there to study the luxury goods—millinery, gloves, lace, jewelry, and furs—offered by the individual proprietors.

It was a showy place obviously designed to draw the highborn and wealthy, providing them with a luxurious space in which to shop in style and comfort. For this evening's benefit, a small orchestra played in one corner while well-dressed waiters circulated with champagne on silver trays.

Atlas recognized many of the same faces from the duke's ball and Roxbury's garden party. "I do not understand the point."

"The point of what?"

"Every day there is another party with the same people. The only element that changes is the locale. It seems rather pointless."

"It does, doesn't it?"

"Do the routs bore you?" He was genuinely curious. After all, this was the world she'd been born into, and although she moved within it as seamlessly as she did everything else, he wondered how she viewed the ton after her extended absence from it.

She lifted one elegant shoulder. "This is how polite society passes its time. Perhaps I should be grateful to my late husband for sparing me from the social swirl for ten years."

He grimaced at the thought of giving that bastard credit for anything. She responded with a quiet laugh. He felt relief that they still dealt easily with each other, despite the intimacy they'd shared less than an hour before in her sitting room.

Earlier, on the ride over in Charlton's borrowed chaise, they had not spoken of it. She did not seem to regret what had passed between them, and he most certainly did not. In fact, satisfaction rifled through him. After sampling the tentative inexperience in Lilliana's kiss, he felt fairly certain Roxbury, her suitor, had not enjoyed the same privilege.

Lilliana scanned the floor and tilted her head back, looking upward to search the gallery. "I do not see Miss Archer."

"Nor I." He looked around as well. "Are you certain she means to attend?"

"Yes, her note to me this afternoon indicated as much."

"Then I suggest that we enjoy ourselves"—he reached for two glasses of champagne from a passing waiter and handed her one—"until Miss Archer makes an appearance."

She accepted the champagne and sipped from it. "I find I cannot help but be in sympathy with her even though I should not be, particularly if she is indeed a murderess."

He understood her sentiment. "We've only confirmed that Miss Archer had an affair with Davis. We do not know for certain that she poisoned him."

"But you believe she did?"

He thought of the no-nonsense, proper young lady he'd met in Clapham, who was well-read enough to be familiar with his father's works. "I haven't formed an opinion on that," he answered honestly.

"My dear Lilliana." Atlas recognized the voice before he and Lilliana turned to find the Marquess of Roxbury approaching them. Fashionably dressed in a royal-blue evening coat with white breeches, the marquess took Lilliana's hand in his and bent over it, his lips lingering against her gloved hand longer than Atlas would have liked.

"Roxbury," she said, "what a delightful surprise."

"I could say the same. You are a vision this evening." His eyes shone with adoration but hardened behind a polite veil when he turned to greet Atlas. "Catesby."

Atlas bowed. "My lord."

Roxbury's focus returned to Lilliana. "Had I known you were in need of an escort, I would have been pleased to fill the role."

"There was no need," she replied easily. "Atlas is here with me as part of the investigation."

"Is that so?" The marquess's eyes went to Atlas. "I cannot imagine why a footman's death would bring you to a charity benefit at the exchange."

"It is a lead I am following up"—Atlas was reluctant to reveal anything of import to Roxbury—"which could easily come to nothing." Miss Archer might be Lady L, but the marquess remained a viable suspect. It was eminently plausible that the threatened ruination of Roxbury's only daughter could have driven the man to murder.

Roxbury said to Lilliana, "If you are serious about this matter, perhaps you should engage a runner."

"Atlas has made significant progress. He is very clever."

"Of that there is no doubt," Roxbury said smoothly. "But surely a professional would be better able to establish whether Davis was murdered."

"Possibly," Atlas agreed, all amiability. It was nothing to him if Roxbury thought him unequal to the task before him. He preferred to be underestimated. It worked to his advantage.

"Papa, there you are." A young lady in a pristine white gown appeared at the marquess's side. "I've been looking all over for you."

"Have you?" Roxbury regarded his daughter, who shared her father's even features and fair complexion, with obvious fondness.

She took his arm. "There are some lovely white leather gloves that I simply must have."

"The dozen pairs you already possess aren't enough?" he teased.

"A woman can never have too many gloves," Lilliana said. "Hello, Adora."

"My lady." Adora Bradford dropped into a graceful curtsey.

Lilliana gestured toward Atlas. "Allow me to make Mr. Catesby known to you."

"How do you do?" Adora regarded him with thinly veiled curiosity. "I believe Lady Lavinia mentioned meeting you."

Lilliana's lips twitched. "Did she now?"

Atlas preferred not to imagine what Merton's daughter might have said about him. He sketched a bow. "My lady. I trust Lady Lavinia is well."

"You can see for yourself," she said pertly. "Lavinia is in attendance this evening."

He suppressed a groan at the thought of spending the evening trying to evade the child's amorous intentions. On the other hand, most of the people on his list of suspects were present that evening, which might prove useful.

Adora tugged discreetly on her father's arm. "Won't you come and purchase the gloves for me, Papa?" she entreated. "After all, it is for a worthy cause."

"I am certain that helping the less fortunate is what motivates your desire to acquire the gloves." The marquess gave a farewell nod to Lilliana as he allowed Adora to steer him away. "Do excuse me. I'll come and find you later."

Lilliana's answering smile was welcoming and gracious. "I shall count on it." Atlas scowled once the marquess turned away and drifted into the crowd.

"Do put yourself at your ease," Lilliana said once she caught sight of Atlas's dark expression. "It is a light flirtation and nothing more."

Atlas gritted his teeth and said nothing, even though he doubted Roxbury saw his interactions with Lilliana as harmless flirtation. The man wanted to marry her, and they all knew it. Just then, something on the gallery level attracted his notice, causing him to forget his foul mood.

"Look, there's Miss Archer."

Lilliana followed his gaze. "So it is." She set her almost-empty champagne glass down on the nearest available surface. "There's no time like the present. Let's go and speak with her, shall we?"

Atlas took one quick last gulp of his drink before handing his empty glass off to a passing waiter and quickening his pace to catch up with a brisk-moving Lilliana, who'd already started up the stairs that led to the gallery.

Once they reached the gallery, they saw that Elizabeth Archer was accompanied by her father. The two of them stood close together, examining a painting depicting the old London Bridge some fifty years prior, before all of the houses and shops on the medieval span had been demolished.

"Good evening, Miss Archer." Lilliana spoke first. Archer and his daughter turned to greet them, Elizabeth's eyes widening slightly, while Archer kept his composure.

"Lady Roslyn." Miss Archer curtseyed. "May I present my father, Mr. Archer?"

"Mr. Archer." Lilliana acknowledged the man with a regal dip of her chin. "I understand you are acquainted with Mr. Catesby."

"Indeed I am, my lady." He spoke stiffly and carefully, without the confidence Atlas had seen at their first meeting. Lilliana's icy majesty seemed to be having an effect on the elder Mr. Archer.

"You are looking at one of my favorite depictions of the London Bridge," Atlas said.

Archer glanced back at the painting. "It shouldn't be long now before the new bridge is built." A design for a new bridge over the Thames had been approved a decade earlier with construction expected to begin in a few years' time.

"I should have liked to see an iron arch spanning the river," Atlas said. He'd been intrigued by the proposal of a metal bridge, but it had been rejected as impractical. The winning design consisted of five stone arches, a more conventional approach.

"I myself feel safer on stone," Archer said. "Who knows if the iron will hold?"

Lilliana had apparently had enough of their polite chatter. "May I borrow your daughter for a few minutes, Mr. Archer?"

Curiosity lit Archer's eyes. "Certainly, my lady."

She rewarded him with a radiant smile. "My brother is a patron of the Society. I am very interested to hear how his donations are being used."

"Of course, my lady." Archer turned to his daughter. "My dear, I will go and find Mama."

"I'll join you after"—she glanced uncertainly at Lilliana—"my conversation with Lady Roslyn."

Once her father strode down the hall and vanished down the steps, Elizabeth licked her lips. "How may I help you, my lady?"

Atlas interjected. "Perhaps we should remove to a more private location."

"I don't see the need for that," Elizabeth said in a steely tone. Atlas suspected she did not care to be alone with him and Lilliana.

Lilliana came straight to the point. "We have discovered the identity of the young woman who wrote intimate letters to Mr. Davis."

The girl swallowed visibly. "I cannot think what that has to do with me."

"It was everything to do with you," Atlas put in. "Because you are she."

Elizabeth's lips thinned. "As I have already told you—"

Lilliana stepped closer. "Do not bother to deny it," she interrupted. "We have compared the writing on your notes to the penmanship on Lady L's intimate letters."

"They are one and the same," Atlas said.

Panic filled Elizabeth's eyes. "No." She retreated, shaking her head in denial, until she'd almost backed into the painting behind her. "Perhaps the writing is alike, but it wasn't me."

"Miss Archer." Atlas spoke in soothing tones. "We are not here to censure you for a love affair, nor do we intend to share what we've learned with anyone."

Lilliana laid a gentle hand on Elizabeth's arm. "We are simply attempting to determine who killed Mr. Davis."

"It wasn't me. It's not true." Elizabeth was still shaking her head. "It isn't."

Atlas did not care to see any woman in distress, particularly one as young and vulnerable as Elizabeth seemed at that moment, but he forged ahead, reminding himself that she could very well have poisoned Gordon Davis. "I have spoken to your former maid. She says you exchanged letters with Davis, that he visited you at your home, and that you were alone with Davis in the laundry with the door closed."

An exclamation of distress erupted from Elizabeth's mouth. "Sara is a liar." She searched for words, speaking in panicky short breaths. "A liar and a thief. You would take the word of a thief?"

"You will recall," he reminded her, "that Mr. Davis's neighbor also saw you with Mr. Davis."

"Two people have seen you with Mr. Davis," Lilliana interjected, but her jaw was tight, and she too seemed shaken by the depth of the young woman's disquietude. "And your penmanship is identical to Lady L's."

"I think," Atlas added, "that if we continue to search, we will find others who have seen you in Mr. Davis's company."

Elizabeth's eyes watered, and she began to shake, her desperate gaze bouncing between Atlas and Lilliana. "My father cannot know. And Mr. Montgomery mustn't ever hear of this."

Their conversation had begun to draw the notice of people around them, the patrons who were taking a turn around the gallery. Lilliana neared the girl and put an arm around her, offering comfort. "Calm yourself. We have no desire to hurt you."

Atlas stepped closer, using his bulky form to shield the girl from observers. "People are beginning to take notice," he murmured. Lilliana gave a sharp nod and guided the girl to the nearest alcove, out of the sight of the other guests.

"Sit." Lilliana urged the girl onto a painted wooden bench in the recessed space. Atlas remained in the aperture to thwart any inquisitive eyes.

"You don't understand," Elizabeth whispered, a hunted expression on her pale face. "I loved Gordon. I thought we were going to be married."

"Of course you did." Lilliana sat on the bench next to the girl. "That much was very obvious from your letters."

"I was foolish. Young and stubborn. I should have listened to Sara. All along, she had the right of it." Tears streamed down Elizabeth's cheeks. "She warned me that my father would never accept Gordon as my husband. I should have listened."

Atlas stepped forward to offer his kerchief. "Did Gordon behave . . . dishonorably toward you?"

She accepted the linen and swiped it under her reddened nose. "He wouldn't return my letters when it was over. I begged him to. But he refused."

Lilliana held the girl's hand. "Why did Mr. Davis refuse to return the letters? Did he say?"

"He had heard that I was betrothed to Mr. Montgomery. Gordon was so very angry." She looked entreatingly from Lilliana to Atlas. "I wasn't being inconstant. It was just that I came to accept the reality of my situation. When Mr. Montgomery began to pay his addresses, I realized that I must wed a man my father approved of. And besides, I had begun to hear things."

"What sorts of things?" Atlas asked.

"I received an unsigned note that said Gordon had taken up with a woman in that house where he lived. And Sara heard he was involved with a grand lady in Mayfair. He denied it all, of course."

Frustration churned in Atlas's gut. He knew where to start in regard to the lady who lived in the same house as Davis, but the identity of Davis's married Mayfair *amour* seemed more elusive than ever.

Lilliana pushed a stray curl of Elizabeth's back into place. "Did you believe Davis when he told you he was faithful to you?"

"I had no way of knowing. But he was such a handsome man, and I am . . . rather plain." She sniffled. "I began to wonder whether what Sara said was true . . . that Gordon wanted to wed me to better his position in life and not because he loved me."

Atlas's thoughts went back to the mysterious note. "Did you ever learn who sent the unsigned letter alerting you to Davis's supposed indiscretion with a fellow boarder?"

"No, I did not." She wiped away more tears. "By then, it hardly signified. I was betrothed to Mr. Montgomery."

Lilliana patted the girl's hand. "Why did you keep up a correspondence with Mr. Davis even after you'd become betrothed to Mr. Montgomery?"

"He still had the letters." A new rush of tears poured down Elizabeth's splotched red face. "He threatened to ruin me. When I asked for the letters back, he said he would only return them directly to my father's hands."

"That scoundrel." Atlas's neck burned. "He took terrible advantage of you."

"It was my own fault. I behaved so badly." She pressed Atlas's now-rumpled kerchief hard against one watery red eye and then the other. "Now my life is ruined."

Lilliana squeezed her arm. "Mr. Catesby is correct. Davis was a cad who took terrible advantage of a young, sheltered, and inexperienced girl."

"Why are you being so kind?" Elizabeth looked from Lilliana to Atlas in bewilderment. "Especially now that you know the terrible things I've done."

Atlas wondered if the terrible things Elizabeth referred to included poisoning her revengeful ex-lover. "Miss Archer, aside from your maid, who else knew of your association with Davis?" Had her father or her brother been driven to extreme measures to protect Elizabeth's honor and reputation? Atlas would certainly have called out any man who had acted in such a dishonorable way with one of his own sisters. "Did anyone in your family know? Your father or brother, perhaps?"

"No!" Her eyes widened, her alarm apparent. "And they must never learn of this."

"Rest assured," he responded, "they will not hear of it from me."

"Nor from me," Lilliana said.

"Elizabeth? Elizabeth?" Mr. Archer appeared behind Atlas, concern stamped on his face. "I heard you were ill."

Lilliana rose. "Miss Archer must have eaten something that upset her constitution." She spoke with smooth command. "However, she does seem to be better now."

Elizabeth smiled shakily. "I am fine, truly, Papa. I hope I didn't distress you."

"Not at all, my dear." He hurried forward to offer his arm to his daughter. "I'll fetch Mama and we can depart."

Elizabeth pushed to her feet and clung to her father's arm. "I am rather weary."

"I owe you both my thanks for looking after my daughter," Archer said as he prepared to escort his daughter away.

Guilt flashed through Atlas. "We did nothing—"

"That is not true." Elizabeth returned Atlas's kerchief to him. "You have been very kind." He shoved the damp cloth into his pocket, watching as father and daughter made their way toward the stairs.

Behind him, Lilliana sank back down on the bench. "I feel terrible for distressing the girl so."

He joined her on the bench. "That was rather unpleasant."

She looked at him. "But what Elizabeth has just told us suggests she had a very strong motive for murder."

Chapter Nineteen

Atlas saw Lilliana home shortly after Elizabeth's departure and returned to his apartments for a long hot bath. Afterward, he pulled on a comfortable old banyan he'd picked up in France many years prior, before the war, on one of his first journeys after Cambridge.

He dismissed Jamie soon after, eager to settle in at his game table before the window to work on his puzzle. With the frame now complete, he focused on the faces in the crowd, trying to decipher which pair of eyes belonged to which floating mouth and lower jaw. As he worked, the familiar sense of calm settled over him, clearing his mind.

He worked in the blissful quiet except for the sounds from the street below, the roll and clatter of carriages and the clopping hooves of the beasts that pulled them. Through the window, he could hear the chatter of young bucks gallivanting along Bond Street, many visiting the discreet sporting hotels where beautiful women were available for a generous sum.

He was having trouble with one particular part of the puzzle, the collage of people in the market. He tried one piece after the other, determined to find the correct one.

A knock at his door broke Atlas's concentration. He was tempted to ignore it and continue with his puzzle, but curiosity pulled at him. He had few visitors late at night. He rose and padded barefoot to the front hall to find a moderately disheveled Charlton standing on the landing outside his dark-paneled front door.

"Charlton?" he said with surprise.

Charlton grinned. "Who the devil did you think it was this late at night? Your buxom and most agreeable landlady? Or perhaps the elegant Lady Roslyn?"

Atlas moved aside to allow his friend to enter. "Do shut your mouth before I'm forced to teach you some manners," he said mildly. "Why are you here?"

Charlton ambled in, heading toward the sitting room. "If you tempt me with that heathen smoking pipe of yours, I shall tell you why I am here."

"And if I don't prepare the *nargileh*, you will go home and leave me in peace?"

Charlton walked over to the game table and stared down at the half-completed puzzle. "I promise that you will want to hear what I have to say."

Atlas eyed his friend. He rarely observed Charlton in a disordered state. The man was normally fastidious about his appearance. However, this evening, his golden hair was rumpled, his waistcoat only half buttoned, and his cravat nonexistent. "Are you foxed?"

"Not at all. But I do feel a pleasant buzz from the few glasses of champagne I consumed this evening."

With a shake of his head, Atlas went to prepare the hookah. Removing the stem from the vase, he filled the receptacle with water.

Charlton picked up a puzzle piece and dropped it back onto the table. "This looks impossible to decipher."

"If it were easy, it wouldn't be worth doing." Atlas sprinkled the *shisha* tobacco in the contraption's clay bowl, making certain it was loose enough for air to pass through.

Charlton turned away from the puzzle and stumbled into a small table piled high with heavy books, noisily upending it. "So sorry," he said, stooping to right the table and collect the scattered books.

"Try not to wake the neighbors, will you?" Atlas lit the coals and inhaled on the hose for a minute or so to ensure that the *nargileh* was properly lit. "My landlady's apartments are downstairs. She lives behind the shop."

Charlton settled into his favorite stuffed chair as Atlas handed him the hose. Charlton dropped his head against the back of his chair and inhaled long and slow. "This is bloody good."

Atlas took his usual seat opposite his friend. "Where have you been? You look as if you've just crawled out of bed."

"I have. Just not my own." Charlton waggled his brows. "If you take my meaning."

"You could not make it more obvious."

Charlton handed the hose over to Atlas. "I say, is your sister's husband still in Town?"

"Palmer? I believe he departs on the morrow." He drew on the hookah, inhaling the rich, mellow flavor. "I haven't seen much of them. They tend to stay home together most evenings when Palmer is in London."

A morose expression settled on Charlton's face. "I expected him to be an old troll with one foot in the grave."

"Did you truly have hopes in that direction?"

"It seemed possible once. But no longer." Charlton grimaced. "Not only does Palmer not have one foot in the grave, but with all of that tiresome farmer vigor and strength, he'll likely outlive us all."

"I wouldn't be surprised if he did."

Charlton's eyes met his. "He treats her well?"

Atlas nodded. "Yes, I believe so. Even though theirs is an unusual arrangement, it seems to suit them both."

Charlton sighed heavily, as if the weight of the world were upon him. "I suppose I should turn my attentions toward finding a countess. We're not getting any younger, you and I."

Atlas handed him the hose as he exhaled. "You certainly have a nursery to fill and a title to pass on."

Charlton sucked on the hose. "If there were an available woman that I cared for the way you care for Lady Roslyn, I would certainly marry her."

"Not this again—"

His friend interrupted. "Yours are not insurmountable odds." Charlton blew the thick silvery smoke toward the ceiling. "Unlike mine."

Up until now, Atlas would have heartily and irritably dashed any suggestion that he could wed Lilliana, but now he wasn't so certain. After the intimacy they'd shared in her sitting room earlier that evening, things between them felt different, although he couldn't immediately articulate how. "I suppose none of us can say what the future holds," he said.

Charlton studied his face. "Has there been a new development in that arena?"

Atlas avoided answering. "Are you here solely to discuss our lusterless love lives, or did you have another reason for visiting?"

"Ah, yes, I did have a compelling reason for rushing over here in the middle of the night."

"Do you care to share it?"

"I have found the wealthy, titled married lady you are seeking."

Atlas straightened. "The lady who had a liaison with Davis?"

Charlton smiled smugly. "The very one."

Anticipation pulsed through Atlas's veins. "Who is she?"

Charlton puffed on the water pipe hose before answering. "Lady Susan Woodford, Countess of Brandon."

Atlas had never heard of the woman. "Are you acquainted with her?"

"She's a beauty. And about thirty years younger than Brandon, her husband."

"How did she meet Davis? They would hardly have moved in the same circles."

"He was the neighbor's footman."

Atlas slammed his palm down on the arm of his stuffed chair. "That's why we couldn't find her."

Charlton exhaled a long steady stream. "Lady Brandon isn't known to be particularly free with her favors."

"How do you know she is the woman we seek?"

Charlton grinned. "I did as you suggested. This evening's pillow talk yielded some very fruitful results."

His eyes went wide. "Were you with Lady Brandon?"

"No." Charlton chortled. "I just told you the lady is not known to be free with her favors . . . although Davis appears to be the exception."

"If Lady Brandon is truly the lady I seek, I must thank you. I'm most appreciative."

Charlton smirked. "My information is well worth indisposing you to prepare the *nargileh,* wouldn't you agree?"

"I would," he allowed. "Tell me more about this Lady Brandon."

"She's young, beautiful, respectable, and of good family . . . a marquess's daughter. The lady was the shining light of her Season. She had her pick of suitors. Brandon was the wealthiest of them all. She has maintained an impeccable reputation since her marriage a few years back."

"She sounds like a paragon. But you're certain she was Davis's lover?"

"There is no doubt. I have it on excellent authority."

They were interrupted by a knock on the door.

Atlas frowned in the direction of his front hallway. "Who could that be?"

Charlton waggled his brows. "If you truly are expecting an illicit late evening visit, you should have told me as much."

Atlas scowled over his shoulder at the earl as he made his way into the front hall. "I anticipated nothing this evening beyond solitude and time to work on my puzzle."

He opened the door to find Olivia Disher, clad in a silky salmon-colored dressing grown with her honey-colored curls loose and flowing.

"Olivia," he said with surprise.

"Hello, Atlas," his landlady said. "I do hope I'm not disturbing you."

"Not at all. Please do come in." He stepped aside to allow her entry. Following her into the sitting room, alarm stirred within him that Olivia might wish to rekindle their very brief affair. "I must caution you that I am not alone."

"No, indeed," Charlton called out cheerfully as he rose to his feet. "How delightful to see you again, Mrs. Disher."

She blushed prettily. "Good evening, my lord. Forgive my intrusion."

"Not at all," Atlas said.

She looked from one man to the other. "It is just that I heard a terrible bang coming from Mr. Catesby's apartments and wanted to ensure all was well."

"I do beg your pardon, Mrs. Disher." Charlton had the grace to appear chagrined. "I knocked over a table and some books. Very clumsy of me. I hope I didn't disturb you too terribly."

"Not at all, sir. I was not yet asleep." The hookah caught her attention. "Is this your water pipe, Mr. Catesby?"

"It is. I seem to recall your interest in experiencing the *nargileh*."

"Care to try?" Charlton held out the hose. "There's no time like the present."

She paused for a moment and then stepped forward and took the hose from him. "I suppose it wouldn't hurt to sample it."

"Go easy since this is your first time," Atlas advised.

She drew on the hose, held the smoke in her mouth for a moment, and then blew it out. "That's delightful."

"I would agree," Charlton said.

She puffed a few more times before handing the hose back to the earl. "Perhaps I should order a hookah pipe for the shop," she said, referring to the glass-fronted back room where her customers came to relax and smoke their recent purchases.

"I would certainly frequent your establishment if you did." Charlton drew on the hookah, exhaling the thick smoke as he spoke. "That way I would not always have to wait for Catesby here to offer it."

She regarded him with interest. "Then I shall have to seriously consider adding a water pipe. Having the Earl of Charlton visit my smoking room would certainly draw new patrons."

Charlton chuckled. "Happy to be of service, Mrs. Disher."

"If you are serious," Atlas said to Olivia, "I do have an extra hookah pipe stored somewhere at my sister's house. You are welcome to make use of it for your smoking room to see if the *nargileh* would be a profitable addition."

"That is very generous." Her pretty face lit up, then grew more serious. "But I wouldn't wish to indispose you."

"Nonsense." Atlas dismissed her objections. "If it were any trouble at all, I would not offer."

"Do take Catesby up on his offer, Mrs. Disher," Charlton urged. "He is a man who speaks plainly. If he says the loan of his heathen pipe is no inconvenience, you may take him at his word."

"If you are certain," she said with some hesitation.

"I am," Atlas said. "It's settled."

"Very well, then. I accept." She favored him with a grateful smile. "Now I shall leave you both to it. I do apologize for the intrusion, but the visit was most worthwhile."

Atlas gave her a slight bow. "I am pleased you found it to be so. And it was no intrusion. I should apologize for having disturbed you."

"I think I shall go as well." Charlton put down the hose and rose to his feet. "I have imposed on Catesby enough for one evening. I'll walk you down, Mrs. Disher."

She dimpled prettily. "That would be lovely."

Atlas saw them out. As he closed the heavy door behind his guests, the sounds of Charlton and Olivia chatting animatedly as they went down together filtered up the stairwell.

* * *

Lady Brandon lived in a mansion on Park Lane in Mayfair. Hoping the countess would grant him an audience, Atlas walked to the majestic Brandon town home the morning after learning her identity.

He gave his card to the butler and waited just inside the front entrance, a marbled and balconied front hall that rose three stories. There was no denying the lady had wed into a great deal of wealth.

The butler returned and bade Atlas to follow him. Susan Woodford was apparently not a woman who stood on ceremony, given that she received Atlas in her private sitting room.

Lady Brandon was standing by the window when he was shown in, and he saw immediately that Charlton had not overstated the countess's charms. Susan Woodford was a beautiful woman with golden hair and stunning forest-green eyes that appeared even more brilliant against the moss shade of her gown. A sizable emerald cut in fine points dangled from her neck.

"Mr. Catesby," she greeted him as the butler withdrew, leaving them alone. "Do come in."

"Lady Brandon." He bowed. "Thank you for seeing me. I beg your pardon for this intrusion."

"Not at all. I have been hoping you would come."

That surprised him. "Have you?"

"Let us be frank, Mr. Catesby," she said pleasantly. "One hears things in Mayfair."

"And what have you heard?" he asked, unsure of where the conversation was headed.

"I understand you are investigating the death of Gordon Davis."

"I am."

"Then I will do everything in my power to be of assistance." She sank down on a paisley upholstered chair and gestured for him to take the matching seat opposite her. "Do join me."

As he drew nearer, he saw that she was not as composed as her erect posture and fluid, self-assured voice would suggest. Lady Brandon's eyes were red, as if she'd been crying. He settled the chair and waited for her to speak.

"Ask any questions you would like, and I will answer them if I'm able. I trust the more . . . intimate details will be kept private."

"You have my word as a gentleman on that."

"Very well," she said. "Your reputation as an honorable man precedes you."

"Were you well acquainted with Mr. Davis?"

"Yes, we were lovers."

Her directness took him aback. "When did your intimate relationship begin?"

"Before my marriage. He was a footman in a neighboring house. We met and fell in love."

"I see. Were you betrothed to Mr. Davis at some point?"

Her smile was wistful. "Yes, I was mad in love with Gordon and was ready to run off to Gretna Green to marry."

"What happened?"

"The Earl of Brandon asked for my hand."

So much for true love. "How did Mr. Davis respond when you jilted him?"

"He was hurt and furious. But I am the daughter of a marquess. I realized I could not live a frugal life. You comprehend that I have never struggled nor sullied my hands a day in my life. I would have been a burden to Gordon."

"What occurred after that?"

"Gordon left, and I did not see him again until several months after my wedding."

"What did he want?"

"Me, of course. And I wanted him. We loved each other deeply. If circumstances had been different, we would have married and been quite content together."

"By different circumstances, you mean if Mr. Davis were wealthy?"

"You may think me a shallow woman, Mr. Catesby, and perhaps I am." She ran a hand down the smooth column of her throat. "But I am also practical. The truth is that the social chasm between us was too large."

"So you resumed your affair?"

"Yes, we did."

"May I ask, was your husband aware of your liaison?"

"I believe he was, but it's hardly the sort of thing one discusses."

"How did Lord Brandon feel about your having an affair?"

She smiled, appearing truly amused. "Surely you are not a naïve man, Mr. Catesby. Such liaisons are not uncommon among the ton. To be jealous would be unseemly, and I assure you Lord Brandon would never behave in a less than decorous manner."

"I see." As long as he lived, Atlas did not think he would ever become accustomed to the cavalier approach peers of the realm took to marital vows and promises of fidelity. "Did your husband not worry you would bear another man's child?"

"My husband is childless. I am his second wife." She ran a light finger over the large emerald resting in the valley between her breasts. "The first Lady Brandon had no children. I have promised my husband never to bear another man's child, and I intend to always honor that vow."

"How often did you see Mr. Davis?"

"Two or three times a week."

"Where did you meet him?"

"Difference places. When my husband was away in the country, Gordon would visit me here. I would leave the side door unlocked for him, and he would be gone in the morning before the servants awakened."

It seemed Lady Brandon was as bold as her deceased lover. Both seemed to take what they wanted and damn the consequences. "Did this affair continue until Mr. Davis's death?"

"No. He broke off with me about three months before he died." Her eyes clouded. "He was secretly betrothed to the daughter of a wealthy merchant and was determined to remain true to her at least until they were wed."

So she knew about Elizabeth Archer. "Did Davis tell you whether he loved this merchant's daughter?"

"No. He did not love Elizabeth Archer. He loved only me, as I have only ever cared for one man—Gordon." Her voice came perilously close to breaking. She paused and composed herself. "But he wanted to bring himself up in the world, and I could not blame him."

"And that's what wedding Miss Archer would do. It would raise him up in society."

She nodded. "He realized it would be almost impossible to wed a noble girl, even if he did manage to seduce her. He did attempt to ensnare Lord Merton's daughter, but the girl wasn't interested in the least. That one has her eyes on a title. And even if Lady Lavinia had been willing, her father most certainly wouldn't have been. Few lords would allow their precious daughters to marry a footman."

Profound distaste for the morally challenged Davis began to stir in Atlas's chest again. "But the daughter of a merchant was easier prey."

"Yes, but pray do not think too harshly of dear Gordon. He truly intended to be a good husband to her. He told me as much."

Atlas considered the lady's words. The man she'd loved for many years had left her for another woman. Atlas supposed people had killed for less. "Were you terribly angry when Mr. Davis ended your affair?"

"Are you wondering whether I was disappointed enough in Gordon's desertion to be driven to murder? No, of course not. I knew he would eventually come back to me." Her chin wobbled, and her face came close to crumpling with emotion. "He always had before. His death means he can never return to me."

Either she was a spectacular actress or her grief was genuine. "Can you think of anyone who wanted him dead?"

"Gordon could be a scoundrel, as you must know by now. I imagine there were more than a few angry papas who would have preferred to have Gordon out of the way permanently."

"Did you know Miss Archer had become betrothed to another man? That she'd broken with Mr. Davis?"

Her eyes widened. She seemed truly surprised. "I find that difficult to believe. Especially after . . ." She stopped herself.

"After?"

"He and Miss Archer were very close. Particularly so."

"Are you suggesting he seduced her?"

"He might have," she hedged. "It would have been a way to ensure a wedding did take place. He'd hoped to get her with child, but it didn't come to pass. I'm afraid I cannot tell you much about the final weeks of Gordon's life. What little I learned about how he fared came from a mutual friend in whom Gordon had taken to confiding."

"Would you mind telling me who this friend is?"

"He is a barrister by the name of Huggins. He keeps a set of chambers at Gray's Inn."

Atlas mentally filed the name away. "Have you spoken with Mr. Huggins since Mr. Davis's demise?"

"I have not." Lady Brandon studied Atlas's face. His distaste for the entire business must have been apparent because she added, "You must not think too harshly of Gordon, Mr. Catesby. He had everything: looks, charm, intelligence."

"Everything but money and social standing."

"Exactly. You and I were to the manor born. He wanted the life you and I take for granted. In his place, you or I might have behaved the same."

He flushed. "No, Lady Brandon. I can assure you I would never seduce a young lady for the purpose of trapping her into marriage."

"Ever so gallant," she mused. She rose and glided over to a small bow-fronted mahogany sideboard. Lady Brandon walked in a way that emphasized the womanly curves of her hips. "You are the talk of Mayfair, Mr. Catesby."

He doubted that. "Am I?"

Picking up the crystal decanter, she filled two glasses and brought one over to him. "Sherry?"

"Thank you." He accepted the glass and was startled when her fingers lightly brushed his.

She drank deeply from her glass, her emerald eyes regarding him over the rim of the glass. "Your courtship of Lady Roslyn Sterling has not gone unnoticed."

He stiffened. "Lady Roslyn is as fine a woman as I have ever met, but I am not courting her."

"Are you not?" She sank down into her chair. "You have been seen escorting her to several gatherings."

He could not begin to explain his relationship with Lilliana. Nor was he about to try with this woman. He had met Lilliana at the lowest point of her life and had been in a position to help her. That shared past was their deepest bond. "I am assisting her and his grace."

"Ah, yes. The investigation."

"Mr. Davis's sister is Lady Roslyn's lady's maid. She is distraught over her brother's death."

"I am glad of Lady Roslyn's interest in Gordon's death. Otherwise it might have gone unnoticed and his killer unpunished."

"Do you believe Mr. Davis was murdered?"

Her gaze met his. "I do not know. But I trust you will find out."

He drank the last of his sherry. "I will certainly do my best." He rose and bowed. "I've taken enough of your time. Thank you for your candor."

She surprised him by standing and accompanying him to the door.

"Mr. Catesby?"

He paused. "Yes?"

"You're a very interesting man." She stood near enough that he could smell her perfume. Something flowery yet not cloyingly sweet. Up close, her jewel-toned eyes were even more captivating. She placed a light hand on his arm. "Perhaps you will come again. A personal call."

He did not mistake the intent behind her invitation. With her former lover dead, it appeared Lady Brandon was looking for a new paramour.

"That would be unlikely, my lady." He gently took his arm away. "Good day."

Chapter Twenty

After his conversation with Lady Brandon, Atlas went by his sister's house to pick up the water pipe for Mrs. Disher's tobacco shop. He was pleasantly surprised to find Lilliana visiting with Thea.

While his sister went to retrieve the pipe—Atlas had stored several boxes at his sister's during the time he'd stayed with her while convalescing after breaking his foot—he filled Lilliana in on the identity of Davis's wealthy married lover.

"Lady Brandon?" She was incredulous. "Are you certain?"

Atlas nodded. "She told me so herself."

"You talked with her?" Her brow wrinkled. "When? Where?"

"Her house on Park Lane. I've just come from there."

"You visited Lady Brandon at home?"

"Yes, and she was nice enough to receive me."

"I'm certain she was," Lilliana said dryly.

"The lady was surprisingly forthcoming." He was eager to share what he'd learned. "She readily admitted to having a long-term affair with Davis, begun before her marriage and continuing shortly after she wed." He filled her in on the rest of the conversation—except, of course, for the very last part of it.

"Do you think Lady Brandon is a suspect?" Lilliana asked. They were in Thea's breakfast room. The main table was littered with papers and books rather than dishes and glasses. Behind it stood a black chalkboard filled with white chalk equations.

"We certainly cannot rule her out as a suspect," he said. "Davis did jilt her in his quest to climb the social ladder, which makes her a woman scorned."

"And we know what they say about scorned women," she said. "As if a scorned man isn't far more dangerous."

Her late husband certainly had been. "I cannot argue with that," he said. "Once I learned the identity of Davis's highborn lover, I tasked Jamie with learning all he can about Lady Brandon from her servants. He's proving surprisingly enterprising with other tasks that I've assigned to him."

She smiled. "Jamie is a bright boy. I am not at all surprised he is flourishing under your guidance." Lilliana rose and went to sit at Thea's table. "There are so many moving parts in this investigation that it is becoming difficult to keep track of them all." She found a pencil and looked for something to write on.

"What are you doing?" he asked, coming over to see.

"Making a list." She wrote down Elizabeth Archer's name. "Do we add any other Archers to the list?"

He pondered the question. "Perhaps Mr. Archer and his son, Trevor, should be on a secondary list of less likely suspects. We have no proof they were even aware of Elizabeth's indiscretion."

"I agree." She started a second column with their names at the top.

"You can also add Walter Perry, Davis's jealous neighbor to the list."

She looked up. "Which list? Primary or secondary?"

"That's a good question. I'll have to visit the Perrys again before we can decide which list they belong on."

She absentmindedly tapped the side of her pencil against the table's edge. "Someone did send that unsigned note to Elizabeth accusing Davis of carrying on with someone who lived in the same boardinghouse."

"They could be referring to Mrs. Perry or someone else entirely."

"Maybe we should put Mr. Perry aside for the moment." She went back to her task. To the primary suspect list, she added Roxbury and Merton's names.

"And do not forget Lady Brandon."

She looked at him. "And which list does she belong on?"

"I should think the primary list, at least for now. And Lord Brandon on the secondary list."

"Her husband? Do you suspect him?"

"It is an avenue that should at least be explored. He could be a jealous husband who turned violent."

"True." She continued writing. When she was done, he stood over her shoulder, and they examined the list together.

Suspect List

Primary	*Secondary*
Elizabeth Archer	Noel Archer
Lord Roxbury	Trevor Archer
Lord Merton	Lord Brandon
Lady Brandon	Mr. Perry (?)

She carefully wrote out a second identical list. When she was done, she folded each list and handed one to Atlas, which he slipped into his outside pocket while she rose and went to put her list into her reticule. Dropping her reticule on the chair, she leaned back against the table, resting her hips on the edge. "What is next? Will you go and visit the Perrys?"

"Eventually, yes. But first I need to visit the barrister who Davis took into his confidence." He counted off each task on his fingers. "And I need to learn more about Lord Brandon to see if his wife's affair might have driven him to murder her lover. Then there's Lady Brandon. We'll see what information Jamie turns up about her before I make any more inquiries in that direction."

"I'm pleased to see you were not so blinded by Lady Brandon's beauty," she said archly, "that you failed to be objective about her possible complicity in Davis's death."

There was something in her tone, a certain flintiness, which took him by surprise. His cyes went wide. "It almost sounds as if you are . . . jealous."

She crossed her arms over her chest and refused to meet his gaze. "Nonsense."

"Is it?" He moved closer until he stood right before her and placed his palms facedown on the table on either side of her hips. Being completely forthright with her now seemed almost natural. "Are you certain?"

Her crystalline gaze met his. This close, her scent—an intriguing mix of flowers and spice—drifted over him. "Why do you ask? Perhaps it is because you are not indifferent to Lady Brandon's charms."

"She does not appeal to me." He had not been tempted in the slightest by what the countess had so blatantly offered. "No one compares to you, Lily."

Her beautiful eyes widened slightly. "Is that so?"

"Yes, it is."

"Lily." She smiled softly. "You called me Lily."

"You asked me to once." Many months ago, she'd requested that he call her Lily when they were in private. Prior to these past few days, he'd never expected to again have the opportunity to do so.

"I remember."

His gaze swept over the lovely lines of her face. "Have I overstepped?"

"No." They were still for a moment, so close that their breaths almost intermingled.

"I finally found it," Thea's voice carried as she breezed into the room, examining the package in her hand. "I believe this is the pipe you are looking for."

Atlas pulled away from Lilliana and moved to take the box from his sister. "This looks like the correct crate," he said, relieving her of the burden.

"What do you need it for?" Thea asked. "Is the one you currently use faulty?"

"No, this is for my landlady's tobacco shop." He placed the wooden crate on the table and lifted the lid. "She's thinking to add it to her smoking room."

"Your landlord is a she?" Thea asked. "Since when?"

"My previous landlord, Mr. Disher, perished while I was in Jamaica. His widow, Mrs. Disher, now runs the shop." He unwrapped the brash pipe. "Yes, this is the one."

"How does she even know you own a hookah?" Thea asked.

"Mrs. Disher orders the special *nargileh* tobacco for me." He searched the inside of the box. "I thought I had purchased some extra mouthpieces, but I don't see them here."

"There are more boxes in the storeroom. I can ask Miller to take a look. If he finds them, I'll have them sent over to you."

"I'd be much obliged," he said. "I'll be on my way then. I'm meeting Charlton for supper at his club." He gave Thea a farewell kiss on the cheek before turning to Lilliana. His intent gaze held hers as he gave her a bow. "Lady Roslyn."

She favored him with a regal nod. "Mr. Catesby."

⋆ ⋆ ⋆

When Atlas reached home, he went first into the tobacconist shop to deliver Olivia the *nargileh*. He found Charlton standing at the long, narrow counter chatting with Olivia.

Atlas set the box on the counter. "Your *nargileh*, Mrs. Disher."

She appeared delighted as she pulled the top off and lifted the water pipe out of the wooden box. "You must show me how to prepare it."

"I would be happy to do so." He turned to Charlton. "Am I late, or are you early?"

Charlton checked his fob. "I suppose I am early, but fortunately, the lovely Mrs. Disher has kept me company while I waited."

"Such a charmer," Olivia said with a laugh. "You're liable to turn my head."

Atlas and Charlton left her to go up to Atlas's apartments. As they went up the stairs, Atlas asked, "Tell me, what do you know of Lord Brandon?"

"There's not much to tell really." Charlton pursed his lips while considering his answer. "He's something of a dull fellow. Brandon prefers life in the country, his dogs, and the hunt."

Atlas paused at the top of the stairs. "Is he the type to be violently jealous of his wife's affair?"

"That scenario is difficult to envision. Brandon's a stolid fellow who doesn't appear overly interested in his wife."

They entered Atlas's apartments to find Jamie stoking the fire in the front wall. "Bring the earl a drink while I dress, will you?" Atlas said to the boy, leading Charlton into the sitting room and then heading on to his bedchamber.

"Of course, sir."

Charlton pulled a few shillings from his pocket. "I could use a coffee. Run and get us some."

Jamie pocketed the money. "Certainly, my lord."

Once the boy was gone, Atlas paused in the doorway to his bedchamber and looked expectantly at Charlton. "Well?"

"Well what?"

"You obviously sent the boy away so we'd have some privacy. He won't be gone long. What is it?"

Charlton cleared his throat, his discomfort apparent. "I must ask you a question, and I hope you will be frank."

Atlas pulled off his cravat. "I will certainly try to be."

"You and Olivia . . . Mrs. Disher, rather . . . is your *affaire d'amour* truly over?"

"It was hardly a love affair." Atlas rested a hand against the doorframe and learned into it. He wondered where Charlton was going with this line of questioning. "I esteem the lady, to be sure, but our dalliance was a mistake, and I regret the indiscretion."

"It's just that . . ." Charlton's gaze floated around the sitting room. "What I mean to say . . ."

"Bloody hell, Charlton, spit it out." Atlas was somewhat bemused by the earl's uncharacteristic discomfiture. "Jamie's liable to return before you reveal what's got you twisted into knots."

"Very well." Charlton straightened. "I am interested in seeing Mrs. Disher on a more . . . erm . . . personal basis."

"Truly?" Atlas dropped his hand and straightened. Olivia might not be a lady, but she was a respectable woman. "She's not one of your opera singers or actresses."

"I am well aware." Charlton ran a hand over the back of his head. "It's just that I am weary of those kinds of liaisons. What I mean to say is that paying for companionship eventually loses its luster. I'm interested in . . . something different."

"I cannot fault you there." Atlas had never paid for female companionship. The idea that such transactions were commonplace among the aristocracy had always struck him as sordid. He felt the exchange demeaned the buyer far more than any woman he might pay for her company. "But it's not as though you can make someone like Olivia your countess."

"No, of course not. However, Mrs. Disher has indicated she has no intention of remarrying. I should like to enjoy her company. I have reason to believe she enjoys mine."

Atlas shrugged. "You are both adults. She's a widow who can do as she pleases."

"You don't mind, then, given that the two of you were once intimate?"

Atlas shook his head. "Olivia and I are friends who lapsed one evening when we were both lonely and had imbibed too much. I have no claim on her. If you are interested in pursuing your acquaintance with Mrs. Disher, it is none of my affair, and I have no objection whatsoever."

"If you are certain."

"I am." Unbuttoning his waistcoat, he turned and made his way into his bedchamber. "Now allow me change so we can get to the club for supper."

Less than an hour later, Atlas and Charlton entered the Voyager's Club and were surprised to find Ambrose Endicott walking through the front entrance hall.

"Endicott," Atlas greeted the runner. "Don't tell me there's been another burglary here."

"Nothing of the sort," the runner responded. "The stolen candlesticks have been recovered. We've just returned them."

"Where did you find the silver?" Charlton asked.

"A fence in White Chapel had them. We are still tracking the burglars, but this is a start." He buttoned his coat. "Good evening, gentlemen. I do hope you enjoy your meal."

Atlas and Charlton bade the runner good-bye. As they were about to head into the Eating Room, Endicott paused. "What do you think of the misfortune that's befallen the Archer family?"

Atlas frowned. "What misfortune?"

"You haven't heard? You are acquainted with the Archers, are you not?"

"Yes, I have met some members of the family." Had Elizabeth's scandal become public? "But I have no knowledge of the misfortune you speak of."

"Practically the entire family was poisoned yesterday." Endicott appeared surprised that Atlas hadn't heard the news. "It appears to be arsenic."

Chapter Twenty-One

"Poisoned?" Charlton exclaimed.

"The devil you say!" Atlas's lower jaw dropped. "Was anyone killed?"

Endicott's expression was grim. "The youngest daughter, Harriet Archer, is in a very bad way. The doctor isn't certain she'll survive."

Atlas recalled meeting Elizabeth's lively and precocious young sister when he'd called upon the Archers. Anger burned in his chest at the thought of someone deliberately harming the child. "And the others in the family? How do they fare?"

"The elder Mr. Archer and Mrs. Archer did not seem too terribly affected. The son, Trevor Archer, also had a bad time of it, like his sister Harriet, but he's pulling through."

"And the other daughter?" Atlas asked after Elizabeth. "How is she?"

"Fit as a fiddle." Endicott gave him a meaningful look. "She was the only person in the family who did not appear to suffer any ill effects at all. By all outward appearances, Miss Elizabeth Archer did not ingest the poison as the rest of her family did."

Atlas exchanged a look with Charlton, unsure of what to make of that revelation. The sole Archer left untouched by poison was Elizabeth, the one family member who had admitted to previously purchasing arsenic. "Do you know how they all—with the exception of Miss Elizabeth—came to ingest the poison?"

Endicott shook his head. "Not as of yet. I have some men searching the poison books to see if they find anything interesting."

And find something they would. Jamie had located Elizabeth's name on the poison register. It was only a matter of time before the runners discovered it too.

* * *

The following morning, Atlas set out for Clapham to visit the Archer family. The maid showed Atlas into the same sunny drawing room with large sash windows as when he'd first visited.

"Mr. Catesby." Noel Archer crossed over the gleaming paneled flooring to shake Atlas's hand. "I'm pleased you have come. I was thinking of sending a note this morning asking you to call."

Atlas masked his surprise, wondering why Archer would summon him the day after his family had been poisoned. "How may I be of service?"

Archer gestured toward the shiny new sofa where a plumper, older version of Elizabeth Archer sat with a distressed expression on her face. "This is my wife, Mrs. Archer."

"Madam," Atlas said with a slight bow. "Please allow me to express my sincere sympathies for the recent misfortune that has befallen your family."

She gave him watery smile. "Thank you. I hope you will be in a position to assist us."

"If I am able," he said, still confused as to what the Archers wanted from him. "How is Miss Harriet faring?"

Mrs. Archer's face crumpled, and Mr. Archer said, "There has been no change. The doctor says there is nothing further he can do. We must wait and pray for Harriet's recovery."

"I shall say a prayer for Miss Harriet as well. And your son, Trevor, how is he?"

"Much better," Mr. Archer said. "He is up and walking around today."

"And Miss Elizabeth Archer?"

"Physically she is fine, but she is most distressed about what has occurred," her father said.

Mrs. Archer blotted another tear. "Libby is particularly distraught about Harriet."

Archer nodded. "She spent all night nursing both Harriet and Trevor once she was assured her mama and I were just fine."

"We are being most inhospitable, Mr. Archer," his wife said. "We have left Mr. Catesby standing for far too long. Please take a seat."

"How may I be of assistance?" Atlas asked once they'd all settled.

"You have been investigating Gordon Davis's poisoning. He worked at my factory. I cannot help but wonder if the two cases are related. I thought, perhaps, during the course of your private inquiry, you might have uncovered information that could shed light on who wants to harm my family."

He would not share what he'd learned about Davis, Elizabeth, and her purchase of arsenic. Not until he was certain she'd poisoned her own family. "Do you have any idea how all of you ingested the poison? Was it in your meal perhaps?"

Archer wiped a hand down his face. "We all took tea and supper together. It makes no sense that Elizabeth wasn't sickened in any way. We all ate the same thing."

The maid came in with the tea tray and set it on the table before the sofa.

"No, no." Mrs. Archer scooted forward on the sofa to serve the tea. "Not this old sugar bowl." The porcelain container was cracked and had clearly known better days. It did not match with the rest of the tea service. "Please take this one away and bring the new one."

As the maid hurried away to do as she was bid, Mrs. Archer glanced apologetically at Atlas while she poured the tea. "One of the kitchen maids broke our usual sugar bowl. We had to make use of this one yesterday."

The maid returned with the new sugar bowl, which was shiny and new, like almost everything else in the Archer household. Mrs. Archer lifted its delicate lid. "How many sugars, Mr. Catesby?"

"Just a little, please." He noted the Archers' sugar had been very finely shaved off the cone. Instead of lumps, the sugar was smooth and almost granular.

He accepted his tea from Elizabeth's mother and watched as she prepared cups for herself and her husband. Neither of them took much sugar, just the slightest bit. Something nudged in Atlas's brain. "Miss Elizabeth does not take sugar in her tea."

"No, indeed she does not," Mrs. Archer said. "She has no interest whatsoever in anything sweet."

"The old sugar bowl. When did you use it?"

"Just yesterday after the bowl we normally use broke."

"How does Miss Harriet take her tea?"

"With lots of sugar," her father said. "My girl adores sweets."

"Sometimes, we catch her sneaking sugar straight from the bowl," Mrs. Archer added.

"And Trevor," Atlas said. "I gather he too is fond of sweets."

"Yes, indeed," said Mrs. Archer. "He is almost as bad as his sister."

Mr. Archer studied Atlas's face, his expression serious. "Why do you ask?"

"Because I think we've just discovered how your family was poisoned. The arsenic is in the sugar. The question now is, who put it there?"

* * *

Atlas spent the next hour questioning the servants.

"The old sugar bowl was pressed into service when clumsy May here dropped the fine porcelain bowl the family normally uses," said Mrs. Becher, the family cook, a stern-faced woman and undisputed ruler of the kitchen and those who worked within it.

May, a pale-faced young girl, nervously wrung the fabric of her flounced apron. "I was drying the porcelain. 'Twas an accident, it was."

"The cost of replacing it should come from her pay." The cook spoke in a biting tone. "But Mrs. Archer is too kindhearted and wouldn't hear of it."

"I'm grateful." The girl visibly cringed under the cook's tongue lashing. "Truly I am."

Atlas surveyed the enormous kitchen. Everything was as pristine and new as the rest of the Archer house, with spotless flagstone floors, freshly painted shelves upon which copper pots and pans were neatly lined up, and a black cast-iron cooking range with brass accents filling the enormous hearth.

"Where do you store the sugar?" he asked.

"The sugar for the master and the family is in the confectionary," Mrs. Becher told him.

"The confectionary?"

"The pastry larder." Mrs. Becher directed him to a cozy shelf-lined room just off the kitchen. A marble-topped dresser stood at the center of the wooden-floored space.

"Here it is." She pulled open a deep drawer, revealing the coarse granulated sugar within. "Powdered for the master and the family." She pointed to the drawer beside it. "The flour is there. We store most everything needed for making pastries in here."

"And this is where all of the sugar is kept?" he inquired.

"No, powdered sugar is far too precious. The servants use cones." She bustled over to another door off the kitchen. "We keep sugar for the servants here in the larder with the spices." She unwrapped a hard cone of sugar. Servants would break off chunks as needed for their tea. "At times we mix this sugar with water for baking."

"But the sugar in the pastry larder is what the family uses for their tea?" He went back to the confectionary, with Mrs. Becher following, and examined the door. "Do you lock this door?"

"Not during the day. We lock up the kitchen at night."

"Who has the keys?"

"I have a one, and Mrs. Archer has one."

He pulled the sugar drawer open, wondering whether the entire supply was tainted. "Have you used the powdered sugar since the family took their tea yesterday?"

"Oh, yes, we made pastries that the family ate in the evening after supper. Everyone ate them but poor Miss Harriet, who had already begun to feel poorly. And Miss Elizabeth, of course. She is not one for sweets. And any pastry that remained was eaten this morning."

"Did Mr. And Mrs. Archer partake?" They both had appeared hearty to him. If the entire sugar store were tainted, they'd have taken ill after eating the pastries.

"Yes, they both enjoy apple pastry, particularly Mr. Archer. He ate several of them."

"Who filled the old sugar bowl once May broke the one the family normally uses?"

"I'm not certain," Mrs. Becher said. "We had the hardest time locating it. The old thing wasn't in its usual cupboard."

"Where did you find it?"

"It was hidden away on one of these shelves." She pointed to where she'd found it. "Someone had placed it behind the pans, and it was already filled with sugar."

"Is that unusual?"

"Most unusual. We wouldn't want roaches, weevils, or other varmints to get into the sugar. The bowls that aren't regularly in use are usually kept empty until we have need of them."

"Maybe one of the servants filled the bowl?"

"If they did, none of them confessed to it when I expressed my displeasure at the sugar being wasted so. But I examined it, and the sugar looked fine, so I sent it in to the family on the tea tray. Mr. Archer does not like waste."

He thanked her and made his way back to where the Archers awaited him.

"I advise you to throw out all of the powdered sugar," Atlas told Mr. Archer. "I doubt the entire drawer is tainted, but were I you, I would not take the chance."

"I will instruct Mrs. Becher to do so immediately," Mrs. Archer interjected.

"What do you make of it?" Mr. Archer asked Atlas, his expression worried and haggard. "Why would someone target my entire family? Perhaps they wished to punish me."

Atlas wasn't sure what to think. "Do you have enemies?"

"Not that I know of. Not to the extent that they would endanger my loved ones." Archer seemed genuinely perplexed. "I do try to do right by people."

"Mrs. Archer," Atlas inquired, "may I ask where you keep the keys to the kitchen?"

"In a drawer in the chest in the front hall," she said.

"It is common knowledge that you keep it there?"

"My children certainly know. When Trevor comes in late, he is sometimes hungry and will go to the kitchen for something to eat. Elizabeth uses it as well. She'll be up late reading and desire refreshment before sleeping."

Atlas did not care for the direction in which the evidence pointed. Elizabeth Archer had purchased arsenic, had ready access to the household sugar supply, and was the only person in her family to escape eating the tainted sugar.

Was it a coincidence? Or was Elizabeth Archer the most cold-blooded of murderers, capable of killing her own family?

⋆ ⋆ ⋆

Atlas returned home to an unexpected visitor.

He found Lilliana sitting before his game table, the window framing her aristocratic profile and lithe figure in sharp relief. He watched her for a moment, her face the picture of concentration as she contemplated his unfinished puzzle.

He broke the silence. "This is a surprise."

She turned at the sound of his voice, concern etched on her face. "Atlas. Finally." She rose and came toward him in a cranberry-colored gown that complemented her ivory complexion and dark hair. "How are the Archers? How is Elizabeth?"

"Miss Elizabeth Archer is well." He'd sent Lilliana a note informing her of the Archers' misfortune before going out to Clapham. "She is the sole member of the family to be spared."

Lilliana studied his face. "What are you suggesting?"

"I?" He flattened a hand against the expanse of his chest. "I have suggested nothing."

"Surely you don't think she poisoned her own family."

"Here are the facts." He verbally listed what they knew thus far. "There was arsenic in the sugar. Bow Street believes the family was poisoned by arsenic. We know Elizabeth Archer purchased arsenic. Gordon Davis, who was intimately acquainted with the young lady, was poisoned with arsenic."

Crossing her arms over her chest, she paced slowly as she considered his words. "I just do not see it."

"The circumstances do seem to suggest Elizabeth is the culprit."

She turned to face him. "Did you see her?"

"No, she was nursing her sister. Elizabeth was apparently up all night tending to her ill siblings."

"Which shows she's likely a loving sister."

"Or," he countered, "that she is consumed with guilt."

"Do you really believe that?"

"I have reached no conclusions, but I do believe Gordon Davis's death is somehow related to the poisoning of the Archer family."

"It does seem likely."

He watched her pace some more. "Will you take a seat?"

She slipped into one of the stuffed chairs, and he took his usual seat opposite her. Lilliana's gaze wandered around the sitting room, from the crimson carpets and orange wallpaper to the chairs and sofa covered in sky-blue paisley chintz. "You can certainly learn a great deal about a person by visiting his home."

Lilliana had been there once before, late at night during a time of great distress, and had only stayed for a few minutes. He liked having her there now, sitting with him, as they discussed the case. "Is it the bright colors?" he asked. "The decoration is not my choice. The apartments came furnished."

She smiled. "Ah, that explains it." She turned her attention to the small table at her side, running a light finger over the flat wooden fragments Atlas had arranged into a perfect square. "And this?" She picked up one of the precisely cut shapes. "What is this?"

"Something I picked up in Greece. It's called an Archimedes' Box."

She rearranged the pieces, sliding them around on the table. "And what is the challenge?"

"To put the pieces together to form a box. If one is particularly adept, you can also shape the pieces into various animal figures or other objects."

"Another one of your puzzles," she mused. "Will you make me an animal?"

He rose, went over, and quickly arranged the shapes.

"An elephant!" She clapped her hands together. "What else can you make?"

He smiled and moved the pieces around again and waited for her to react.

"It's a ship," she said. "Like the one that will soon take you away to India?"

He heard the question in her voice. "Perhaps. I have not made any definite plans." He looked around. "Where is Jamie?"

"He was taking your laundry to Charlton's when I arrived. I told him he did not need to stay and attend me. I hope you don't mind."

"Not at all." He hadn't realized Jamie still took his dirty linen over to Charlton's to be laundered. "It's an unexpected pleasure to find you here."

She smiled at that. "What is the next step in the investigation?"

"I'm not certain of how to proceed where the Archer poisonings are concerned. But I do have an appointment on the morrow to go and see Huggins."

"Who is Huggins?"

"The barrister in whom Davis confided about his liaison with Elizabeth."

"Will you come and see me after you've spoken? To tell me what you learn."

"I would be pleased to call upon you."

"Excellent." She stood and went over to the window overlooking the street. "I must go. Somerville's coach is here. The boys will be done with their lessons soon."

"What have you decided to do about sending Peter away to school?"

She exhaled wearily. "I haven't yet. My indecision is plaguing me."

He followed her out to the front hall and opened the door for her. "I am certain you will make the correct choice for you and your son."

She paused. "Sometimes you have more faith in me than I have in myself."

He accompanied her down and saw her into her coach and on her way. When he returned to his apartments, he went over to his game table. Something was different. He let out a small amused huff of surprise when he realized what it was.

Lilliana had completed the difficult section of the puzzle, the one that had plagued him for days. What he'd spent hours on, she'd apparently deciphered in a matter of minutes.

"Extraordinary," he said aloud to himself. "Simply extraordinary."

⋆ ⋆ ⋆

Gavin Huggins kept a set of chambers at Gray's Inn, the ancient lodging quarters at the intersection of High Holborn and Gray's Inn Road near St. Paul's Cathedral, which was frequented by barristers, students of law, and literary-minded men.

The barrister, a small-framed man who exuded energy and intelligence, was forthcoming, particularly after learning of the Duke of Somerville's interest in the matter.

"Yes, I was acquainted with Mr. Davis." Huggins settled behind his desk and invited Atlas to take the seat across from him. "I knew him for about three years. I also know Miss Archer and her family, although not terribly well. I am acquainted with Mr. Archer mostly due to various business concerns, and I have seen the Archer family on occasion at various social events."

"Were you aware that there was an ongoing correspondence between Mr. Davis and Miss Archer?"

"Yes, Davis confided as much to me." Huggins made a moue of distaste. "I advised him to go to Miss Archer's family and tell them of his attachment. It was the most gentlemanly course of action."

"And what did he say?"

"That Miss Archer was opposed to telling her father, who already held Davis in dislike because Davis had introduced Trevor, Miss Archer's younger brother, to the gaming hells."

"Was Trevor aware of his sister's attachment to his friend?"

Huggins shook his head. "I don't believe so. Davis seemed to think his association with Miss Archer was completely unknown to her family."

Atlas pondered Huggins's words. If neither father nor brother was aware of the liaison, that effectively eliminated them both as suspects. "When was the last time you saw Mr. Davis?"

"He came to my office several weeks before his death. By then Miss Archer was betrothed to Mr. Montgomery. When I mentioned the engagement to Mr. Davis, he became very agitated and said it wasn't true. He informed me that he too had heard the rumor but that Miss Archer had assured him that it was false."

"Did he believe her?"

"He seemed to suspect she was being less than honest with him. That was when Mr. Davis told me that even if the rumor was true, he had documents in his possession, evidence that would be sufficient to prevent the reading of the banns."

"Their correspondence."

Huggins's expression was grim. "I believe so, yes."

"Were you aware that Mr. Davis took arsenic?"

"Yes, I saw him take some on more than one occasion in my presence."

"Did he tell you why he took it?"

"He said he needed it because he could not sleep. I admonished him because I personally believe taking a great quantity of arsenic is unsafe."

"Did he tell you he took it regularly?"

"I assumed as much when he insisted one could take it in small doses. I believe the situation with Miss Archer was causing him a great deal of distress to the point that it was impacting his health. He looked very unwell the last time I saw him."

"Unwell how? Was he ill?"

"I asked him as much, but he denied it. He complained of terrible headaches and body aches that he blamed on the stress caused by the uncertainty of his association with Miss Archer. I advised him to see a doctor. I recommended my own doctor, and Davis said he would go and see him."

"What is the name of his doctor, if I may ask?"

"Dr. Young. He works at Guy's Hospital in Southwark."

"Do you know whether Davis ever went to see him?"

"I believe he did." Huggins paused, his expression uncertain.

Sensing there was something the barrister was holding back, Atlas leaned forward. "Is there something more?"

He exhaled an overburdened breath. "I do not wish to spread tales."

"I hope you will share whatever it is you know with me, particularly if it has a bearing on this case."

"Davis suspected that Miss Archer was poisoning him."

"Why did he think that?"

"He used to go and visit her in the evenings or on Sundays when the family was away. She would prepare chocolate for them. He said he felt ill after those meetings. Particularly after the rumors of Miss Archer's betrothal to another man began to circulate."

"I see." A chill arrowed up his spine. Davis's landlady, Mrs. Norman, had also mentioned that Davis believed his mystery ladylove was poisoning him, and Davis himself had suggested as much in the diary he'd kept the last few weeks of his life. The evidence against Miss Archer was certainly mounting.

Huggins rose. "If that is all. I am expecting a client in a matter of minutes."

Atlas came to his feet. "My thanks. You've been most helpful."

⋆ ⋆ ⋆

The last person Atlas expected to find at Lilliana's was Miss Archer herself.

She was already in Lilliana's private sitting room when Atlas arrived. Miss Archer stood by the window, looking out, her back to the room.

Lilliana rose and came toward Atlas as soon as Hastings announced his arrival. "Miss Archer is here. She says she has something important to tell us."

"Indeed?" He scanned the room, his attention hitching on the tea tray set on the table before the sofa. Alarm and dread shot through him. He took both of Lilliana hands in his—they were softly warm—and urgently studied her face. "Are you well? Did you take tea with her?"

"What is the matter?" She squeezed his hands in a reassuring manner. "Of course I am fine."

"Are you certain?" How long did it take before arsenic affected a person? "Did you drink the tea?"

She gave him a puzzled look. "No. I did order it, as you can see, but we did not take tea. Miss Archer is too upset."

He crossed over to Miss Archer and spoke to her back. "Why are you here?" His tone was curt, rude. "What do you want?"

"Atlas!" Lilliana came to his side. "What is the matter? Why are you being so harsh?"

He kept his hard gaze on Elizabeth. "I don't want this woman anywhere near you."

Beside him, Lilliana gasped. "I've never known you to be discourteous."

Elizabeth finally turned to him. Her appearance shocked him. Her face was ravaged by grief, her eyes red and anguished. "Mr. Catesby has the right of it. I am not fit for decent company."

Lilliana looked from Elizabeth to Atlas. "What is going on here?"

Elizabeth answered for them both. "He doesn't want me here because he knows I killed Gordon Davis and poisoned my own family. And now he fears you will be my next victim."

Chapter Twenty-Two

Atlas stared at her in shock. "You admit to killing Gordon Davis?"

"Why do you appear so surprised?" Elizabeth asked tearfully. "You believe me to be a murderess, do you not?"

"It is your admission that shocks me," he said stiffly, "not your culpability."

A sound of surprise escaped Lilliana's throat. "I cannot fathom it," she said to the young woman. "You purposely poisoned your own family? Your own sister almost died."

New tears rushed down Elizabeth's face, her red face crumpling with grief and guilt. "I am responsible for their misfortune, but it was an accident. I swear to it. The servants weren't meant to bring in the old sugar bowl. Mama never uses it anymore. She only likes new things, shiny things." She broke off on a sob. "I hid the bowl in the pastry larder behind several pans and supplies. I didn't expect anyone to find it."

Lilliana went to the girl, directing her to the sofa before settling next to her. "Take a deep breath and, when you are ready, explain to us what happened."

On edge and alert, Atlas remained standing. "You say your family was poisoned by accident." He wasn't certain he believed her, but he decided to focus on the crime she readily admitted to committing. "But you say you did kill Gordon Davis. Tell us why."

Elizabeth inhaled and visibly attempted to collect herself. "Gordon threatened to show the letters to my father. I couldn't face having my father know what I'd done." She looked entreatingly at Lilliana. "Mr. Montgomery would never have had me after that. And I no longer saw Gordon in the same light. He seemed frightened, almost desperate, the last time I saw him."

"Davis's suspicions were correct," Atlas put in. "He kept a diary in the last few weeks of his life. He believed you were poisoning him."

She did not deny it. "Yes, I mixed the arsenic I'd purchased with sugar in the old sugar bowl and served him from it." She dropped her face into her hands, crying bitterly. "I'm a terrible person. I killed him."

"How many times did you put poison in Davis's chocolate?" he asked.

"Just that once. I think he even suspected it. Gordon said the chocolate tasted strange. He looked me in the eye and asked if I had put something in it. It was almost as if he knew."

"What did you say?" Atlas asked.

"I denied it, of course. But I think he knew what I had done. He died a few weeks later." She looked at him with haunted eyes. "They said he suffered terribly. I didn't realize. I thought it would be quick."

But Davis had suspected Elizabeth of poisoning him over a period of time. His diary had said as much, and Huggins, the barrister, seemed to confirm those suspicions when Davis reported feeling unwell on several occasions after visiting her. "Are you certain it was just that once?"

"Yes. I couldn't have done it a second time." She shivered. "It was awful. Knowing I'd given him poison and sitting with him and watching as he drank it. I have nightmares about it every night. I deserve to be punished. I killed him."

He wondered about that. "Exactly how much arsenic did you put in Davis's chocolate?"

"I mixed it in with the sugar. I cannot say exactly how much. I was so nervous I barely remember anything about that evening." She sniffled. "But however much I gave Gordon, it was clearly enough to kill him."

"You knew Davis had the letters," Lilliana said. "Did you not fear what would happen to them after Davis died?"

"I never signed my true name to those letters. Whoever found them would not know they were from me. However, if Gordon had brought those letters to my father, Papa would have recognized my handwriting."

"Why have you decided to confess to us now?" Atlas asked.

"Because I must be punished for what I have done. When Harriet was at her lowest point and we feared she would die, I vowed to confess my crime if the lord spared my sister." Her expression brightened, and she seemed at peace with her decision. "The doctor says Harriet is through the worst of it. She is recovering. And so I must keep to my side of the bargain."

Hastings appeared. "Miss Archer's coach has arrived, my lady."

Elizabeth looked expectantly at Atlas. "I will go now to Bow Street to confess my crime. I know I have no right to ask this of you, but will you accompany me? I fear I am too much of a coward to go alone."

Atlas shook his head. "I think you should go home and be with your family, Miss Archer."

"Why?" She gaped at him. "I have confessed. Now I must be punished."

"I'm not so sure about that."

Lilliana's brow furrowed. "What are you saying?"

He doubted a single dose of arsenic could kill a man who took the poison regularly. "I am not convinced Miss Archer killed Gordon Davis." He spoke directly to Elizabeth. "And until I am, I think you should go home to your family and speak of this to no one."

* * *

A note to Ambrose Endicott, the Bow Street runner, resulted in Atlas learning the name of the physician who'd performed the autopsy on Gordon Davis.

Atlas visited Dr. Frederick Corbett at his residence, a brick town home hidden away in an alley off Fleet Street. A maid in a black uniform and flounced white apron ushered Atlas through the cozy front hall, where several patients sat waiting to see the physician, her heels clicking efficiently against the wooden floors as she directed him to Corbett's office, where the doctor awaited him.

"Yes, there was an arsenious acid in the deceased's body." Dr. Corbett returned a tome to his glass-fronted bookcase and closed its latticed door. It had not been difficult for Atlas to secure the appointment. A brief mention of the Duke of Somerville's interest in the case once again proved to be the only calling card he needed.

"The arsenic is the common type one would find in shops." Dr. Corbett moved to his desk. "It consisted of colorless crystalline particles."

"So it was definitely not sooty arsenic."

"No, it was not." Still standing, Corbett organized some papers on his desk as they spoke, sorting them in separate piles after giving each sheet a cursory examination. "But it was of a quantity considerably more than sufficient to destroy life."

"How much arsenic does it take to kill a man?"

"That depends on the person ingesting the poison. As little as two grains can cause death in some, but it usually will take four to six grains." He paused from his paper sorting to give Atlas a significant look. "There were almost forty in Mr. Davis's stomach."

Atlas doubted Elizabeth could have given Davis that much arsenic in one cup of chocolate. "If someone were to mix arsenic with sugar and dilute in a single cup of chocolate, would that be sufficient to cause death?"

Corbett appeared skeptical but only said, "It is hard to say for certain, but if I were to venture to guess, I would assume not."

"Mr. Davis was known to ingest arsenic for medicinal purposes and believed it was safe to take the poison in small doses."

"That is true," Corbett acknowledged. "However, it was no small dose that I found in Mr. Davis's stomach. There was enough arsenic in him to kill a half dozen men. A dose that large would have sickened him immediately and killed Mr. Davis within a few hours."

Atlas rose to go. "Thank you for your time." He'd gotten the information he'd come for—that it was highly unlikely

Elizabeth Archer was responsible for her lover's death. "I see you have a waiting room full of patients. I won't keep you from them any longer."

"I'm pleased to be of assistance," the doctor said.

Atlas paused when one final question came to him. "Aside from the arsenic you found in his stomach, I presume Davis was otherwise a healthy young man."

"Not exactly."

"What do you mean?" Atlas recalled Huggins, the barrister, relaying that Davis had appeared ill during their final meeting a few weeks before the man's death. Atlas had assumed arsenic was the cause of the man's ailment. "Was Mr. Davis ill?"

"I observed sores in the deceased's groin area."

"Sores? What kind of sores?"

"If I were to venture a guess, I would say the man had syphilis."

Shock rippled through Atlas. "Are you certain?"

"No, nor did I not explore that avenue any further. I was retained to determine what killed the man. And there is no doubt that Davis died of acute arsenic poisoning."

Atlas blinked, still trying to digest this new information. "Did you see any other signs of syphilis?"

"None. If the deceased had contracted the disease, he was clearly in its very early stages. He might not have even known he had it. I saw no signs of mercury in his system."

"Mercury?"

"The common treatment for syphilis."

"I see." Atlas thanked the doctor and departed, still rattled by this newest revelation.

As he walked toward Bond Street, he wondered whether Davis had known about the syphilis, a cruel and agonizing disease that twisted a person's looks into something grotesque. He remembered meeting a syphilitic man whose nose had caved into his face. It had been a gruesome sight.

Gordon Davis had been a man intent on parlaying his handsome visage into a better life for himself. Atlas wondered how someone like Davis, who'd traded so heavily on his good looks, would have reacted upon learning he was about to lose the only true currency he possessed in life.

* * *

Atlas found Lilliana and his sister practically on his doorstep when he returned home. They were standing on the stone walkway in front of the tobacconist's shop.

"Are you coming to see me?" he asked after greeting the two ladies.

"Yes." Thea handed him a wrapped package. "My footman found the mouthpieces for your landlady's water pipe."

"We were just on our way to Hatchard's," Lilliana added.

"Precisely," Thea said. "We thought to bring the package to you as long as we were in the area."

"Thank you," he said. "I'm certain Mrs. Disher will be most pleased."

Thea peered through the shop's window, where Olivia stood behind the counter waiting on a customer. Turning, she reached for one of several large square-shaped glass jars filled with snuff lining the shelf behind her and set it on the counter.

"Is that your landlady?" Thea asked.

"Yes, that is Mrs. Disher."

"Introduce us, will you?" Thea started for the shop entrance. "Mrs. Disher sounds like an interesting woman."

"Does she?" He held the door open for both ladies. The smooth rich scent of unburnt tobacco assailed them as they entered the shop. "How so?"

"Few women operate their own businesses on Bond Street. And I find it compelling that she is trying out the water pipe to see if it will increase business." Thea paused to examine the wooden statue of an American Indian carrying a large smoking pipe and waited while Olivia concluded her business with her customer. At the moment, she was carefully scooping snuff out of its glass container for the gentleman at the counter.

Stepping in behind the ladies, Atlas murmured to Lilliana, "May I call on you tomorrow?"

Her eyes widened. "Have you learned something new?"

"Yes, and if true, it is quite shocking."

"Then I absolutely cannot be expected to wait until tomorrow. Join me for supper this evening?"

"I'll need to speak with Tacy."

"I'll make certain that she's there," Lilliana assured him.

Olivia's customer thanked her and stepped away from the counter carrying his purchase. With a polite nod to Atlas and the ladies, he slipped past them, the bell above the door sounding as he went on his way.

Atlas ushered the ladies to the counter and introduced them to Olivia.

"My thanks for bringing the mouthpieces," Olivia said to the ladies. "Allow me to send for some refreshment." Olivia seemed slightly awed to be in the presence of a duke's sister, and Lilliana's natural reserve did little to put her at ease.

"Goodness, no," Lilliana said as she surveyed the shop. "You are clearly occupied at present, and Mrs. Palmer and I are on our way to Hatchard's."

"How is the water pipe being received?" Thea asked Olivia.

"Quite well thus far," Olivia said. "The patrons seem interested in sampling it. And I've had some assistance in that area."

"I've never tried it," Thea told her. "Perhaps you might host an evening at the smoking room for ladies only. I would come. Lady Roslyn would accompany me, wouldn't you?" she added to Lilliana.

Lilliana was diverted by something at the far end of the narrow shop. "Is that Charlton?" She stared back at the glass-fronted smoking room, where about a half dozen male patrons were enjoying a smoke in the haze-filled space.

"Where?" Thea asked, glancing out of the shop's front window.

"There"—Lilliana gestured toward the back of the shop—"in the smoking room."

It was indeed Charlton holding court with a number of gentlemen as he passed the hookah pipe hose around for his companions to sample.

"Yes, that is Lord Charlton," Olivia said with a smile. "He has been most helpful in urging the patrons to try the *nargileh*."

"It is no surprise he is partaking," Thea said acidly. "The man does enjoy indulging himself."

Charlton spotted them and appeared to excuse himself before rising and stepping out of the smoking room, closing the door behind him. The smoky scent of burning tobacco followed him out.

"Lady Roslyn and Mrs. Palmer," he said as he approached them. "Do not tell me you've decided to take up smoking. How scandalous."

Thea shot him disdainful look. "It is unlikely that either of us has the time to diddle away our afternoons as you appear to be doing."

"Lord Charlton has been most kind," Olivia interjected. "At first, no one would try the water pipe, but then the earl began appearing each afternoon to indulge. He now draws a crowd eager to join him." She favored the earl with a warm smile. "Lord Charlton has been very good for business."

"It has been my pleasure, Mrs. Disher." Charlton caught her eye and smiled back, blatant flirtation shining in his gaze. "The truth is, this has all been a ruse to win your favor."

Olivia blushed and dimpled prettily. "How you do go on, my lord."

Thea frowned, her questioning gaze bouncing from Charlton to Olivia and then back again. "We've taken up enough of Mrs. Disher's time," Thea said abruptly. "Shall we go, Lilliana?"

Farewells were said all around before Atlas escorted the ladies from the shop. Once they were back out on the stone walkway, Thea glanced back through the bow-fronted window, where Charlton remained within, leaning against the oak counter, engaged in conversation with Olivia.

"There are times Charlton takes harmless flirtation too far." Thea's eyes were still on the earl and Olivia inside the shop. "Poor Mrs. Disher will think he is serious."

"Actually," Atlas said, "I believe he might be. He seems to hold Mrs. Disher in high regard."

Thea swung her head around to look at him. "What does that mean?"

"It appears the Earl of Charlton has decided to grow up, at least a little." He gave her a look. "That is what you've always wanted of him, is it not?"

Thea blinked. "Well, of course."

"I imagine you'll be pleased not to have Charlton constantly underfoot." He fell in step alongside the ladies as they began to stroll in the direction of the bookshop. "All you do is complain about the man."

Thea paused. "Yes." Her tone turned brisk. "It will be a very great relief indeed."

Chapter Twenty-Three

"I cannot remember the last time I ate this well." Atlas spooned another helping of game pie onto his plate.

Lilliana plucked a grape from her dish. Supper had turned out to be a private affair in her sitting room, where numerous shining candelabras bathed her fine-boned features in soft amber light. "Are you suggesting that Jamie hasn't learned to cook?"

He gave her a look. "The boy can't even tie a cravat, and you want me to give him access to the kitchens?"

Lilliana smiled that haughty crooked smile of hers and, with a wave of her hand, dismissed the attending footman. "I've been more than patient," she said once they were alone. "What is the shocking news about Gordon Davis?"

Atlas reached for a strawberry. The cozy table was dressed with the finest porcelain, twinkling crystal, and gleaming silver. There were endless dishes to choose from—succulent roasted lamb and venison and pheasant smothered in a rich cream sauce, along with a colorful assortment of vegetables and fruits. A boisterous fire crackled in the hearth, cloaking the elegant chamber in toasty warmth. All in all, it was a delightful meal in very agreeable company.

Atlas hadn't known whether they'd be dining with the duke. He had not expected the children; he knew they took their evening meal early and that their mother made a habit of joining them. As it was well past nine o'clock in the evening, he presumed the boys were asleep.

"Well?" Lilliana said impatiently. "Out with it."

He popped the strawberry—sweet, plump, and delectably perfect—into his mouth. "It's possible he had the French disease."

"The pox?" she exclaimed. "Are you certain?"

"No." He sliced a neat bite of lamb. "Which is why I'd like to speak with your lady's maid as soon as we are done with supper." As they ate, he recounted his entire conversation with Dr. Corbett, sharing the details about Davis's autopsy.

Lilliana hung on every word. "Based on what this Dr. Corbett told you," she remarked when he finished speaking, "it appears that Elizabeth didn't poison Davis."

"She poisoned him all right, but it's very possible she did not deliver the fatal dose." He reached for a dessert biscuit. "Surely you are not leaving me to eat dessert alone?"

"I'm afraid you'll have to manage on your own." She plucked another grape from her plate. "I do not have a fondness for sweets. Do you believe Elizabeth only tried to poison Mr. Davis that one time?"

"I'm not sure what to believe. Miss Archer's story is inconsistent with what Davis wrote in his diary." He placed a slice of almond cake on his plate. "He also told at least two people—Mrs. Norman, his landlady, and Mr. Huggins, the barrister—that he believed his beloved was slowly poisoning him."

"Could he have possibly been referring to Lady Brandon?" Lilliana nibbled on a piece of cheese. "He mentioned the lady he loved was poisoning him, and it appears Lady Brandon was the only woman he truly loved."

"Lady Brandon claimed not to have seen Davis in the last few months of his life. He broke with her, intending to be faithful—at least for the moment—to Miss Archer." He took a bite of the rich moist cake. "Are you certain you won't have some of this? It's excellent."

"No, I am fine," she assured him.

Atlas cast a skeptical look at the fruit and cheese on Lilliana's plate, which he supposed was her idea of dessert. Being rather fond of sweets, he did not agree.

"Do you take Lady Brandon at her word?" she asked. "About her not seeing Davis in those final months of his life."

"I had Jamie inquire into it, and he returned with some very helpful information." At her look of surprise, he said, "The boy is quite enterprising when it comes to garnering intelligence from his fellow servants."

She half smiled. "I guess I am not terribly surprised. Jamie does have an endearing way about him."

"That he does." Atlas had never thought of his valet in that way, but now that Lilliana mentioned it, Jamie's surprising success at gathering information began to make sense. "I confess to being baffled by Jamie's ability to uncover some rather helpful findings, but I can see now why people might feel comfortable opening up to the boy."

"What did Jamie learn about Lady Brandon?"

"Her servants all but confirmed the affair. By all accounts, she did try to be discreet about sneaking Davis into her home, but servants seem to know everything."

"They certainly do," she murmured.

"According to the Brandon servants, Davis stopped visiting the house on Park Lane at least two months before his death, which confirms what Lady Brandon told me about Davis breaking things off with her. They said Lady Brandon was deeply upset when she learned Davis had met his end."

"And what of Lord Brandon . . . is he a jealous sort?"

"He does not appear to be." Atlas polished off the last bit of the cake on his plate. "The servants report that the earl and his wife maintain a cordial relationship and seem to be rather fond of one another."

"What a strange relationship," she mused. "Did she not say that her husband did not mind her infidelities?"

"She did." Atlas could not imagine any man being indifferent to a wife's extramarital affairs, even though he knew it was the way of the ton.

"While we are on the subject of interesting relationships"—she favored him with a sly look—"I must say, Mrs. Disher appears to be a lovely woman."

"I suppose," he answered vaguely, not wishing to discuss Olivia with Lilliana, even though his lone intimacy with his landlady was firmly in the past.

"Is Charlton truly taken with her?" she asked.

"So it would seem."

She almost seemed disappointed. "What of his infatuation with your sister?"

"I believe meeting Mr. Palmer in the flesh—and witnessing the man's obvious youth and vitality—had a sobering effect."

"Ah, that makes sense." She sipped her wine, her eyes on his empty plate. "Are you done? Shall we call for Tacy?"

They rose from the table, and Atlas salvaged the plate of dessert biscuits—which he brought over to the sitting area with him—before the footmen reappeared to remove the remainder of the food and dishes. Lilliana's lady's maid entered as the footmen were departing.

"Gordon ill?" Tacy said when Lilliana inquired. "No, never. Even as a young boy, that one was always as fit as they come."

"And he did not speak to you of anything relating to ill health?" Atlas asked.

She shook her head. "No, sir. He did look rather peaked the last time I saw him, but Gordy insisted he was well." Her eyes shined with emotion. "He never liked to worry me even if he was ill; it would be like Gordy to try to spare me."

"Did you believe him when he told you he wasn't ill?"

"Oh, yes, Gordy was very particular about his health. He couldn't abide sickness of any sort. I think he felt so strongly because of how Ma died."

"And how was that?" Atlas asked.

"It is not something we are proud of." Tacy stared at the ground. "Gordy made me promise never to speak of it to anyone."

"Please be frank, Tacy," Lilliana said gently. "It could have an important bearing on the case."

Tacy looked from her mistress to Atlas. "Our ma died of the French pox."

"Your mother had syphilis?" Atlas exchanged a look with Lilliana before asking, "When, pray tell, was this?"

"When Gordy was very young. He was ten when Ma died. I looked after him after that."

"He was fortunate to have you," Lilliana said. "He must have been terribly affected by your mother's death."

"It was something awful." Tacy shuddered. "She went mad right before our eyes. She was a beauty, Ma was—Gordy got his good looks from her—until she got sick." Tacy's voice trailed off.

"I understand it's very difficult for you to speak of," Lilliana said, "but it might help Mr. Catesby to learn who killed your brother."

Tacy nodded and visibly swallowed before continuing. "At first, we didn't know she was sick. She had open sores and blemishes, but we didn't know what was causing it. It upset her terribly because Ma depended on her looks to . . ."

Tacy did not have to spell out what she meant. Atlas surmised that Tacy and Gordon's mother had supported her children by entertaining men for a certain price.

"Then she started acting strangely, and in the end, her face was so . . ." She hugged her arms around herself. "She didn't look anything like herself, and in those final months, Gordy was so afraid of Ma that he wouldn't go anywhere near her."

Atlas could only imagine how awful it must have been for a young boy to witness his mother's horrifying decline. "Thank you, Tacy," he said to the maid. "You have been very helpful."

"Well," Lilliana said after the maid was gone. "How perfectly terrible."

"Indeed," he said, deep in thought, considering what they'd just learned.

"How does this new information impact how you view the investigation?" she wanted to know.

"I'm not certain." He reached for another dessert biscuit and bit into it. "The big question at the moment is whether or not Davis knew he had contracted syphilis and, if so, how that might have impacted his behavior."

"Didn't you say that Mr. Huggins, the barrister, recommended a physician for Gordon Davis to go see?"

"Yes, that's right." Atlas straightened. He searched his memory. "Huggins said he sent Davis to see a Dr. Young. The barrister said the good doctor works at Guy's Hospital in Southwark."

"I guess I know who you will be speaking with next."

"You have the right of it." Realizing the evening had grown late, he came to his feet. "I'll go and see Dr. Young tomorrow." After he bowed and bade her good night, Hastings, the butler, showed him out. As Atlas paused in the front hall for his hat and coat, a footman appeared with a large wicker basket covered with a pale linen cloth.

"What is this?" he asked when the footman handed it to him.

"It is compliments of Lady Roslyn," Hastings said. "She asked Cook to prepare a basket of food for you."

"That was very kind of her." Atlas took the basket from the footman and was surprised by how heavy it was. There seemed to be enough food for several men. "But I do wish she hadn't gone to the trouble."

"It was no trouble at all, sir," Hastings said.

The massive carved front door opened, and the Duke of Somerville swept in, his double-caped greatcoat swirling about his trim frame. He arched a regal brow when he spotted Atlas. "Catesby, we meet again."

Atlas bowed. "Your grace."

"And once again I find you in my front hall." Somerville shrugged out of his coat, revealing an exquisite embroidered ivory silk waistcoat under a beautifully cut navy tailcoat. "Making a habit of it, are you?" The butler promptly handed off his grace's greatcoat to the nearest footman and melted back into the shadows.

"Lady Roslyn was kind enough to invite me to take supper with her."

"Was she? I see my sister is determined to test Roxbury's patience." The duke's gaze slipped to the basket in Atlas's hands. "And you've raided my kitchens as well."

Atlas felt himself flush. "Your sister had a basket prepared for me. I suspect she's taken pity on a bachelor who finds his meals where he can."

"Lady Roslyn tells me the investigation is continuing apace." The duke ran a hand over his artfully tied cravat. "And that you've developed some very interesting suspects."

Atlas wondered just how much Lilliana had shared with her brother. "We've certainly learned the dead man had no shortage of people who thought ill of him."

"One hopes you identify the culprit in all haste so that my sister can return her attention to less morbid matters." Somerville turned to Hastings. "Has the tailor arrived?"

"Yes, your grace. Mr. Nash awaits your pleasure in your dressing room."

"Very good."

Atlas was not surprised that Kirby Nash, the proprietor of an exclusive Pall Mall tailor shop, attended Somerville at all hours. The custom of a personage as esteemed as the duke was not to be underestimated. And there were other pertinent reasons for Nash's house calls that were unknown to almost everyone. Atlas had discovered them himself quite by accident.

"Well, Catesby." Somerville regarded Atlas with an arrogant look. "As you heard, Mr. Nash awaits."

"I would not want to keep you." Atlas looked the duke in the eye. "Do give Mr. Nash my regards."

"I shall." The duke looked away. "Good evening then."

"Good evening, your grace."

⋆ ⋆ ⋆

Atlas met Dr. Young at Guy's Hospital in Southwark in central London, where the man worked as an assistant physician.

The hackney let Atlas off at the hospital's wrought-iron gates. He passed under the iron scroll overhead and crossed through the stone courtyard, which was flanked by three red brick hospital buildings. He immediately spotted the statue of the hospital's founder, where he was to meet Young, at the center of the courtyard. He waited there for a few minutes in the brisk chilliness of the day, taking care to stand outside the shade in order to enjoy the subtle warmth of the sun, which had made a rare appearance.

"Mr. Catesby, I presume?" The man striding across the yard was younger than Atlas expected, about his own age and clad in the formal black clothing physicians preferred. "Mr. Huggins told me to expect you."

Atlas greeted the doctor and thanked him for agreeing to meet.

"I cannot stay long," Young informed him. "I do have an appointment, but I'll answer what questions I can."

Atlas came straight to the point. "I understand Gordon Davis was under your care."

"He was." The long, narrow face held a somber expression. "But not for very long."

"Why was that?"

"He did not care for my diagnosis."

Interesting. "Why did he come to see you?"

"He was feeling extremely agitated. I gather a love affair that meant a great deal to him was ending badly. He came to see me on the advice of Mr. Huggins, who, as you know, is a mutual friend."

"Did you ever prescribe arsenic to Mr. Davis to help relieve his frenzy?"

"Certainly not. I do not advocate the use of poison." He buried his hands deep into his coat pocket. "What Mr. Davis needed was mercury, which he refused to take."

Atlas began to see why Davis hadn't cared for the doctor's diagnosis. "And the reason he needed mercury?"

"Mr. Davis had syphilis. He was in the very early stages of the disease."

So Davis had known he was ill. "And you told him as much?"

"I did. The patient refused to accept my assessment of his condition. He was very angry and departed before our appointment was completed. I never saw him again."

"How certain are you that Mr. Davis was afflicted with syphilis?"

"Fairly sure, but there was no way to tell for certain when he came to see me. One diagnoses the disease by evaluating the visible symptoms. I did not observe any other signs of syphilis on Mr. Davis's person."

"What other signs would one look for?"

"Within weeks, he would have developed a rash as well as pain in his joints and muscles. The pocks would have spread all over his body. Then there are the mental changes—possible delirium, depression, and violent mood swings."

"When did you last see him?"

"I believe it was about five weeks before his death, just a few days after Mr. Huggins recommended that he come and see me." Young checked his fob. "If that is all, I have a consultation with another physician."

Atlas stepped aside. "I won't keep you then. Thank you for your time."

Chapter Twenty-Four

After speaking with Dr. Young, Atlas hailed a hackney, which took him to the narrow lane off Great Russell Street in Bloomsbury where Davis's lodging house was located.

Mrs. Norman, the landlady, remembered Atlas and treated him with cordiality. "Do come in," she said. "It is not every day that a gentleman graces us with his presence."

Atlas wondered how Mrs. Norman would react had she known a duke's daughter had already visited her establishment. On their last visit, Lilliana had declined to use her title.

She showed him into her private sitting room, a cozy space not unlike the ones kept by housekeepers in grand homes. "I hope you haven't come to look through poor Mr. Davis's room again. It has long since been rented out to another boarder."

"No, it's nothing like that." He took a seat on her sofa, trying not to take up all of the space on the petite piece of furniture, which made him feel like an awkward giant. "I was hoping you could tell me a little more about the state of Mr. Davis's health in his final days."

"He was very excitable in his last days. I believed his distracted state had to do with the young lady he had hoped to wed."

Atlas wondered if Davis's deteriorating mental health meant his syphilis had worsened. Dr. Young had mentioned depression and mood swings as possible signs that the disease had taken a greater hold on its victim. "The medical examiner found that Mr. Davis had a very large quantity of arsenic in his stomach—enough, in fact, to kill several men."

"Oh, dear." Mrs. Norman pressed her lace kerchief against her lips. "How very awful. Someone obviously gave it to him. And I think we both know who it was."

"Do we?"

"It was that young lady of his! I just know it," she insisted. "He told me she was poisoning him."

"But we also know that Mr. Davis took arsenic regularly."

"So you say, but after his death, when I cleaned out his room, I did not see any arsenic, nor any empty containers where he might have kept the poison."

Atlas's brow furrowed as he thought back to when he and Lilliana had gone through Davis's things. There'd been no sign of arsenic then either. "I assumed that you or the doctor who had attended Mr. Davis in the end had thrown out the arsenic after Mr. Davis's death."

"No indeed." She shook her head emphatically. "That's just it. I found no arsenic in his room, none at all. I am telling you that Mr. Davis did not accidentally take too much arsenic. It's that young woman he'd hope to wed who did this awful thing to him."

Atlas pondered her words. Where was Davis's arsenic? If none had been found in his room, either he'd stashed his supply elsewhere or he likely had not ingested a huge amount of the poison on his own. "Are Mr. and Mrs. Perry at home?" he inquired.

"Mr. Perry is at work. I saw Mrs. Perry arrive after running her errands a short while ago."

"Thank you for your time, Mrs. Norman." He rose. "Now I should like to have a word with Mrs. Perry, if I may."

Mrs. Perry was indeed at home in the shabby but tidy rooms she shared with her husband. She greeted Atlas amiably and invited him to share the tea she'd just prepared.

"Have you made progress in learning who killed Mr. Davis?" she asked once they'd settled at the worn circular table.

"Some." He sipped his tea. It was somewhat weak—tea was precious to those with limited means—but he enjoyed the libation's fragrant heat. "However, many unanswered questions still remain."

"Oh?" Curious eyes watched him from over the rim of Mrs. Perry's cup.

"Were you aware that Mr. Davis took arsenic?"

"Goodness. Whatever for?"

He wasn't about to share the true reason. "He believed it helped maintain good health."

She pursed her mouth. "I never saw him take any arsenic. And on the rare occasion I stopped by his room to drop off the post or to share a baked treat, I never saw any sign of arsenic."

Atlas wondered why Davis would keep his arsenic-eating habit a secret from Mrs. Perry. He certainly hadn't been shy about disclosing his arsenic usage to other acquaintances. "How did he appear to you in those last weeks of his life?"

"He wasn't himself. I believe I mentioned that to you when we last met."

But they'd been interrupted by her husband before Mrs. Perry had been able to explain what she meant. "Perhaps you could elaborate on that now."

"He seemed troubled, almost feverish at times. He was too good for her, much too good."

He did not need to ask to whom she referred. "You believe the young lady he wished to wed was the cause of all his troubles."

"I do. Mr. Davis was the picture of vigor and health when I first met him. He was such a charmer and so very handsome. But after he took up with his young lady, things changed. He seemed very pleased at first because he was convinced his life was about to change for the better. But after a few months, she seemed to lose interest in him."

"Did Mr. Davis tell you that?"

"He mentioned briefly once that he detected a cooling in her ardor. It was an agony to him. I'm convinced that is what caused Mr. Davis's decline."

Either that or the ravages of syphilis. "Did he ever mention that name of the young lady?"

She shook her head. "No, he only said that she was gently raised."

"Someone sent this young lady a note suggesting Mr. Davis was engaged in a . . . friendship . . . with a fellow boarder. Was there a young lady here that Mr. Davis showed interest in?"

"No, none that I saw. It was probably just gossip."

"That's certainly possible," he allowed.

"Or they could have believed Mr. Perry's ridiculous claims about Mr. Davis having designs on me." The rosy pink in her cheeks deepened. "It was nonsense, of course. I am several years older than Mr. Davis and rather plain."

Atlas took in the woman's features, which were faded except for the rather pointed nose that dominated her thin face. She seemed an unlikely candidate for a sexual indiscretion, yet she made Atlas think of Elizabeth Archer.

Had Davis had a certain pattern when it came to women? While Lady Brandon, the woman he had professed to love, was an undeniable beauty, Elizabeth Archer was anything but. If Davis had taken up with his neighbor's homely wife, it would not have been the first time he had seduced a woman of unremarkable looks. The reason for the game he'd been running on Elizabeth was obvious, but what could an older married woman with neither money nor status have had to offer?

* * *

Atlas returned home to an unexpected visitor.

"The Marquess of Roxbury's been waiting for you," Jamie whispered in an awed voice the moment Atlas stepped into the front hall. "I served him coffee and biscuits."

"Well done." He handed his coat and hat to the boy and proceeded into his sitting room, where he found Roxbury standing at the tall window next to the game table with his hands clasped behind his back.

"Ah, Catesby, there you are." Roxbury turned as Atlas entered the room. "I do hope I am not intruding by calling without prior notice."

"Not at all." It came as no surprise the mannerly marquess might abandon strict etiquette in his dealings with the lowly fourth son of a baron. "I hope Jamie has adequately seen to your comfort while you awaited my return."

"He has indeed." Roxbury gestured toward the full cup of coffee and biscuits Jamie had put out. As the marquess drew nearer, the biscuit tray seemed to capture his attention. "Lady Roslyn often serves those for tea. Somerville's pastry chef is known to make the best dessert biscuits in the metropolis."

"I am rather partial to them." Atlas wondered just how often Roxbury was having tea with Lilliana these days. "Lady Roslyn was kind enough to send the biscuits home with me. She's taken pity on a bachelor whose meals are less than regular."

The two sat, Atlas in his usual spot and the marquess in the plush chair that Charlton favored.

Roxbury studied Atlas for a moment. "I am told you are an honorable man."

"I endeavor to be."

"You certainly behaved gallantly with Lady Roslyn during her most dire hour."

Atlas nibbled on his biscuit and said nothing.

Roxbury continued. "People have taken notice of the attentions you pay to her."

"We are friends." That wasn't entirely accurate, but it was also no one's business aside from his and Lilliana's.

Roxbury cast a glance around the room, which was, of course, far more rudimentary than the accommodations to which the marquess was accustomed. "Do you find yourself in a position to offer for Lady Roslyn?"

"If and when I do," Atlas said stiffly, "you can be assured that the lady—and not you—will be the first to hear of it."

"I am prepared to take the honorable course where Lady Roslyn is concerned." Resting his elbows on the chair's armrests, Roxbury settled back and steepled his fingers just below his chin. "I hold Roslyn in great esteem, and before you returned from your journeys abroad, I felt quite certain she was prepared to accept my suit."

"Oh?" He had not realized Lilliana had come so close to wedding Roxbury. "Then you've discussed marriage with her?"

"Most certainly. At length. And she promised to consider my proposal."

Icy disappointment encased Atlas's spine. "I was not aware your courtship had progressed that far."

"Indeed it has. I've engaged in preliminary talks with Somerville regarding the marriage settlements."

Atlas set his half-eaten biscuit down. The bite remaining in his mouth tasted like pebbles and sand when he considered that Lilliana was already practically promised to Roxbury and had neglected to inform Atlas of that fact. This revelation certainly explained why the duke had invoked Roxbury's name after learning that Atlas had dined with Lilliana.

Atlas studied the marquess, regarding him in a new light. The man had a right to be territorial, considering he was all but betrothed to Lilliana. If anything, Roxbury had shown great restraint. Certainly far more than Atlas would have in his place. "You didn't mention your claim on Lady Roslyn when we last spoke on this topic."

"Without a formal betrothal announcement, my discussing the matter with you would have been both premature and indiscreet."

"What has changed?"

"The matter has come to a head." Roxbury crossed one knee over the other, a relaxed yet superior posture that suggested he was completely at ease in the home territory of his presumed rival. "Roslyn has put me off of late, and I suspect it is because you have confused her."

Not half so confused as Atlas felt at the moment. "How so?"

"Only a fool would fail to see there is a bond of some sort between the two of you. Perhaps it is an inevitable result of the manner in which you met. She clearly feels grateful to you."

Atlas's patience was beginning to run out. "What is it you want from me, Roxbury?"

"I'd like for you to release Roslyn so that she will feel free to accept my offer of marriage."

"Release her?" he said irritably. "She can do as she pleases. I have no hold on Lilliana."

Roxbury's brows lifted at Atlas's slip, his informal use of Lilliana's Christian name. "I think we both know that is not true. I also believe you will do right by Roslyn." He rose. "I won't keep you any longer. I'll see myself out."

Atlas sat for a moment after he heard the door close and listened to Roxbury's light steps going down the stairs. If the marquess was to be believed, Atlas's ill-timed arrival in London had cast Lilliana's future, and her complete return to respectability, into doubt.

Becoming Roxbury's marchioness could assure Lilliana's future in a way that even Somerville—or Atlas, for that matter—never could. No fortress would be greater for Lilliana than wedding a peer and attaining a rank of her own. She and the children would be shielded should the ruinous revelations of what had occurred in Buckinghamshire ever become public.

Remorse snaked through Atlas's gut. By indulging in a flirtation with her, he had selfishly put Lilliana and the boys at risk. He must put her first, however distasteful the task.

There was one decisive way for Atlas to quit the field and clear Lilliana's path to wedding Roxbury. He rose and jotted down a note to his friend, Edward Hughes, inquiring whether passage was still available aboard the East India Company ship due to leave London in a few weeks. He'd just finished sealing the note when Jamie appeared to remove the refreshments he'd laid out for Roxbury.

"When you are done with that," Atlas said to him, "please have this note delivered to the East India Company."

"Very good, sir." Jamie paused. "The East India Company? Will you be traveling again so soon?"

"Yes." He set the sealed note down on the game table. "I believe I will be."

Jamie nodded and stooped to clear away the coffee and biscuits. "His lordship didn't touch the refreshments. Do you suppose the marquess found them unworthy?"

"Hmm?" Prodded from his musings, it took Atlas a moment to answer. "No, I'm certain he found everything most acceptable."

Jamie peered into the cup. "He didn't have any of this either. It would be a shame to let fresh coffee go to waste."

"Help yourself." Atlas pushed heavily to his feet. "I'm going to change."

"I'll assist you," Jamie said promptly.

"No need." Atlas spoke over his shoulder as he entered his bedchamber. "Drink your coffee, and then see to having that note delivered."

He shrugged out of his tailcoat and tossed it on the bed. Tugging at his cravat, he wandered into his dressing room and froze. Pivoting, he returned to the bedchamber and surveyed his surroundings. Everything was as it should be yet also not quite in its proper place. His shaving implements and tooth powder were not arranged in their usual way. The cover pane on the bed was neat, except for a couple of ripples near the footboard. To an outsider's eye, everything would appear neatly arranged. But he wasn't an outsider. This was his home, and something was amiss.

He crossed back into the sitting room and appraised the space with a more critical eye. His almost-completed Hogarth puzzle was as he'd last left it. Nothing else was disturbed. Walking back to the bedchamber, he went to the small desk and pulled open a drawer, then another. *Ah.*

Comprehension dawned. Someone had gone through his things, and although an effort had been made to leave everything as the intruder had found it, the disturbance was apparent to someone like Atlas, who paid attention to the details. "Jamie!"

The boy appeared immediately, coffee still in hand. "Sir?"

"Have you been here all day?"

"Yes, sir."

"Are you certain? Did you perchance run some laundry over to Charlton's or undertake some other such task that took you from home?"

"No, sir. I've been here all day."

Atlas's attention slipped to the half-empty coffee in the boy's hand. "But you left to get coffee."

"Oh, yes, I did." He flushed. "I should have remembered that. I do beg your pardon."

"Never mind about that. Whose idea was it for you to go out and fetch coffee? Was it yours or Roxbury's?"

"I asked if he'd like something." Jamie considered the question for a moment. "And the marquess said he wanted fresh coffee from a particular shop on Bond Street."

"You didn't fetch the coffee from Mr. Waters as you usually do?" Jamie always bought Atlas coffee from Waters because it was close by—next to the tobacconist—and Atlas preferred his coffee hot.

"No, sir. His lordship specifically instructed me to go to Hookham's. He said he can only abide coffee from there."

Hookham's was several shops away, almost at the opposite end of Bond Street from Atlas's apartments. It would have taken

Jamie much longer—fifteen minutes at least—to go there, fetch Roxbury's coffee, and return. Enough time for Roxbury, who'd found a way to conveniently be left alone, to search the premises. But for what?

Jamie frowned. "It's a bit odd, don't you think, sir, for a man to ask for coffee from a specific shop and then not touch the drink at all after you've gone to the trouble and expense of acquiring it?"

"It is odd," Atlas agreed. "Unless it wasn't the coffee Roxbury was after."

"Sir?" Jamie asked, obviously puzzled.

"Never mind." He wandered back into his dressing room. "Go and finish your coffee."

What had the marquess hoped to find? Did he think Atlas might have proof of Roxbury's daughter's scandalous trip to Holywell Street? Or possible evidence that Roxbury had killed Gordon Davis?

Of course, it was entirely possible that something as mundane as jealousy had motived the marquess. Maybe Roxbury hoped to unearth scandalous information about Atlas that might prove to Lilliana that Atlas wasn't worthy of her esteem.

Atlas had an impulse to call upon Lilliana and work out this latest piece of the puzzle with her. She had a keen brain and was far better acquainted with the way Roxbury's mind worked than Atlas was. Discussing the marquess with Lilliana, as well as going over the details of his visit to the boardinghouse, would help him sort out all the facts.

He turned and strode back into the bedchamber, ready to call for his coat and hat, but stopped dead. Visiting Lilliana at Somerville House, enjoying her company, was not a habit he should fall into. He stifled a curse. Blast Roxbury and his smug self-assuredness that Atlas would do the right thing by Lilliana.

Bloody hell. Fury burning in his chest, he stomped into his dressing room, stripped off his clothes, and reached for his banyan.

★ ★ ★

On Tuesday afternoon, Atlas waited across the street from the General Annuity Society where Elizabeth Archer volunteered each week. He wondered if she would come on her usual day or whether her distress over poisoning her family would keep her from her customary activities.

He paced while keeping watch, his thoughts drifting back to Roxbury's visit, as they often had over the past few days. Atlas had not seen Lilliana since. He'd sent her a brief note detailing his boardinghouse visit but had not called in person.

If Roxbury had had nothing to do Davis's death, then Atlas's path was clear. It was obvious to him that Roxbury cared for Lilliana and could offer her and the children the protection and comforts they deserved. Atlas, with his limited income and constant travel, would make a poor husband and stepfather. Across the street, the front door to the Society opened, diverting Atlas from his thoughts.

Elizabeth Archer, clad in no-nonsense navy clothing, marched out, stiff-postured and trailed by her maid. Atlas strode across the muddy black road, taking care to try to avoid the worst of the filth, and reached the young lady just as she was about to climb into the waiting carriage.

He tipped his hat. "Good day, Miss Archer."

"Mr. Catesby." She halted and regarded him with solemn eyes. "Is it time then?"

"No." He wasn't marching her over to Bow Street just yet, if that's what she thought. "I wonder whether you would care to walk for a moment and perhaps answer a couple of questions."

She nodded crisply to her maid and waiting coachman. "I'll return presently."

When they were out of earshot, Atlas asked, "How is Miss Harriet?"

"Much better. The doctor says we can expect a full recovery."

"I'm pleased to hear it. And Trevor and your parents?"

"They are well, thank you." Which was more than could be said for Elizabeth. She did not look at all well to Atlas. She seemed to have lost weight, and her wan face held no color.

"You look unwell," he said to her. "It will not serve your family if you make yourself ill with guilt."

"My complexion has never been very fine. I have always been pale." The corners of her mouth turned down. "I suppose that is why Mr. Davis encouraged me to buy arsenic."

He halted and faced her. "Davis wanted you to buy arsenic?"

She nodded. "He said it would improve my complexion."

"Are you saying you purchased arsenic at Davis's direction?"

"Yes, he said arsenic had done wonders for him and that I should try it because it would make me a bit less plain." Atlas silently cursed that reprobate Davis for his cruel treatment of the young woman. "I promised to send my maid to purchase some, but he insisted that I should go myself."

"Did he say why you should be the one to purchase the poison?"

"He was very adamant about it. He said servants were known to steal arsenic and replace it with something else. I told him Sara would never do that, but when he became angry with me, I promised him that I would go and purchase the arsenic myself."

Atlas's mind whirled. Why would Davis insist Elizabeth purchase the poison herself? Had he wanted her name to appear on the poison registry that all apothecaries kept?

"Why?" She studied his face. "Does it signify?"

"I'm not certain." He turned to continue walking, and she quickened her step to keep up with him. "I was wondering how Davis seemed to you the last time you saw him." At her quizzical glance, he elaborated. "Did he seem at all ill to you?"

"He seemed highly excitable, but surely that was understandable in the situation in which we found ourselves. I was betrothed to another man, and Gordon had refused to return my letters as an honorable man should."

"I am interested in whether, physically, his outward appearance seemed as usual."

"Yes, I think so." She paused as if she'd remembered something. "He did have a rash on his arm. It caused him some discomfort."

A rash. Another known symptom of the pox. "You saw this rash, I presume."

"Yes, Gordon kept scratching it, and when I asked what was the matter, he showed it to me. The rash was all over his arm." She bit her lip. "He said it was my fault. That my betrayal was causing him to become ill."

The guilt coating her words communicated that she believed it as well. That bounder Davis had done everything he could to ruin the young girl's life. Atlas swallowed down the acid that suddenly rose in his throat. Davis might still possess the power to deliver one last devastating blow to Elizabeth from beyond the grave.

"I am going to ask you a very personal question," he said carefully, "and you must answer me honestly."

"I will. I swear it."

"Do you recall the last time you were . . . erm . . . intimate with Mr. Davis?"

She flushed, the first sign of color he'd seen in her all afternoon. "It was several weeks before he died. Once Mr. Montgomery began to court me, I ceased my intimacies with Mr. Davis." She lowered her gaze. "At first, I was afraid to be completely truthful with Gordon. I feared what he might do if I cried off, so I pretended I wanted to wait until we were wed."

"And how did Davis respond to your decision to abstain?"

"He was very unhappy and tried many times to change my mind. He said if I truly loved him, I would succumb to him."

"And what did you say?"

"I told him that a man of honor would not ask such a thing of his intended."

He was pleased to see she'd shown some backbone with Davis. "I gather you did not give him what he asked for."

"I did not. I had begun to develop a high regard for Mr. Montgomery. It meant a great deal to me that my father liked and accepted him." She sighed. "Of course now, given what I've done, there will be no future of any kind with Mr. Montgomery."

Dread pooled in Atlas's stomach. In so many ways, Miss Archer remained an innocent. Beyond her lost betrothal to Montgomery, Davis might very well have snatched away any future at all that Elizabeth might have. Only she did not know that yet.

Atlas prayed she would never find out.

* * *

Later that afternoon, Atlas was at home working on the puzzle when he noticed that Jamie, who'd gone on an errand while Atlas was out, had left a note for him by the game table.

Atlas broke the seal and unfolded the note. It was from Charlton, informing Atlas that he'd gone to Bath for a few days. Atlas suspected the earl had a traveling companion; Olivia had mentioned just yesterday that she would be away visiting family for several days.

Charlton certainly seemed charmed by Atlas's fair landlady. On a couple of occasions over the past several days, as Atlas had come and gone from his apartments, he'd spotted his friend at the tobacconist's, immersed in conversation with Olivia. And two mornings ago, from his window overlooking Bond Street, he'd observed Charlton leaving quite early, before the shop opened, in a state of dishabille.

His musings were interrupted by a knock on the door. Perhaps Jamie had forgotten his key. He crossed into the front hall and was surprised to find a footman on his landing. He wore the black-and-gold livery and possessed the handsome good looks common to all of Somerville's footmen.

"Mr. Catesby, sir." The man handed him a letter. "I am to await a reply."

Atlas took the note. "Come in then while I read it and craft a response."

The footman stood perfectly postured in the front hall while Atlas continued into the sitting room. He broke the seal, recognizing Lilliana's script at once.

If it is not too much of an inconvenience, please attend me in person at your earliest opportunity.

She hadn't signed the note, a clear indication of her displeasure that he had neglected to visit her for several days. He had been avoiding Lilliana, and she had noticed. He let out a long labored sigh. She deserved a visit from him, if only to set things to rights once and for all.

He went back to where the footman awaited his reply.

"Please inform Lady Roslyn that I will attend her within the hour."

Since the weather was fair enough, Atlas decided to walk to Somerville House. Stepping briskly along the busy stone pavement, he went past a group of parading dandies only to come upon Roxbury exiting a Bond Street jeweler's shop with a small wrapped package in his possession.

"Catesby," the marquess greeted him with icy courtesy.

"My Lord," he returned, glancing at the package tucked beneath the other man's arm.

"I have purchased a significant trinket for Lady Roslyn," Roxbury informed him. "One that I hope to present to her as a betrothal gift."

"Is it official then?" Atlas forced himself to ask.

"Not as of yet, but I hope it will be soon." He paused. "I do appreciate your deciding to stand aside."

Atlas's chest heated. "I am solely interested in what is in the best interests of Lady Roslyn and the children."

"I do understand that." Roxbury looked him in the eye. "And I assure you that I shall always treat her with the care and respect she deserves. I will never give you cause to regret your decision to remove yourself from the playing field." With a parting nod, Roxbury turned toward his waiting carriage.

Atlas stepped in his path. "Why did you search my apartments when you visited the other day?"

Roxbury drew himself up. "I did no such thing."

"You did, and we both know it." Atlas set his jaw. "I do not intend to give you a clear path to Lady Roslyn until and unless

I am convinced you had nothing to do with Gordon Davis's death."

"The footman?" Roxbury stared at him in obvious disbelief. "You cannot seriously believe I had anything to do with that!"

"Why did you search my rooms?" Atlas pressed. "Do you think I have evidence against you or your daughter?"

"No, of course not." Roxbury flushed and even appeared a bit embarrassed. "I didn't kill that cad. I'm not a heathen."

"Then why?"

He waited a beat. "I wanted to confirm for myself that you don't have nefarious motives where Roslyn is concerned. That you are truly a man of honor. Even Somerville suffers your constant presence at his sister's side." He eyed Atlas with suspicion. "Why is that?"

As it happened, Atlas did have information that could destroy Somerville, but that had nothing to do with his relationship with Lilliana. "It is as you have said." Atlas spoke carefully. "What occurred in Slough created a bond between Lilliana and me. There is nothing more to it."

"I have come to believe the sincerity of your words. Roslyn mentioned she rarely sees you these days."

"I have not seen her since you and I last spoke. I intend to leave for India in a matter of weeks."

Roxbury brightened, then tried to mask his relief. "So you are truly going away?"

"I am."

"Let me assure you I had nothing to do with Davis's death," Roxbury said earnestly. "If I had, no one would even know his demise had been orchestrated. I would have made certain it looked like an accident."

That much Atlas could believe. "I envision a man such as yourself might use a bit more finesse in killing a man."

"I daresay that is true." A corner of Roxbury's mouth kicked up. "Besides, poison is a woman's weapon of choice, wouldn't you say?"

"Perhaps," Atlas said mildly, while the less noble part of him hoped Roxbury would mention as much to Lilliana. She'd been indignant when Atlas had said the same not so long ago.

"I am a man who remembers his debts," Roxbury said. "If there is ever a time I may do a favor for you, all you have to do is ask."

Atlas doubted he'd ever ask this man for anything, but he did not say as much. He murmured his farewells and went about his way.

⋆ ⋆ ⋆

"I'm relieved to find you in good health," Lilliana greeted him coolly when he arrived at Somerville House. "I thought perhaps your old injury had flared, rendering you incapable of going out."

"Nothing of the sort," he assured her, ignoring the subtle censure in her tone. She looked quite regal in a royal-blue gown. "I am quite well."

"You certainly have made yourself scarce," Thea agreed. He'd found his sister visiting with Lilliana. "I wondered if perhaps you and Charlton had gone off on one of your jaunts."

Last year, he and the earl had traveled to Bath for a few days. Charlton thought taking the healing waters at Bath might hasten the recovery of Atlas's broken foot. It hadn't, but the excursion had proven to be more than worthwhile anyway. It was on that trip that he'd first encountered Lilliana.

"As a matter of fact, Charlton has gone to Bath for a few days," he told his sister, "while I have been working on the investigation."

"He's in Bath, is he?" Thea said. "With whom?"

"He didn't say." Atlas avoided his sister's sharp gaze. "Charlton might very well be alone, for all I know."

"Yes, no doubt," she said briskly as she came to her feet. "I must go." She stooped to buss Lilliana's cheek. "And do no fret. I'm certain Peter will be fine."

"What's this about Peter?" Atlas asked with concern. "I trust he is well."

"Peter is fine," Lilliana said. "It is just that I have decided not to send him away to school quite yet."

Thea reached for her reticule. "I've no doubt she's made the right decision."

"I agree," Atlas said as he helped his sister put on her wrap. "Peter is very young to go away from home."

Thea made her farewells and bustled out, leaving Atlas and Lilliana alone.

Lilliana gave him an icy look. "You said you've been investigating. Are there any new developments?"

"Yes." He relayed what he had learned from Dr. Young, about Davis's refusal to accept his syphilis diagnosis, and the rash Elizabeth Archer had seen a few weeks later on Davis's arm.

"Whoever killed him could have waited and allowed nature to take its course," she said dryly.

"So it seems."

"Or he could have taken the poison to spare himself the horror of the effects of the disease."

"Yes." Atlas had considered that possibility. He appreciated discussing the case with her; talking it out helped the many seemingly disparate pieces fall into place. "But Mrs. Norman, his landlady at the boardinghouse, says she found no arsenic at all in Davis's rooms."

"Hmm." She crossed one arm over her waist while propping her chin in the opposite hand in a contemplative stance. "And the medical examiner told you Mr. Davis consumed so much arsenic, it would have killed him almost immediately."

"Indeed."

"It seems we are no closer to discovering who administered the fatal dose."

"I will continue looking." He stood. "I should go."

"Hastings is about to bring supper in. Will you stay and take nourishment?"

He was sorely tempted to accept her offer. To join her at the cozy table and bask in both the warmth of her hearth and radiance of her presence. But he had come here to release her, not to further their acquaintance. As much as he would like to do so. "Thank you, but I have an engagement."

"Yes, of course," she said with a reserve so frigid, he'd have required a steel pick to pierce it.

He paused. "Have I mentioned that I shall set sail soon? I'll be off as soon as we discover who killed Davis."

"Is that so?" Her eyes widened momentarily before she hid her surprise behind her bone-chilling composure. "Are you still bound for India?"

"I am," he said.

"That is very far away."

"Yes, the voyage could take up to six months," he affirmed. "I expect to be absent from London for well over a year."

"How exciting." She gave him a closed-lip smile. "I shall look forward to hearing of your adventures from Thea."

"In the meantime, I will keep you apprised of any progress in the investigation."

"A letter will suffice when you have any updates that I may share with Tacy."

"You may count upon it." He bowed and tried to ignore the rising soreness in his throat. "Good evening then."

"I may as well wish you bon voyage now," she said abruptly. "It is unlikely we will meet again before your departure."

A profound sense of loss panged through Atlas. He had not expected this to be good-bye. But Lilliana, ever the daughter of a duke, had seized the last bit of control she had in regards to their final parting.

"So I bid you *adieu,*" she said, and he did not miss the finality in her cut-glass tones. "Godspeed."

"Thank you," he said. "I wish you well . . . you and the boys." He took one last look at her—with her perfect posture and upturned chin—a portrait to frame in his memory of an empress dismissing her adoring subject.

As he departed, his heart like lead in his chest, it dawned upon him that the next time he laid eyes on her, Lilliana would be wed to Roxbury and safe from all harm. And while this was the resolution he'd intended, the thought did not cheer him in the slightest.

Chapter Twenty-Five

Atlas returned home to find Jamie bickering with Bess, the cleaning lady. They were in the sitting room where Bess was mopping the floor by the game table.

"Do not touch the master's puzzle or his papers," he said imperiously.

Bess bustled around Jamie, not even bothering to look up, mopping in long sure strokes. "Move along, boy, before I trample you with my mop."

Jamie jumped out of the way, his face a mottled red. "That's *Mister* Sutton to you."

"Bollocks." She came at him with the mop again, and Atlas suspected it was a deliberate offensive action. Jamie sidestepped out of Bess's path before she hit him. "I'm more likely to turn you over my knee than call you *Mister* anything. I've got slippers older than you."

"Good afternoon," Atlas interrupted. After his parting with Lilliana, he was in no mood for their bickering. And a slight headache had begun to throb behind his left eye.

Jamie stiffened, while Bess paused and dipped a curtsey. "Master Atlas, sir."

"Hello, Bess." He turned to Jamie. "Shall we step out of this room and allow Bess to finish her cleaning?"

Shooting a furious look at Bess, Jamie protectively snatched up a piece of paper from the game table—it was the list of potential suspects Lilliana had drawn up—and followed Atlas with the reluctant, dragging gait one would expect of a convict facing transportation. They went down to Waters for coffee and sweet buns.

Once they entered the shop, where the mingled aromas of fresh rolls and coffee saturated the air, Jamie stood hesitantly by the table.

"Sit," Atlas instructed.

Jamie didn't move. "As your manservant, it is not appropriate for me to sit at table with you."

"Is it appropriate to disobey the gentleman you serve?"

Jamie's brow furrowed. "No, sir, certainly not."

The waiter arrived with the coffee and sweet buns. Jamie watched intently while Atlas reached for a bun and bit into it. "Mmm, delicious. Warm and sweet. Just the way you like them." He sipped his coffee. "But do just stand there if you prefer."

Jamie plopped down into the seat opposite him. "I suppose it is more important for a valet to obey his master's instruction than follow the proprieties." He reached for a bun, tore it in half, and eagerly popped a piece into his mouth. "I suppose I shall have to ask Mr. Finch what a manservant should do in this situation."

"By all means." More instruction on cravat tying was also in order, but Atlas held his tongue on that subject. "Where's that list of suspects you picked up from the table?"

Jamie pulled the paper from his pocket and straightened it out on the table. "Mr. Perry?" He scrunched his eyes as he scrutinized the list. "There's a Mr. Perry on this list."

"Yes." Atlas bit into his bun despite a marked lack of appetite. The one thing he truly hungered for now was forever lost to him. "What of it?"

Jamie pushed the list over to Atlas's side of the table. "There was a Mrs. Perry who purchased arsenic in Bloomsbury, near where that Davis fellow died. I saw her name on the poison registry there."

Atlas stopped chewing. "How can you possibly remember that? Perry was not a name I asked you to look for."

"No, sir." Jamie reached for another bun. "But 'Perry' is my father's Christian name, so I remembered when I saw it on the poison registry."

The hair on Atlas's arms stood up. "Are you certain?" Both Mr. and Mrs. Perry had access to Davis and could have easily poisoned his food or drink. They lived in the same house and took their meals together.

"Yes, sir." Jamie spoke around a mouthful of half-chewed sweet bun. "Quite sure."

"Which apothecary was it?" He could only hope Jamie remembered the name.

"Greenwood's." Jamie gulped some coffee down. "It's off Great Russell just down the lane from the boardinghouse."

Atlas shot up. "I have to go."

Jamie glanced mournfully at the basket of sweet buns. "But we just sat down."

Atlas dug some money out of his pocket and tossed it onto the table. "Stay as long as you wish, but I'm for Bloomsbury."

Atlas had little trouble finding Greenwood's, a small apothecary tucked away on Phoenix Street off Great Russell.

It took a moment for Atlas's eyes to adjust to the shop's dark interior. He crossed the worn stone floors to reach the wooden counter, narrowly avoiding a striped gray cat that streaked across his path. An immense apothecary chest with dozens of small medication drawers stood behind the counter, as did a bearded man of middle years.

"May I help you, sir?"

"Yes," Atlas responded. "I hope so." The feline meowed, arching its back before slinking between Atlas's feet.

"That's Lenny. Don't mind him," the apothecary said.

Taking care not to step on the animal, Atlas returned his attention to the man. "Are you Mr. Greenwood?"

"I am."

"Are you familiar with a Mrs. Perry, who lives near here?"

The man's gaze narrowed. "I am. She comes in from time to time."

"Did she buy arsenic from you?"

"Who are you? And what business is that of yours?"

The man's defensive posture took Atlas aback. "I am investigating the death of a man who lived near here, at the request of the Duke of Somerville."

"I had nothing to do with that."

Atlas studied the man's demeanor with more care. "I did not accuse you."

"She told me the poison was to kill rats up at the boardinghouse. I had no reason not to believe her."

The feline curled up on Atlas's feet. "So Mrs. Perry did buy arsenic from you."

The man nodded. "The next thing I hear is that a boarder ended up dead, poisoned from arsenic. I knew it was her that did it. I just knew it."

Atlas's heartbeat moved a little faster. Here, finally, was the true break in the case he'd been searching for. "Why do you assume Mrs. Perry murdered the man?"

"She bought enough arsenic to poison twenty men."

"If you had your suspicions about Mrs. Perry, why did you not bring them to the attention of the authorities?"

Greenwood rolled his eyes. "And who would have cared? The cove who died was just a lowly clerk with no family to speak of."

"He has a sister. She works for the Duke of Somerville."

"And that's the only reason you are here," he said disdainfully. "Because someone powerful and important wants to know who killed the man."

No, he was there for Lilliana. He didn't give a damn about Somerville. "I would like to find the killer to give the man's sister, who is a lady's maid, a measure of peace."

Greenwood reached for a heavy worn leather book. He paged through it until he found what he was looking for. "Here it is." He pointed to an entry.

Atlas bent over to study the poison registry. There it was in careful penmanship: *Mrs. Maria Perry.* She'd purchased the poison on the fifth of March, about one month before Davis died. Atlas looked up. "Have you seen Mrs. Perry since Mr. Davis died?"

"No, she knows better than to come in here. Mrs. Perry comprehends that I'm aware of what she did. I saw her once after I'd shut the shop for the evening. She crossed the street to avoid me."

"I see." It was time to visit Mrs. Perry again. He turned to go, gently shaking his foot to dislodge the sleeping feline that had taken up residence atop his boots. The animal made a sharp meow of protest at being unsettled. Atlas looked down in time to catch its accusatory stare before the creature dismissed him with an arrogant glance and wandered behind the counter. "Thank you for your time."

Greenwood slammed the poison book shut. "Are you going to see her then?"

"Yes, I am."

"Mind you don't drink the tea."

As he approached the boardinghouse, Atlas found Gordon Davis's landlady sweeping the front stairs.

"Mr. Catesby." Mrs. Norman paused from her task when she spotted him. "I didn't expect to see you again so soon."

"Good day, Mrs. Norman. I hope I am not interrupting your chores."

The woman flushed. "It is not my usual task, you understand. My maid of all work is ill, so I must make do. After all, cleanliness is next to godliness."

"It is indeed," he said agreeably.

She resumed sweeping dirt and debris from the stairs, flicking it out into the street with the broom. "How may I be of help?"

"I've actually come to call upon Mrs. Perry. I hope she is at home."

"I believe she is, but Mr. Perry has gone out." She worked in short efficient strokes. "You are welcome to go on up."

"My thanks." He stepped around her to reach the front door and then paused. "If I may ask . . ."

"Yes?"

"Do you perchance have a problem with rats or mice here at the boardinghouse?"

The broom stilled. "Absolutely not," she huffed, clearly offended. "I keep the cleanest of homes."

"I can see that you do," he said soothingly. "I suppose you never asked Mrs. Perry to procure a large amount of arsenic in order to rid yourself of any rats that might come around."

"No. I have no vermin here." She perched one hand on her hip while the other gripped the broomstick. "We do have the occasional mouse, but that is all."

"That is as I expected." He went on in, treading over the threadbare rugs as he made his way to the stairs. In the parlor, the worn curtains framing the open windows flapped lazily in the gentle breeze.

It was the warmest day they'd experienced so far that season. Perhaps the lingering winter had finally ceded the field to the long-overdue spring. The floorboards creaked beneath his feet in the corridor leading to the Perrys' room. Mrs. Perry answered as soon as he knocked at the door.

"Mr. Catesby." She opened the door wider to allow him entry. "I was just about to have tea and lemon cakes. Won't you join me?" Her manner was open and unguarded; she showed no hint of discomfort in his presence.

"Tea and cake sounds like just the thing," he said, stepping into her rooms. He sat in the hard chair at the small round table and observed Mrs. Perry as she bustled around, plating the cakes and pouring tea from the kettle.

It seemed incongruous that this small homely woman of middle years would have been driven to murder her handsome young neighbor. Had Davis finally come up against a female conquest who had not been content to allow him to callously toy with her affections?

"There now," she said when she'd served the tea and offered him a lemon cake, "what brings you here on this fine day?"

Eyeing the steaming cup she set before him, Atlas grimly recalled the apothecary's warning: *Mind you don't drink the tea.* He bit into a lemon cake instead. It was warm, moist, and flavorful. "This is delicious."

"It is the lemon." She beamed at the compliment. "Just the right amount of fresh lemon and lemon peel makes all of the difference."

"As to what brings me here." He swallowed the last of the dainty cake, which had the slightest bitter aftertaste, and decided to come straight to the point. "I was wondering why you purchased arsenic from Greenwood's Apothecary."

She took a breath and calmly sipped her tea before answering. "I am not surprised you learned about that." She set her cup down. "I expected it was only a matter of time before you looked in the poison book."

"Mr. Greenwood said you purchased a large amount of arsenic."

"I did." Her gray eyes were sharp in her narrow face.

"You purchased the poison to kill Mr. Davis."

She shook her head. "You don't understand at all."

"Please explain it to me."

"I purchased the arsenic because Gordon asked me to," she said in a calm, matter-of-fact manner.

"Why would he do that?"

"He was an arsenic eater. I suspected he was taking it for what ailed him."

"If Davis asked you to buy the poison, why did you tell the apothecary you needed it to kill rats in the boardinghouse?"

She lifted her shoulders and dropped them. "Gordon asked me to keep it a secret, so I obliged him." Her eyes watered. "I realized too late that he wanted the arsenic to kill himself."

"You believe he killed himself?"

"I do, yes."

It made perfect sense. Davis had enough of the poison to kill himself. "There was no sign of the drug in Davis's room after he died. Do you know what happened to it?"

"After he died, I went into his room and retrieved all of the arsenic I could find." Her distress was becoming more apparent, her manner more agitated. "I knew how badly it would reflect upon me if Bow Street found the arsenic in Gordon's chamber and learned that I had purchased it. They would have suspected me of killing him when the truth is I only acquired the poison because Gordon asked me to. You must believe me," she pleaded.

The pieces shifted into place. Atlas suddenly understood why Davis had manipulated both Elizabeth Archer and Mrs. Perry into purchasing arsenic.

"It is Elizabeth Archer's fault." Hate twisted Mrs. Perry's face. "Gordon killed himself because she broke his heart."

He stared at her. "You know about Miss Archer?"

"Of course." Mrs. Perry rose from her seat and paced across the room in an agitated manner. "I followed him once when he went to her house. She's nothing but a strumpet who must pay for what she's done."

A strange sense of euphoria shot through Atlas's veins. He blinked. His body felt weighted down by a thousand stones. "What the devil—?"

"It was the lemon cakes," Mrs. Perry said from behind him. "I sprinkled a little laudanum on them to keep things manageable. You're such a large man. The drug will slow you down."

He blinked, willing himself to keep his eyes open even though his lids suddenly seemed incapable of the task. "I don't understand."

"You should have just drunk the tea. It would have gone much easier on you than this."

He was about to turn around and ask her what she meant when pain exploded against the side of his head and the room went black.

Chapter Twenty-Six

"Atlas. Atlas!"

Lilliana's sharp voice seemed to come from a distance. Atlas felt like he was floating, perhaps in the ocean, because everything was damp. Was he back in Jamaica?

The drifting sensation wasn't at all unpleasant—that was, until he became aware of a pulsating pain in his head so intense that it knocked his breath from his body. He groaned.

"Thank goodness," Lilliana's voice said to someone. "I thought he might be dead."

"Not dead," Atlas managed to murmur, struggling to open his eyes. He blinked, trying to adjust to the light. It took a moment for him to realize where he was. He took in the scarred table, the faded bed covering and remembered he was in Mrs. Perry's rooms at the boardinghouse.

"What happened?" Lilliana's face hovered above his, a furrow in her delicate brows. "How do you feel?"

"Like I ran into a wall." The taste in his mouth was strange; his throat felt dry.

"Well, something most definitely ran into your head." She feathered a finger over his hairline. "Someone hit you. You're bleeding."

"I am?" He brought his hand up to touch his forehead. His hair was damp. So was his face. He must have been bleeding heavily. He held his hand in front of his face but saw no sign of blood. "Why am I wet?"

"Because Jamie tossed a basin of water on you," she replied.

"Why the bloody hell did he do that?"

"To wake you up, of course," she said crisply. "Can you sit up?"

"Here you go, sir." Strong arms, presumably Jamie's, came from behind, gently pulling Atlas into a sitting position before he could answer.

"What happened?" Lilliana asked as she peeled back the hood of her deep-purple cape, baring her dark, upswept hair.

"That's an excellent question." He struggled to remember. "Where is Mrs. Perry?"

"She's not here. Neither is Mr. Perry."

Jamie came into view with a cloth he'd purloined from somewhere nearby. "If you'd like to wipe yourself off, sir."

Atlas took the cloth and gingerly scrubbed his face and hair. The agony in his head had ratcheted down some, tapering off from hellish agony to a painful throb at his temple. When he started to rise, Lilliana and Jamie each took hold of one of his arms to help him stand.

As he straightened to his full height, Atlas caught sight of the lemon cakes on the table. "Bloody hell."

"Sir," Jamie exclaimed, shocked. "I understand you were hit in the canister, but there is a lady present."

Dread flooded Atlas. He gripped the boy's arm. "You didn't eat the cakes, did you?" Jamie was always ravenous.

Jamie's eyes went wide with interest. "What cakes?"

"Never mind," Atlas said gruffly. "Don't eat anything in this room. It could be drugged."

"Did Mrs. Perry poison you?" Lilliana inquired. "Or was it Mr. Perry who did it?"

He shook his head. "Perry wasn't here. It was his wife, Mrs. Perry. She put laudanum in the cakes and intimated she'd put something in the tea as well, but I'd refrained from drinking it."

Jamie surveyed the room with a grim face. "Does that mean she killed Gordon Davis? Is that why she bought the arsenic?"

Atlas stared at Lilliana, trying to figure out how she'd come to be at the boardinghouse. "What are you doing here?"

"I came to make certain you didn't need our assistance, mine and Jamie's."

"I don't follow." His mind was still groggy.

"I went to your apartments, and Jamie told me where you went."

"Did he tell you why I was coming here?"

"Yes, because Mrs. Perry purchased arsenic. I presumed you were going to confront her. I was worried that she and her husband might overpower you. So I commandeered Jamie, and we came as quickly as we could."

"That was foolish." He stared at her in disbelief. "You could have been hurt."

"Yes, but I wasn't, was I?" She looked him over. "But we cannot say the same of you."

Had his mind been functioning properly, he might have formed a suitable response. Instead he didn't even try. He looked at her. "You came to see me?" He hadn't expected to encounter her again for at least a year, possibly longer. "Why?"

"I had something of importance to discuss with you."

He was about to ask what she'd come to see him about when he suddenly remembered his conversation with Maria Perry. Cursing to himself, he started for the door.

Lilliana hustled behind him, with Jamie bringing up the rear. "Where are you going?"

"To Clapham. Mrs. Perry is going after Elizabeth Archer, and I must stop her."

⋆ ⋆ ⋆

After finally emerging from the metropolis's heavy late afternoon traffic, Atlas raced toward Clapham on the Duke of Somerville's borrowed mount.

He'd never ridden such a fine animal—well-muscled, fleet-footed, with just the right amount of spirit. It came as no surprise that Somerville's stables would be filled with superior highly bred horseflesh.

A headache stilled dogged Atlas, but fortunately the blood horse had easily maneuvered around the carts and carriages, fruit vendors, and flower sellers clogging the city's roads and was now hurtling through the open roads toward the Archer home.

He'd ridden from the boardinghouse to Mayfair with Lilliana in the duke's opulent coach. Once they'd reached Somerville House, Lilliana had ordered the duke's swiftest mount saddled immediately for Atlas's use. Maria Perry might have had a running start on him, but she was no doubt making her way to Clapham in a hired rig. No contraption would move as briskly as Somerville's exceptional animal.

He reached Clapham about thirty minutes later and prayed Maria Perry hadn't gotten to Elizabeth first. He had no idea how long he'd been unconscious or how much of a head start Mrs. Perry had on him. Fortunately, a groom appeared as soon as Atlas dismounted. It was the first fine day they'd enjoyed in a long time, and several people were strolling outdoors and along the common, enjoying the warming weather.

He dashed up to the Archers' front door and pounded hard on it. A startled servant opened the door. Atlas did not wait to be invited in.

"Where is Miss Elizabeth Archer?"

"Sir!" the man who'd answered the door—the butler, perhaps—exclaimed, clearly affronted. "This is a respectable home. You cannot barge in here."

Atlas rounded on him. "Where is Elizabeth, dammit!" he roared.

Fear shimmered in the butler's eyes. Atlas was a large man, and he knew what an intimidating picture he could present. "I . . . I . . . ," the man stammered.

"She's in the parlor with a guest," an amused young feminine voice said from behind him. He turned to see Harriet Archer emerging from somewhere in the back of the house with her slingshot firmly in hand. She looked more slender than he remembered, but otherwise her unfortunate encounter with arsenic did not appear to have left a lasting mark. "Good day, Mr. Catesby."

He pointed at her. "Do not come into the parlor," he ordered. "It's not safe."

Without waiting for her response, he spun away toward the parlor. He entered the large sunny room at a fast clip to find Elizabeth and Maria Perry seated on the sofa. Elizabeth brought her teacup to her mouth.

"Don't drink that." He dashed over and hit it out of her hands. It hurtled out of Elizabeth's hands, the tea spraying over the expensive carpet.

"Mr. Catesby!" Elizabeth said with surprise. But he wasn't looking at her. He was focused on the gun Maria Perry had pulled out of her basket.

"How much of it did you drink?" he asked Elizabeth urgently.

"None at all, thanks to you," she said.

"Don't come any closer," Mrs. Perry warned him. Carefully rising from the sofa, the woman kept the weapon trained on Elizabeth.

Elizabeth turned away from Atlas at the sound of Maria's command. A sound of distress erupted from her throat when she spotted the weapon. She shrank back on the sofa. "What are you doing?"

Atlas held out a calming hand. "Do as she says, Elizabeth."

Elizabeth stared at him with fear in her eyes. "She said you sent her. That's why I received her."

Atlas shook his head. "I did not send her."

Mrs. Perry backed up, putting more distance between herself and Atlas. "You needn't have made such a dramatic entrance. I did not poison the tea. Why use arsenic when a pistol is so much more to the point?"

He looked the woman in the eye. "You don't want to kill Miss Archer."

Elizabeth uttered an unintelligible exclamation of shock and surprise. "Kill me?"

Mrs. Perry ignored her. "I assure you that I do." Scorn twisted her narrow face. "She deserves to die like Gordon did. He took his life because she broke his heart." She'd backed up all the way to the massive open window.

Trembling, Elizabeth shot a panicked look at Atlas.

He focused on Mrs. Perry. "You are mistaken," he said to her.

"I told you he killed himself." Mrs. Perry's voice became louder as her agitation level seemed to rise. "I purchased the arsenic because Gordon asked me to, and I gave it to him for his personal use. I knew he took it occasionally, but I didn't think he would take it all at once and kill himself. I would never have hurt him. I loved Gordon, but he only had eyes for her."

"I do believe you." Atlas spoke in a soothing voice, hoping to calm Mrs. Perry. "I know Gordon killed himself."

"What?" Elizabeth said, horrified. "He poisoned himself because of me? No, it cannot be."

"It is." Hate filled Mrs. Perry's voice as she gestured menacingly at Elizabeth with the gun. "You as good as killed him. Now it is only fair for you to die as well."

Atlas inched closer. "Mr. Davis did kill himself, but not because of Miss Archer. He did not love Miss Archer. He loved a lady in Mayfair who he had known for many years, but she is wed to another."

Mrs. Perry eyed him suspiciously. "You're lying."

"I am not," he assured her. "Mr. Davis wanted to wed Miss Archer to better his place in society, but he did not kill himself because of a broken heart."

"Why else would he do it?" Maria Perry demanded. "I don't believe you."

"Mr. Davis killed himself because he had syphilis."

A shocked sound escaped Elizabeth's throat. "No!"

Atlas nodded, his focus on the woman holding the weapon. "I spoke with his doctor and the medical examiner; both agree the man suffered from the pox."

"No, it cannot be." Maria Perry shook her head back and forth in short, quick motions. "He was so beautiful."

"So I have heard," Atlas said. "You can imagine how difficult it would have been for a man like Mr. Davis, who depended upon his good looks, to know he would soon have a visage that repulsed people rather than attracted them."

Mrs. Perry seemed to waver. "But I thought he cared for Miss Archer. I thought she was responsible." She spoke softly, almost to herself. "How can it be?"

"As you can see now, there is no reason to harm Miss Archer." Atlas took a step toward the woman.

"She jilted him," Mrs. Perry said angrily.

"He was neither faithful nor devoted to Miss Archer. I'm certain even you would agree it was not a good match."

"I no longer know what to think." She slumped onto a stool before the open window. "I was so certain . . ." Her voice trailed off.

Something sailed through the window—a rock—and struck Mrs. Perry in the head. Stunned, she reflexively looked out the window. Atlas took advantage of the distraction to launch himself at her, wrapping his large hands firmly around her weapon.

"No, stop," Mrs. Perry cried as she struggled with him, but he easily disarmed her, breaking her hold on the weapon and backing away from her.

"What do we have here?" Ambrose Endicott stood on the threshold of the parlor with two men flanking him. "Lady Roslyn came to Bow Street and informed me there might be trouble at the Archer abode."

Thank goodness for Lilliana's quick thinking. Atlas regarded the runner with relief. "That is Mrs. Maria Perry." He pointed to the woman, who had collapsed back onto the stool and seemed to be paying no mind to what was happening around her. "She drugged me and attempted to shoot Miss Archer here."

"Is that so?" Endicott's bushy brows lifted as he eyed Mrs. Perry with interest. "May I assume she also killed Mr. Davis?"

"No," Atlas informed him. "I believe Mr. Davis killed himself."

Endicott gestured to the two men. "We'll take Mrs. Perry down to Bow Street." He turned to Atlas as the men took hold of Mrs. Perry and began escorting her from the room. "You will need to give a statement."

Atlas nodded. "I will follow shortly."

Endicott readied to leave.

"Which of your men threw the rock to distract Mrs. Perry?" Atlas asked. "That was quite clever."

"Rock?" Endicott looked puzzled.

"It was me." Harriet Archer's smiling face popped up in the window. "As you know, I am very good with a sling. I couldn't hear what that old bedlamite was saying, but I could see her gun. She made for an excellent target in the open window."

"She did indeed." Atlas cracked a smile, the tension of the last few minutes beginning to break away.

Harriet looked beyond him to her sister. "Are you all right, Elizabeth?"

With his focus on Mrs. Perry and the gun, Atlas had almost forgotten about Elizabeth. He turned to look at her. She sat buckled forward on the sofa, hugging her midriff.

"Miss Archer." Alarmed, he went and knelt before her, the movement sending a sharp pain through his head. "Are you hurt?"

She looked up at him with despair in her hollowed eyes. "I have noticed certain . . . signs . . . on my person," she whispered entreatingly, as if willing Atlas to deny the horror she might have ahead of her. "Are you certain Gordon had the pox?"

Sympathy filled him. "Yes." There was nothing else he could say. "I am so sorry."

Chapter Twenty-Seven

Several days later, he went to see Lilliana.

Roxbury's carriage was pulling away when Atlas arrived at Somerville House. Heaviness settled in his chest. Perhaps Lilliana's betrothal was finally official.

She received him in Somerville House's expansive gardens. As he crossed over the wide stone verandah and trotted down the steps leading to the lush manicured lawn, he easily spotted Lilliana—her dark hair and snowy day dress resplendent against the verdant backdrop.

She sat at a table set with crystal and fine china, the remnants of tea and refreshment as elegantly laid out as at any supper party Atlas had ever attended. The crystal caught the sun, adding glimmer to the picturesque tableau.

"Enjoying the fine afternoon, I see," he said as he drew near. It was warm and gently sunny, the most pleasant day so far after a particularly brisk spring.

She looked up from the book in her lap as he approached. "It is a lovely day. I thought to enjoy it." She studied his face. "I trust your health is improved."

"Much, thank you." He had been abed with a headache and some dizziness for the last few days, the lingering effects of Maria Perry's bashing him in the head with what turned out to be a cutting board. Aside from an interview at Bow Street immediately after Mrs. Perry's arrest, Atlas had taken to his bed, seeing few people save Jamie and Charlton, who'd returned with glowing stories of his time in Bath.

"I visited Miss Archer," Lilliana informed him. "I have made arrangements for her to see Somerville's physician."

"She faces a terrible ordeal." He pulled out the iron chair opposite her and settled into the cushioned seat. A half-full cup of tea and a floral china plate with a partially eaten slice of cake sat on the table before him. Roxbury's, no doubt.

"Elizabeth believes it is what she deserves for attempting to poison Mr. Davis."

"I highly doubt Miss Archer gave him more arsenic than he regularly took on his own." A fresh sense of distaste for Davis rifled through him. "But I believe Davis wanted people to believe Miss Archer responsible for his death."

"Truly?" Her luminous gaze regarded him over the rim of her porcelain teacup. "That would explain why he encouraged her to purchase arsenic."

"You'll recall he insisted that she buy the poison herself and not allow the servants to do it."

Comprehension lit her patrician face. "He wanted her name written down in the poison book." Illuminated by the sun, her eyes were an intriguing coppery shade. "Proof for all to see that she'd purchased the poison."

"Imagine his surprise when she decided to put it in his drink."

"So he meant to frame her, and then she actually attempted to commit the crime he meant for her to be accused of?"

He shrugged. "I don't suppose we'll ever know for certain exactly what went on in Davis's mind, but that's how it appears to me. He was threatening to ruin Elizabeth, and thanks to Davis, she had the arsenic in hand while at her most desperate."

A footman appeared with a fresh table setting and whisked Roxbury's used teacup and plate away. "It also explains why Davis only began keeping a journal in the last few weeks of his life," Atlas continued. "It was a way for him to implicate her from beyond the grave. For all we know, he wrote all of those passages in the journal in one sitting."

Lilliana leaned forward to pour the tea. "But why? Because she'd tried to poison him, or because she jilted him?"

"Perhaps both. He'd already been jilted once by Lady Brandon. Elizabeth's rejection could have sent him over the edge. And once Davis realized he was ill, maybe he decided to take his final revenge on her."

"What a terrible man." She shuddered. "To take advantage of a young girl and then attempt to punish her in such a gruesome manner."

He thought of the grim future that Elizabeth Archer faced. "Davis might not have succeeded in having her blamed for his murder, but he has managed to ruin her life all the same."

"Yes," Lilliana said, all sympathy. "The poor girl."

"And then there's the question of why Davis had Mrs. Perry purchase the arsenic he ultimately used to kill himself."

"I should think it is obvious."

"How so?"

She reached for her tea. "If he meant to frame Miss Archer, it would not do for his name to appear in any poison books."

"Quite right." He immediately saw her point. "If his name had appeared in the poison book, Bow Street would have assumed he used the arsenic he'd purchased to kill himself." He drank his tea. "I imagine you've told Tacy what we discovered."

"Yes. Not all of it, of course. There is no need for her to know what an absolute scoundrel her brother was. She is aware that he took his own life because he was ill. It's been very difficult for her, but she is relieved to finally know the truth of how her brother died." She set her tea down. "Do you still plan on setting sail for India soon?"

"Yes, the East India Company has a ship leaving in a fortnight."

Her tone cooled. "And you have secured passage."

"I have." He paused, then added, "I saw Roxbury leaving when I arrived."

"Yes, he came for tea. I never truly imagined he had anything to do with Mr. Davis's death. He is the best of men, you know."

He swallowed down the acid that rose in his throat at her praise of the marquess. "Is a happy announcement soon to follow?"

"That is unlikely. I rejected Roxbury's proposal today."

"What?" His head shot up. "But why?"

She lifted one delicate shoulder in an elegant shrug. "I do not wish to wed him."

"I thought the two of you had an understanding. Roxbury indicated he'd even spoken with Somerville about the marriage settlements."

"Yes, the two of them did seem rather eager to see me wed. As did you," she added archly.

He did not miss the rebuke in her tone. "But Roxbury would have given you everything."

"Not quite. I do not love him."

A frisson of delight shot through him at the confirmation that Roxbury had not engaged Lilliana's affections. "I did not think love was required in ton marriages."

"I doubt I will ever wed again. If I do, it will have to be for a very compelling reason." She gestured around them at the immaculate structured lawn and enormous neoclassical pile towering over it. "As you see, my brother provides very nicely for us; wealth and rank are not incentive enough for me to suffer another husband."

"You said yourself that Roxbury is the best of men," he protested, worried for her future. "He could have protected you and the boys."

She exhaled, long and slow. He was obviously trying her patience. "When will you realize that not all women need saving? I certainly no longer need to be rescued."

"I realize that."

"Do you?" The words dripped with disdain. "You really are an incredibly arrogant man. I don't know how I didn't see it before now."

He stiffened, taken aback by her reproach when all he had ever done was try to do what was best for her. "I only want your happiness." He had sacrificed for her future, and she tossed that aside now as if it were nothing.

"Do you?" she said in a voice rich with scorn. "By happiness, I presume you mean what you believe *should* make me happy, not what would actually bring me joy and contentment."

What the devil was she talking about? "No," he said tightly. "That is most certainly not what I mean."

"Yet you and Roxbury decided between yourselves what would make me happy." Her nostrils flared. "And neither of you saw fit to consult me."

His brow furrowed. "I don't know what Roxbury told you but—"

"He informed me that the two of you conferred and reached the conclusion that he and I should wed. That is why I came to see you the afternoon you confronted Mrs. Perry. To tell you what I thought of your machinations." She gave him a pointed look. "How considerate of you both to spare me the trouble of determining my own future."

"That's not what either of us intended," he began. "You are the daughter of a duke. We both know I am beneath your touch. A woman as fine as you should wed a marquess."

"Very pretty words." She did not appear impressed. "Did it ever occur to you that perhaps I should decide what is best for me?"

"Of course you should."

"And yet you could not give me the courtesy of allowing me to do so."

"You are twisting everything," he said, his temper rising. "Surely you comprehend that I only want what is best for you . . . and for the children."

"I have already endured one husband who saw fit to dictate everything in my life."

She was comparing him to her late husband? "Godfrey Warwick and I could not be more different."

"I certainly thought so once, yet you thought to command my future just as he did in the past." She rose to her feet, regarding him regally over the bridge of her nose. "You must have a great deal of packing to do for your journey. So if we are finished here . . ."

His jaw hardened at her dismissal, as if she were his mistress and he a mere boot boy. "No."

Her eyes widened. "I beg your pardon?"

"As you should." He came to his feet, emotion swirling in his chest. "We are nowhere near finished, and I do not appreciate being dismissed." It was not up to her to determine when it was done between them. It was far from over.

"Is that so?" An expression of polite boredom settled on her face. "I cannot imagine what there is left to say between us."

He stepped closer, pulled Lilliana into his arms, and kissed her for all he was worth.

Author's Note

As hard as it is to believe, arsenic was used for a variety of purposes in eighteenth-century England. The substance could be found in all sorts of everyday items, including clothing, candles, curtains, and wallpaper dyes, because it produced a vibrant shade of green known as "arsenic green." Workers in the factories that produced these dyes, as well as the artisans who used products containing them, often suffered from arsenic poisoning.

Also, like the character of Gordon Davis in this novel, people voluntarily took arsenic for health reasons. Many were convinced the poison improved their health by giving them an energy boost. Cosmetics and face washes containing arsenic were believed to improve complexions.

Murder in Bloomsbury was loosely inspired by a fascinating murder case that riveted Scotland in the mid-1800s. Madeleine Smith, the daughter of a wealthy, well-regarded architect, was accused of poisoning her working-class lover. What made her trial even more scandalous was a series of passionate letters that revealed very intimate details of her secret love affair with Emile L'Anglier, a factory clerk.

Once Madeleine accepted that her father would never allow her to marry Emile, she became engaged to a wealthy merchant and neighbor. Emile did not take her rejection well and threatened to show their intimate letters to Madeleine's father. Emile died shortly afterward after complaining of terrible stomach pains; an autopsy showed he'd been poisoned. (The introduction of syphilis in *Murder in Bloomsbury* is my own invention.)

Madeleine was arrested and put on trial for Emile's murder. The verdict was "not proven," and public opinion was split on whether Madeleine got away with murder or was framed by her vengeful ex-lover. I was fascinated to find the transcript of the entire trial online and borrowed liberally from courtroom testimony and Emile's actual autopsy results. I also referred to Madeleine and Emile's authentic letters when penning Elizabeth and Gordon's fictional missives to each other.

If you're interested in reading more about the Madeleine Smith case, you can find the entire court report online at murderpedia.org.

A few final notes . . . I must acknowledge the extraordinary people who helped make this book possible. My editor, Faith Black Ross, is a dream to work with and makes the editing process a breeze. My agent, Kevan Lyon, guides my professional affairs with an expertise and tenacity that make me continually grateful that she's in my corner. My friend Megann Yaqub is always there for me when I need help keeping a story on track. She and Joanna Shupe each read the earliest versions of *Murder in Bloomsbury* and gave me their valuable input. Thank you!

The wonderful community of readers, bloggers, booksellers, and author buddies all contribute to making writing and publishing such a joy in my life. I love hearing from readers and bloggers. Please keep those messages coming! And thank you for taking the time to spend a few hours in Atlas's world.